UNCERTAIN STAKES

A LUCA MYSTERY
BOOK 9

DAN PETROSINI

Print ISBN: 978-1-960286-21-5
Naples, FL
Library of Congress Control Number: 2023901528

ACKNOWLEDGMENTS

Special thanks to Julie, Stephanie and Jennifer for their love and support, and thanks to Squad Sergeant Craig Perrilli for his counsel on the real world of law enforcement. He helps me keep it real.

OTHER BOOKS BY DAN

Complicit Witness

Push Back

Ambition Cliff

1

———————

Sheriff Chester was in a good mood. I expected as much, making the timing of my request perfect. We hadn't had a homicide in five months, and every crime stat, except driving under the influence, was trending lower. It was a good time to ask for something.

"How old is your daughter, Frank?"

"Jessie is going to be three next month."

"Enjoy it. I'm sure you realize time moves quickly."

"It sure does."

"What did you want to discuss?"

"We're working a cold case. Back in 1989 a man named Whitaker was murdered downtown."

"A thirty-year-old case?"

"Yes, but I feel good about it. I believe we can solve this one."

"It's always nice to clear an old one. What do you need?"

"The way I see it, the case hinges on DNA. I had forensics go over the evidence, and they found five deposits of DNA that aren't the victim's. I believe they belong to the primary suspect in the case. I think he's the killer."

The sheriff eased into his chair. "Okay."

"I'd like to exhume the suspect's body so that we can get a sample and confirm he was the killer."

"He's dead?"

"Yes."

"I don't know why we'd get involved in something like that."

"The victim's family, sir. They've been calling every couple of months since I've been here."

"But it's a thirty-year-old case."

"I understand, sir. But I'm certain we can clear it. Think of how the department would be portrayed in the press."

His face brightened. "We'd look good."

"Good? We'd prove that we don't give up. It'd be a powerful message to the community, including crooks: We'll hunt you down."

"Isn't there a way to do this without disturbing the body?"

Chester had never authorized an exhumation as sheriff. He claimed it got bad press and could turn against us. But I believed it was deeper, maybe a religious conviction or a necrophobia. He also never attended an autopsy, making it likely it was necrophobia.

"We've combed through everything, even what's left of the family memorabilia. There's nothing."

"I have to think about this, if it's worth the risk to solve a thirty-year-old case."

"I understand, sir, but thankfully there is nothing fresh for us to deal with."

"Speaking of that, a friend of a good friend of my wife's been calling about her daughter. She's been missing a couple of days. I'd like you to take a look into it for me."

And just like that he steered our talk from an unsolved

murder case to a missing persons report. Or was Chester offering a trade?

"Certainly, sir. I'd appreciate your consideration on the exhumation matter. I think we'll be able to stamp it solved when we get the DNA."

"I'd rather not waste resources on such an old case, especially one where the primary suspect is dead."

"It's for the family, for the community, sir."

"I'll mull it over." He reached for a pad. "Let me give you information on the missing woman."

***

DERRICK, my partner, peered over his monitor. "What did Chester say?"

"That he'd have to think it over. It's his way of saying no."

"But we could solve a cold case."

"I told him that, but he's never dug up a body since he's been here."

"What are we going to do?"

"He wants us to check into a missing woman."

"A missing person?"

"Yep, a friend of a friend kind of thing. The woman's mother called him."

"How long has she been missing?"

"Sheriff said a couple of days."

"Could be anything."

"I know, but if we're going to have a shot at getting Chester to approve an exhumation, we're going to have to follow this up. I'll call the mother."

I dialed the number the sheriff gave me. A woman picked up on the first ring.

"Beth?"

"This is Detective Luca, Collier County Sheriff's Office. Is this Mrs. Wade?"

"Yes, that's me. I was hoping it was my daughter, Beth."

"Sorry, ma'am."

"The sheriff said you'd be calling."

"When was the last time you saw your daughter?"

"Well, about a week ago, but we talk every day. She never forgets to call me. Something is wrong."

"When was the last time you spoke to her?"

"Day before yesterday. She didn't call yesterday, and I was getting nervous, but then she still didn't call today, and that never happens."

"Did you try to call her?"

"Of course. I called her about twenty times. Stopped leaving messages because her mailbox is full."

"How about anyone she knows?"

"Well, her husband, John, said she didn't come home."

"She's married?"

"Yes, why?"

I avoided telling her that when a missing person turned up dead, most times it was the spouse. "She still kept your last name?"

"Yeah, it's her second marriage. She changed it the first time, but after the divorce she changed it back and never bothered when she remarried."

"I see. I understand you're upset, but there could be any number of reasons why she hasn't called—"

"No, something is wrong. I can tell."

It was never a good idea to doubt a mother's intuition. "Is there anything specific that leads you to believe she may be in danger?"

"I'm not crazy. I just know."

"What about her husband? How was the marriage?"

"They fight all the time."

"Is he someone that could conceivably be involved in her disappearance?"

"Oh my God! You think John did something to Beth?"

"Your daughter is missing two days at this point. Please don't jump to conclusions. Why don't you give me her husband's number, and we'll check into this?"

I jotted down the number and hung up.

"What's the matter?"

I didn't want to tell him I was getting a bad feeling. "Nothing. The mother said they talk every day, but she hasn't spoken to her in two days, and her calls haven't been returned."

"I heard you say something about a husband. You want to start there?"

2

———

THE DMV PORTAL WAS ONE OF THE FIRST PLACES I accessed. I looked at a photo of Beth Wade. The thirty-five-year-old had shoulder-length, brown hair and hazel eyes. Her license said she was five foot three inches, and a hundred and ten pounds.

A 2017 Ford Mustang, white, was registered in her name at 313 St. Croix Boulevard. Googling the address confirmed my belief it was in a rental community on Immokalee Road known as St. Croix. It was a busy area, not far from the ramp to Interstate 75.

I put her name into the law enforcement touch database, and what came up deepened my fear. There were five domestic violence incidents, three with her first husband and two with her current.

I read the most recent report. It was May 20, 2019, just six weeks ago. Two officers responded to the call. To get the situation under control, the officers had to cuff both Beth Wade and her husband, John Frelig. Both wanted to press charges against the other, and they were brought to the station and booked. The charges were eventually dropped.

Booking photos are never flattering, and these were no different. Beth's right eye was swollen shut and her green sweatshirt torn at the neck. Her messy hair reminded me of what Jessie did to Mary Ann's when she play-washed her hair.

With a couple of days of stubble, her husband had scratches down both cheeks and a blood-caked ear. The report made no mention of alcohol or drug use, which seemed odd, given the battle that had ensued.

INCHING my way west on Immokalee Road, I could see the black-tiled sign for St. Croix Apartments. It would take two traffic light changes to go the quarter of a mile. I usually avoided this stretch of road, with the worst traffic in town, but couldn't if I wanted to talk to Beth's husband.

John Frelig was a thirty-eight-year-old who drove a tow truck on an overnight shift. He was out of shape and looked ten years older. He wasn't overweight but flabby. I was tempted to get a ball and ask him if he knew what it was. If Frelig wanted any quality of life twenty years from now, he'd better start exercising.

A car beeped its horn as I followed him into the kitchen. I wondered if the air here had unhealthy levels of car exhaust. Probably. We sat across a glass table that had two long scratches on it. The padding on the chairs was tantamount to the cushion in a Band-Aid.

"You still haven't heard from your wife?"

"No."

"How long has it been?"

"Over two days now."

"Last time you saw her was when?"

"Monday night about seven."

"What was she wearing?"

"Uhm, jeans, she had jeans on, and I think a blue top."

"Blouse? Tank top? Long or short sleeve?"

"It was the one with skinny straps on the shoulder and a couple of buttons. Let me check her closet."

I followed him into the bedroom. The bed was unmade.

He slid a door to the side and ran a hand over the clothes. "Yeah, that was the one. It had three buttons I think, here." He touched the center of his chest.

"Okay, that's good. What did she say before you went to work?"

"She said she was going to the casino."

"The Seminole Casino in Immokalee?"

"Yeah. She liked to play blackjack. She was pretty good at it too."

Was? Did he know something about what happened to her? "She went there frequently?"

"I guess so."

"You don't know?"

"No, she'd go a lot of times when I was working. You know, I work the overnight shift for Baker's Towing."

"Did you hear from her after she left for the casino?"

"Yeah, she texted me. Said she was doing good, had a hot hand."

"What time did you get back home?"

"About six thirty, in the morning."

"And she wasn't home?"

"No."

"Didn't you get concerned?"

"A little. I mean, she said she was doing good, and I figured she played late and got a room."

"She would stay overnight at the casino?"

"Not a lot, but sometimes, you know. They'd comp her a room every now and then."

This guy certainly wasn't the jealous type. "Did you check with the hotel to see if she was there?"

He shook his head.

"Why not?"

"I thought maybe she stayed there and then maybe went with a girlfriend or something. She knew a lot of people there. I just thought she'd eventually show up."

"Had she done something like that before?"

"You mean staying over and going out the next day?"

"Yes."

"One time she did. I work at night, and when I get back, I sleep till, like, two in the afternoon."

"Does your wife work?"

"Yeah, she works for an insurance company, checking into claims that are filed. You know, I knew there was a lot of bullshit claims, but the fraud she tells me about is frigging crazy."

I wasn't discounting that problem, but if he worked on my side of the street, his head would spin. "Where did she work?"

"Accurate Insurance, they're in Fort Myers, but she doesn't go there too much. Most of the time she does everything from home. And it doesn't matter when she works."

"How were things between the two of you?"

"What do you mean?"

"What I mean is that we've responded to two domestic violence calls at this address."

His shoulders sagged. "We got past all that a long time ago."

I knew time was flying, but not as fast as he made it seem.

"Just six weeks ago, the two of you were going at it so bad that you had to be hauled in."

He frowned.

"What were you fighting about?"

"You know, I can't even tell you. The usual stuff."

Couldn't or wouldn't? "I saw the photos. If that's usual, you may need to get help, and fast."

"Everything's okay between us. Really, it is."

He could profess till the sun set, but I'd find out how the relationship was. I took the contact information for his wife's boss and left.

3

The Seminole Casino Hotel had no record that Beth Wade had stayed in one of their rooms. That didn't mean she hadn't. She could have been shacking up with someone who rented a room.

If it turned out this woman had a boyfriend or cheated on her husband, it could mean she simply took off for a couple of days with a lover. Based on the prior domestics we'd responded to, her stepping out on her old man was a distinct possibility.

The thought that she could be trying to get away from an abusive husband crossed my mind. I'd seen it way too many times before, but in this case, Beth Wade's mother claimed her daughter called her every day. If they were that close, I would think she would have tipped the mother off. Or was she too embarrassed by it?

The missing woman was a gambler. It had been a few years since I'd taken profiling classes, but with something like this it shouldn't matter. Most people who frequented casinos, and I'm not talking about seniors out for the day, were risk-takers. They'd discount that the odds were stacked against them. They'd ignore the real risk that they would walk out with less money. Did that neglectful trait extend beyond so-called recreational activities?

My preference was to slow-walk this for a day or two, hoping this woman would show up. But the sheriff had asked me to look into this. If I wanted a shot at approving my exhumation request, I'd have to show him I was pursuing the whereabouts of Beth Wade.

Going to see the mother would provide insight on the missing woman and give me a reason to update the sheriff.

***

JOAN WADE LIVED in a white home in a new community on Airport Pulling Road known as Manchester Square. Located in a busy area, it was a little of, like mother, like daughter; both of them didn't seem to mind traffic where they lived.

Based upon the community's modern sign, I expected the homes in the neighborhood to lean contemporary. They weren't. It was a large development, and her home, on Cambridge Lane, was near Livingston Road. The driveway was lined with little American flags, leftovers from the July 4th holiday. As I walked to the home, I wondered if you could get used to the sound of cars whizzing by.

When she opened the door, the lanai and pool came into view. The wide-open floor plan was nice. Shaking her hand, I tried to estimate what the home went for.

The elder Wade was tall and slender. Her raised eyebrows and tight jawline were giveaways that she'd had work done. She led me past a collage of family photos into a kitchen that was open to the main room. The more I saw, the better I liked the layout.

"Would you like some coffee?"

I hadn't seen a pot. "Only if it's made."

"No problem. I use pods. Regular or decaf?"

"Regular."

She brought a cup over. "All I have is almond milk. Is that okay?"

It wasn't. "Sure." I put in a tiny amount of what they called milk and asked, "Following up with our phone call, I thought it would help to get a sense of your daughter, her relationships, activities, that sort of thing."

"Do you think she's been harmed?"

"We have no evidence of that. I know it's difficult. I have a daughter as well, and if she was missing, I'd be worried sick about her. But the chances are she's with a friend or needed time alone."

"I hope you're right, Detective."

That made two of us.

"Now, I went to see her husband, John. I know they've had some issues in their relationship, and I'd like your opinion on it and on him."

"Beth struggled in her relationships with men. Her father died when she was just nine, and I didn't realize it at the time, but it left a larger hole than I imagined."

Society had to find a way to ensure that a child's search for a father figure didn't trap them in a bad situation. "That's understandable. How did she react?"

"Well, she wasn't the best at choosing a partner. Beth's first marriage, which I tried to warn her about, ended quickly."

"He was abusive?"

She nodded. "Yes, she was too immature, to be honest about it."

Reflection and time had a way of clarifying things. "How old was she?"

"Twenty-three."

That wasn't considered young to get married in the South.

"Tell me about her current husband, John."

"They met about five years ago."

"When she was thirty?"

"Actually, it was before that. I remember John being there for her thirtieth birthday. I threw a little party for her."

"Okay. They hit it right off?"

"You could say that."

"You didn't like him, did you?"

She shrugged. "Not that I had anything against him. I don't want this to sound terrible, but he was a tow truck driver. I was hoping for something better for her."

After a failed marriage, you'd think the mother was looking for happiness, not an image.

"How long have they been married?"

"About four years now."

"You said you speak with your daughter every day."

"Yes, that's why I'm so concerned."

"Do you know about the domestic violence calls?"

She frowned. "Yes. The two of them have bad tempers."

"Many people argue, but it doesn't result in the police responding. What did she say about the physical part of it?"

She shrugged.

"Was it John that started it?"

"You don't think he did anything to her, do you?"

A black cat slipped in and out of the kitchen. Was it some kind of sign?

"I'm just collecting information, ma'am."

She shook her head. "I don't know where she got it from, but Beth was quick to hit someone. All through school she'd get into fights. I sent her for therapy, and it helped somewhat, but she would still get into them."

"She was headstrong?"

"You could say that, but she is a good person. Beth loves babies. You should see her with one. She wants to be a mother. Likes dogs too, but John didn't want one."

"Do you know if your daughter was having an affair or something more casual?"

"No."

"Do you think she would do something like that?"

"I guess so. Do you think she ran off with someone?"

"It would explain her disappearance."

"But why didn't she call?"

"It could have been too uncomfortable for her to talk about it."

"I can't believe I'm saying this, but as long as she's safe, I could care less if she is having an affair."

4

———

The sheriff stood when I entered his office.

"Frank, come on in. You must have good news."

"Just wanted to update you, sir."

"You haven't located her?"

"Not yet."

Chester fell into his chair. "Whatever you have to say should have been put in a report, Luca."

"Since you had an interest in the case, sir, I thought coming in person—"

"I have an interest in all the cases we handle."

"Of course, I was just trying—"

"I've got a busy day ahead."

"Sorry, sir. I've already interviewed the mother, on the phone and in person, as well as the husband. They have serious marital issues that resulted in a couple of domestics."

"Do you believe it's foul play?"

"I hope not. She could have run off with a boyfriend, but if another day passes without a word, and well, let's see what develops. It could be nothing, and we get lucky."

He rapped a knuckle on his desk. "Let's hope so. If there's a major development, I expect to hear from you."

"Yes, sir."

I wanted to ask about the exhumation request, but he reached for a file and said, "That's all."

I never liked to kiss ass, but I'd do anything to solve a murder, especially one that half a dozen detectives had failed at. If Chester wouldn't agree, I'd have to see if there was a way around him. It was dangerous, but I had to. I had promised the family I'd get the killer. Besides, if it stayed unsolved, the three and a half months Derrick and I had put into it would be a total waste.

Taking the stairs down to my office, my mood descended in tandem. It wasn't the old case that had me down, but that I'd misread Chester. I had discounted the woman's disappearance. It was a serious error. I knew that to have any chance of saving her, if she was in trouble, I should have put the pedal to the metal the moment I was handed the case.

I'd wasted two days, and the feeling that something bad had happened to Beth Wade was growing. I hustled down the hallway to my office.

When I entered, Derrick said, "Why don't we put out an alert on the woman's car?"

He beat me to it. Was he taking lessons in telepathy from Mary Ann? "Was thinking the same thing. Get it out there ASAP."

"What did the sheriff have to say?"

"Nothing. I'm going to take a ride out to the casino. See what I can dig up."

"Do we even know if she was there?"

"Not outside of the husband saying that was where she was going."

"That's a long ride."

He was right. I wanted to do something, but taking a forty-five-minute drive without knowing if the missing woman had even been there the night she disappeared might not have been the best choice.

"She liked to play blackjack out there. Worse comes to worse, I'll talk to the people who work there. You never know."

"That's a good idea. We need to know more about her."

He should only know that I hadn't thought it through until he challenged me. The chemo had screwed with my memory, but at least I could still think under pressure.

I CONTINUED east on Immokalee Road. A few miles after passing Oil Well Road, the road narrowed to a single lane in each direction. With a handful of new developments slated, I wondered how long until they doubled the capacity of this stretch of roadway.

Another ten miles east, and there was nothing but farmland and undeveloped land on both sides of the road. The Immokalee area was agriculture based and a major center of tomato growing in America. The road bent to the north, and a sign proclaimed, Welcome to Immokalee, with an explanation that Immokalee meant "your home."

Passing the county's Immokalee jail, I rolled toward Main Street. You couldn't miss the canary-yellow complex that dominated the area with a depressed feel. I pulled into the Seminole Casino Hotel. The place was owned and operated by the Seminole Tribe of Florida. A valet came over and I flashed my badge. He pointed to a spot along the curb that was just past the doorway.

It was the first time I'd been here. Gambling in casinos

didn't appeal to me. You knew it was rigged; how else were they able to build places like this? I enjoyed playing cards. I also bought the occasional lottery ticket when I got a feeling, but the vibes I received never delivered. The messages that did work were the ones suited to solving crimes.

I'd heard that most of the action here came from day-trippers, seniors looking for a little sizzle, and tourists making the drive on a bad-weather day. The casino was connected to a hundred-room hotel for overnight guests and hard-core gamblers—regulars who would be comped a room in an attempt to give them something of value as the casino siphoned the guest's dollars at a gaming table.

Just outside the entrance, I picked up a cane that had fallen out of a man's hand as he nodded off. I propped it against his chair and turned toward the entrance.

A blast of cold air infused with cigarette smoke greeted me as the casino's doors slid open. Stepping in provided a 360-degree view of people playing slots the size of soda machines. The screens were oversized and colorful. It was all set on a carpet so red you'd have trouble seeing blood on it.

The combination of hundreds of machines making clanging sounds, on top of a sound system blaring pop music, amounted to an aural assault. If you weren't hard of hearing, you would be.

I circled the floor, noticing a sign but not a partition of any kind that separated the smoking and nonsmoking sections. There had to be over a thousand slot machines and three or four dozen gaming tables. There was an exclusive area called the Player's Club, making me wonder how much you had to lose to be a member.

Protocol called for me to check in with management before talking to anyone.

5

I FOUND THE SECURITY OFFICE. IT WAS WALL-TO-WALL VIDEO coverage of the gaming tables. I explained about the missing woman, but they seemed more concerned about customers cheating than customer safety. Saying they'd call the management office, they asked me to wait outside.

I watched a couple of old ladies relentlessly feed slot machines until a man in an off-the-rack sports jacket approached. He was grinning from ear to ear. I figured the place was having a better than usual take that day.

"Gus Bender. I'm the day-shift manager for the casino."

His skin was a couple of shades darker than mine. He didn't look like a Native American, but it was possible, as the top jobs were usually reserved for tribe members.

"Detective Luca."

He didn't look me in the eye when we shook, something that always bothered me.

"How can I help you today?"

"I'd like to talk to a couple of employees about a missing woman."

"A missing woman? And what does that have to do with the casino?"

"Probably nothing, but her husband said she was here the night she disappeared."

"First I'm hearing about it."

"Her name is Beth Wade. She liked to play blackjack. From what I understand, she was a regular."

"Her name don't ring a bell, but I work days."

"The night in question is July seventh. For all we know, she never came here and ran away with a friend of some kind."

"Well, if she was here and playing, we'll likely have her on camera."

"Good, but I'd like to chat with a couple of dealers, see if they knew her and if she was even here."

"I don't know. There's a process that—"

"It's nothing formal. I just want to see if someone can tell me they saw her with another man or mentioned going away. She didn't have the best marriage, and if you ask me, I think she was stepping out on him. I get confirmation; I drop it and leave you alone."

"We can't have you talking on the floor."

"I understand. Like I said, it's just a couple of questions that I need to ask."

"All right, then. Follow me, but please keep it short."

He brought me to an employee lounge where dealers and cocktail waitresses could get off their feet on a break. A TV was playing a soap opera. There were three women sitting in low-backed chairs and a blond man heating something in a microwave.

"Listen up, folks. This is a detective. He's interested in a woman who may play blackjack here, more than likely at night, if she does. Who was working Monday night?"

A woman in black pants and a white shirt said, "I was dealing blackjack Monday."

Another woman in a silver sequined bodysuit, whose high heels were on the floor in front of her chair, said, "I was on too."

I said, "Why don't we sit over there?" I pointed to a corner table.

"I'm Detective Luca, with the Collier County Sheriff's Office."

The cocktail waitress said, "Maggie Prine. Nice to meet you."

The dealer said, "Dolores Espina. Who are you interested in?"

"I'm looking into a woman named Beth Wade. She told her husband that she was coming here Monday night." I showed them a picture of her.

The server said, "Yeah, I've seen her around here a bunch of times."

"Monday night?"

"You know, I'm not sure. It was busy that night. Some kind of convention was here. Right, Dolores?"

"It was packed. I know her too. She's played at my tables. She was nice, knew how to play the game."

"Did she play Monday?"

She shrugged. "I don't remember exactly. I worked five days in a row. Just got back on today, as a matter of fact."

"But you saw her recently?"

"Yes. It could've been Monday."

"It'd be helpful if you'd think about it. You said Monday was a busy night, so it was different than other nights. Do you think she was here Monday?"

"It's possible. We see a ton of people, and unless someone

wins big, the nights kind of flow into each other, if you know what I mean."

Why weren't people more observant? If they'd take the time to make a simple connection, what they were wearing, the weather, or something that happened, it increased your ability to recall. It would make witnesses more confident in remembering what they saw and my job easier.

"Okay. You said Wade was nice and a good player."

"She was."

"What else can either of you tell me about her?"

The cocktail waitress said, "One day she came in with a big bruise on her face. I was like, what happened? And she said she and her husband had a fight and he hit her. We're not supposed to say anything to the customers that's personal. But I was, like, that's crazy, you know?"

"Were there any other times she came in banged up?"

They shook their heads.

"How often would she come in?"

"I'd say at least once a week. Right, Dolores?"

"That's about right."

"Was she friendly with anyone? Somebody who works here or a customer?"

"She was nice to everybody that was playing at my table. Sometimes a guy playing would try to hit on her."

"Did she ever—engage them?"

"I saw her at the bar a couple of times talking to men but don't know if anything more came of it."

"Did she ever come in with someone?"

"Not that I saw."

"Me either."

A beep sounded, and the other people in the room rose and got ready to go back on the floor. The cocktail waitress said, "I've got to get my shoes on."

I thanked them and walked back into the casino. Three men, all wearing cowboy hats, were setting up on a small stage in the Zig Zag Lounge. I circled through the gaming tables and exited through the hotel entrance.

A bus was unloading a group of seniors. The parking lot was across the entrance. I went around the motor coach and headed into the rows of parked cars looking for Beth Wade's vehicle.

A FILM of dust made the Mustang appear off-white. It was parked in the rear of the self-park lot, next to a red pickup truck. As most places did, the closest spots were either designated for the handicapped or used by the valet service.

For those who parked their own cars, the walk to the casino was an unsubtle way of making you feel like a cheapskate. I didn't consider myself cheap, but why spend money you didn't have to? I didn't need the valet's confirmation I was a good guy by handing over a fiver.

Peering inside the car, there was nothing that raised an alarm. I circled the car, begging it to give me a signal.

I looked toward the casino. It was more than two football fields away. It must have been a busy night. Or had she parked out here for privacy? A dense, wooded area encircled most of the lot. It was only steps away from her car. Could an attacker have been hiding in there? It took me a minute to roll a couple of scenarios around.

Going back to my Cherokee, I grabbed a tool kit we used to open car doors. I opened the door in less time than it takes to tie a shoe. Gloves on, I searched the glove compartment. Besides the owner's manual, there was nothing but a handful of old insurance cards, Burger King napkins, and two pens.

Under the driver's seat was an empty water bottle; on the passenger's side, just a dirty quarter. I popped the trunk. A satchel bearing the logo of State Farm sat next to a pair of sneakers and a couple of Publix shopping sacks.

I unzipped the State Farm bag. It contained a light blue blouse, a beige bra, a pair of jeans, and a thong. They appeared to be freshly laundered. Wade had a change of clothes. Why? Was she expecting to stay over at the casino's hotel? Or somewhere else?

Finding her car changed everything. It was now likely something bad had happened to Beth Wade. The question was if she was still alive. It was weird; I found myself hoping that she'd been kidnapped.

What else was strange was the need for a tow truck since her husband drove one for a living. We needed to protect the car. The sheriff's office had a good working relationship with the Seminole Tribe, but it was on the casino's property, and if the vehicle contained any evidence, I needed to maintain the integrity of its custody.

The possibility that Wade was trapped somewhere elevated the urgency. Time was not in our favor. Most kidnapping victims were killed soon after being abducted.

I made the call to transport the car before getting approval from the casino. I didn't expect pushback and didn't get any, but that didn't mean the Seminoles would give me carte blanche as we ramped up the investigation. Chester needed to know we'd found her vehicle and be ready for a tussle over jurisdiction.

6

Sheriff Chester was sitting at an oval table signing a document. He peered over his reading glasses as I entered his office.

"That time of the year. The state seems to add a new certification each time. They added yet another one on diversity training. I read it twice. It's almost a carbon copy of the original from two years ago."

"Keeps the lawyers busy."

"Probably a lawsuit had them change a word or two. Sit down."

There was only one chair without papers on it, and it was right next to Chester. As I sat, I picked up the smell of his eucalyptus-infused breath. Was he coming down with a cold? I scooted my chair a few inches away.

"As I mentioned, it appears Beth Wade might be in trouble."

He tossed his pen aside. "I hope you're wrong, Frank."

"Me too, but there's only two explanations for why she left her car behind, and I'm leaning toward abduction."

"You believe someone kidnapped her in the casino's parking lot?"

"Yes, it's likely. Of course, she could also have been killed there and her body moved. But there's no evidence, at least the blatant type, to support that."

"No other theories?"

"There is a slight chance she left with someone, but why leave her car there? Why no call to your husband or your mother, who said they talk every single day? Unless Wade wanted to disappear completely, but there's nothing in her background to suggest she needed or wanted to run."

"If she wanted to make a new start, it's possible she'll reach out to the mother later, after things settle down."

"Possibly, but I'm getting a feeling she's in trouble. We need to dig in, see if there's any hint of a scandal, crime, major money issues, something that would motivate her to run."

"I hope for her and her mother's sake that she took off."

As the father of a daughter, it was tough to imagine hoping your kid took off without a warning. "Of course. Given what appears to have happened, time is of the essence. I'm not saying the Seminoles are going to give us a hard time, but it'd be helpful if you could speak with them."

"We have an excellent relationship with them. Are you implying that someone in the tribe may be involved?"

Before Chester became sheriff, relations with the Seminoles were poor. He improved communications and policing in Immokalee tamping fears crime would spread to Naples. The success of his policies earned him a second term. "I have no reason to believe so, sir. I'm trying to avoid any stonewalling."

"If this is an abduction or worse, the Major Crimes Act

would give jurisdiction to the federal courts, meaning the FBI would probably be running things."

"I know, sir, but what I am looking for is their cooperation. We're going to need access to all their CCTV footage."

"I'll reach out to Chairman Osceola. He's always been helpful. I can't see it being a problem. After all, we handle their policing."

He was right, to a degree. The casino was on the Immokalee Reservation, one of six owned by the Seminole Tribe. It was a tiny reservation, just about a square mile, and it was all about the casino. If there was even the hint that someone with the casino was involved or that they had covered anything up, I was certain they'd try to freeze us out. There was simply too much money involved.

DERRICK WAS EATING raw vegetables and hummus at his desk. What the hell kind of a lunch was that? After getting bladder cancer, I altered my diet, but I couldn't go that far.

"What did the boss have to say?"

"He's calling the tribe leadership, to make sure we're not going to run into anything."

"You think she's been kidnapped?"

"We don't know enough. She could've run, but that's as rare as an empty restaurant in season. Run a credit check on her, and find out what you can from her employer and coworkers."

"I'm on it. Kidnapping is pretty rare, no? Most of the ones we had in DC were parents taking their own kids."

"There's a quarter of a million kids taken each year, the far majority of them by a disgruntled parent. Most of them end up okay, but three quarters of children abducted by a stranger are murdered, and quickly."

"Bastards."

"Scum of the earth. A lot of adult kidnappings are sexual in nature. They're grabbed and raped, sometimes for long periods, but usually end up dead."

"And most of the time a family member is involved. It's frigging disgusting."

"Mental illness is the only way to explain this shit. It's seems like it's easier to kill than to imprison someone."

"Hell of a lot riskier."

"That's why they end up dead."

"So, we're looking at a male?"

"Not quite a hundred percent, but probably. Before you check on her job, put in a warrant request for Wade's phone records. I'm going to see one of her girlfriends."

I SLIPPED on the wet driveway, and a dog began yapping. Was that its way of laughing? Paws on a glass sidelight, the cocker spaniel had proven to be a good alarm.

The door swung open before I could ring the bell.

"Behave, Tinker Bell! You want to get locked up?"

"Cybill Gates?"

"Yes, you're the detective looking for Beth?"

I nodded and showed her my badge as the dog ran circles around my legs.

"Come on in. He gets excited when anyone comes in."

Wade's friend wore cranberry capri pants and sandals. Gates was thin, had short black hair, and pearl earrings. It might have been the dog's name, but her nose brought to mind Peter Pan.

"She still hasn't turned up?"

"Not yet, ma'am."

She pushed the dog's bed away with her foot. "Is sitting over here okay?"

"It's fine."

We sat around a bistro table for two. Tinker Bell had grown bored and curled up under the table.

"What can you tell me about Beth Wade?"

"Well, we met about five or six years ago. We met at LA Fitness."

"She worked out regularly?"

"We both did. I mean, we still do."

"What about her relationships?"

"I didn't know her first husband, but from what she said, he was no winner."

"What about John Frelig?"

"They had problems, no doubt. Beth wanted to have a baby, but it wasn't a good situation and she was frustrated. Some days she'd say she went to the gym to deal with her anger."

"I understand she'd get physical at times."

"I never saw her do anything, but she told me that when she was in school, she used to get into fights."

"We've responded to a couple of domestic violence calls involving Beth and her husband."

"Like I said, they don't have the best marriage."

"Did she mention leaving him?"

"A couple of times."

"Was she seeing anyone else romantically?"

"She'd flirt with guys in the gym, especially Jerry, but I don't know if it went anywhere."

"Jerry? What can you tell me about him?"

"He's one of those bodybuilders. To me, they're really gross, but Beth loves the way they look."

The first thing that popped in my head was someone like Jerry using steroids and how they could make people violent.

It turned out that Cybill Gates didn't know Beth outside of the gym. I left with the gym's address and questions as to why the mother gave me her name.

7

———

Hanging up the phone, I made a U-turn and pressed the accelerator. The call from Derrick had me exceeding the speed limit. He'd uncovered two leads related to Beth Wade's job, where her responsibilities were reviewing large insurance claims that adjusters had approved.

It was a method many companies used to combat fraud. While it frustrated policyholders, it was necessary, as adjusters and claimants could work together to inflate claims.

I was on Golden Gate Boulevard heading east to see a man upset with Beth Wade. He had submitted a large homeowner's claim that an adjuster had approved. The dollar amount exceeded the company's ten-thousand-dollar threshold, and it was sent for review. It was assigned to Wade, who reduced the claim by more than half.

Making a left on Everglades Boulevard, I took the first right onto Second Avenue NE. There was no need to check the address; I was certain it was the home, with a pair of blue tarps tacked on.

There was no way to tell for sure, since a tarp was

blocking the view, but it appeared that the right section of the home was tilted. Had it broken away? Walking up the drive I saw aluminum support beams piled up in the backyard; the lanai cage had been destroyed.

A light breeze was fanning a section of aluminum siding as I rang the bell. The door squeaked as a burly man in a tank top opened it. The hair on his shoulders made me question his choice in shirts.

"Mr. Anderson?"

"Yeah, want do you want?"

He blinked when I showed him my badge. "Detective Luca, with the Collier County Sheriff's Office. I have a couple of questions for you."

"Me? What about?"

"Can we do this inside?"

"I'm in the middle of something."

"It won't take long."

He hesitated before moving aside. "All right, then."

Cracks in the wall running from floor to ceiling had me wondering whether entering was a good idea. I followed him into the kitchen. It was all white and updated. A TV hanging under a cabinet had a game show on. We sat around a table that had on it a water bottle and a newspaper opened to the sports page.

"What's this all about?"

"Your insurance claim with State Farm."

He shifted in his chair. "It was a legitimate claim. You should be hassling them."

"Tell me about it."

"What's there to say? They took my damn premiums for years, and then when I have a claim, they screw me over."

"What was the nature of the claim?"

"The hurricane. It destroyed most of this place. They sent a guy right away, and I thought everything was going okay. It was too good to be true. The adjuster, he was good; he saw everything was a mess and approved the claim, but then, all of a sudden, what he said didn't count, and they denied most of it."

"Why was that?"

"You ask me? It was that frigging woman reviewing the claim. I heard these people get a piece of how much they reduce the payout. She was a real bitch."

"What was the reasoning behind it?"

"Like I said, it was all about the money. It was a big claim, and she'd get a lot of money by screwing me."

"What were the specifics behind the denial?"

"I lost my roof and half the siding, and they didn't have any problem with that. But my family room, office, and bathroom, it frigging separated from the house. We can't even use them. It has to be torn down and rebuilt with a new foundation and all. The adjuster pegged fixing it at eighty-three thousand."

"And the hurricane did that?"

"What else could it be? That bitch said it was faulty workmanship, a bunch of bullshit about the foundation."

"Was it an addition to the house?"

"Yeah, about eight years ago I put it on. They didn't have a problem charging me more money to insure it. They said the house was worth more and jacked up the premium. I'm telling you, those bastards got some racket going."

"The reviewer was a woman named Beth Wade?"

"Yeah, that's her. Frigging crook."

"Did you meet with her?"

"Just once. What a cocky bastard."

Maybe her overconfidence is what kept her playing black-jack. "Did you meet here? And what happened when you met?"

"Yeah, she came here, but it was a waste of time. She didn't want to hear it. She wouldn't budge on the extension, and I had to twist her arm to get her to give me something for the pool cage."

"And what happened after that meeting?"

"Nothing. I was screwed. Look at this place. I ain't got the money to fix it, and the county is up my ass threatening to condemn it. Can you believe it? They want to throw me out of my own house 'cause I can't get the money to fix it back up."

It sounded unfair, but I didn't have the facts. My role wasn't to referee an insurance claim but to see if the insured had anything to do with the missing woman.

"Have you ever been in trouble?"

He hesitated. "Look, I'm almost fifty, stuff's come up, but nothing serious."

"You don't consider getting arrested for assault serious?"

"Hold on now. What would you do if you bought a car and a couple of days later it needed a whole bunch of under-carriage work? They sold me a lemon. I bought the used-car warranty, and they wouldn't make good on it. They're nothing but crooks. You know, all that shit they say about used-car salesmen? Well, it's all true."

"That doesn't give you the right to beat the guy with a chair."

"He took my fucking money for the warranty but wouldn't honor it."

"The record shows that you damaged the car by running over something."

"That's bullshit, and what difference would it make? Huh? They should just make it right."

Tony Anderson was one of those people who never took responsibility; it was always someone else's fault. The way he justified the assault made him someone we needed to know more about.

8

THE LA FITNESS ON VANDERBILT AND US 41 OCCUPIED what had been a grocery store. It was a massive gym with banks of treadmills, cycles, and other exercise equipment. In a section packed with benches and free weights, four men were doing overhead presses.

All of them were shirtless and had bodies Arnold Schwarzenegger would be proud of. I pulled my shoulders back and approached the group as they shouted encouragement to an older man who was bench-pressing a couple of soda cans.

Even without my sports jacket, I stuck out. The musclemen looked my way, exchanging a couple of words. Did they think I was with the DEA?

"Sorry to interrupt, gents, but I need a word with Jerry."

A slab of granite that could have been carved by Michelangelo stepped forward. "Who's asking?"

His hands were manicured, and there were so many veins on his forearm it looked like a Google map. "A friend of Beth Wade."

He hesitated. "I'm in the middle of a workout."

"It won't take long."

"I'm training for a competition. I can't break the cycle."

"No more than five minutes."

"I'll be right back. Johnny, do your scrunchies."

I felt the heat coming off him as we walked into the locker room. His body had more definition than a dictionary. The weightlifter's skin was flushed, a telltale sign of steroid use.

"That's a ton of weight for an overhead lift."

"Came in second in the county last year."

A couple of teenagers were hurrying into their bathing suits. Guess they wanted to walk the beach while the workout pump lasted.

Jerry Belcher had acne on his chin and jawline, another sign of steroid usage. "When was the last time you saw Beth Wade?"

"I don't know, a couple of days ago."

"Where?"

"Here, in the gym."

"What day was it?"

"Monday."

"How was she?"

"What do you mean?"

"Was she acting unusual?"

"I don't think so."

"Did you and her have something going on?"

"What do you mean by that?"

Was he all muscle and no brain, or stalling? "Did you see her outside the gym? Go on a date?"

"A couple of times."

"Doing what?"

"We screwed around some."

"You had sexual relations with her?"

"Yeah, that's right. There's no law against that."

"Did you know she was married?"

As he shrugged, his shoulder muscles grazed his ears.

"Do you know where she is?"

"No. Why would I know?"

"She's gone missing."

"I got nothing to do with that."

"So, you don't know where she is?"

"No clue, man."

"You juicing?"

"No, never. Look, I got to get back to training, man."

He was lying about the steroid use. Was he also lying about Beth Wade?

COMING in from the parking lot, I saw Derrick from behind.

"Where are you going?"

He turned around. "Perfect timing. Come on, we're going up to FCU."

I followed him into the stairwell. "What's going on?"

"Looks like Wade was trying to get a loan."

"How large?"

"Perez didn't say."

The Financial Crimes Unit was in a separate room on the second floor. The secluded space wasn't the only thing that differentiated the division. Everyone working there was more like an accountant than a cop. After Jessie was born and Mary Ann was moving off the street to a desk job, I wanted her to work here rather than the Cyber Sex Unit she ended up in.

The office was library quiet. Victor Perez was a fireplug in size but not demeanor. He was hidden behind a pair of monitors. At any of the social functions the sheriff's department had, Perez kept to himself.

Derrick said, "What do you have for us, Vic?"

Perez gave us a nod. "Both Equifax and Experian reported two inbound requests for credit on Ms. Wade."

"Do we know how much she was looking to borrow?"

"Without a warrant, we only have a range."

I said, "And what range was that?"

"Mid five figures."

"About fifty thousand dollars?"

"That is the middle."

Derrick said, "Where did she go to borrow the money?"

"Without a warrant, we can only ascertain the type of institution a prospective borrower approached."

"Were they banks?"

"Yes."

I said, "With a warrant, what kind of detail can we obtain?"

"That depends on what is in the request."

I wanted to choke Perez. "Could we get the application?"

"Yes."

———

DERRICK SAID, "You think we should get a warrant?"

"We need to know what she wanted the money for. It couldn't be for a home; you'd go for a mortgage. Wade lives in an apartment, so it's not for renovations. Did she want it to finance a new start?"

"Fifty grand is a lot of money, but you're not going to disappear with it."

"She may have had a gambling debt that needed to get paid off."

"Maybe whoever she owed it to grabbed her at the casino and is holding her until they get paid."

"No ransom calls at this point, and it's getting late in the game."

"She could have told them she was waiting on a loan."

"Why abduct her?"

"Maybe it's not the first time she said that."

"How long does it take for something like a personal loan, 'cause that's what it sounds like it was."

"Should be just a couple of days. We need to know when she applied and what she put down as a reason. It could be she was being blackmailed."

"Over an affair?"

"She was fooling around with Mr. Universe. You never know."

"You think someone could have filmed her during sex?"

My mind went straight to the second case I had worked down here. "That's a real possibility. It's happening a lot these days."

"Cameras are so tiny."

"You really have to be careful what you say and do today."

"She shouldn't have put herself in such a position."

"We don't know she did anything. Let's collect facts first. Draft up a warrant request for all documents and communications on the loan."

9

―――――

JESSIE RAN TOWARD ME AS I WALKED IN THE HOUSE. "DADDY, Daddy, Mommy and me made you a cake, for your birthday."

She said birthday like burp-day, but it was wonderful and the only thing positive about my descent into middle age. I'd been thinking a lot about the passage of time, and none of it was good. Jessie was the best thing in my life, but how quickly she was growing was a constant reminder that Father Time was undefeated.

Scooping her up, I said, "You made me a cake? What kind?"

"Chocolate with mnms."

"M&M's are my favorite. Can I have a piece now?"

"Me too, Daddy."

"After dinner, guys. Tell Daddy we also made his favorite meal."

"You did? What did you make?"

"Pasta and spada."

Pasta e pesce spada linguine and swordfish had leapfrogged other macaroni dishes after making a recipe I found online researching Sicilian wines. Swordfish was so prevalent in Sicily, it was surprising they didn't have it for breakfast.

"Oh wow! This is the best birthday, ever."

"And we got you a present. A hat for the beach."

"Oh boy. I can't believe it. Thanks so much."

Forty-five didn't feel good. I pushed myself to choose one of my better wines to have with dinner. It was to dull reality, not to celebrate.

Dinner was good, but the best part was getting Jessie to help blow out the candles. Luckily, Mary Ann had refrained from numerical candles and had stuck three in the center of a chocolate-frosted cake dotted with M&M's.

"No, Jessica. Use your fork, not your hands." Mary Ann moved the cake out of her reach.

"It's okay. We'll wash her up."

I didn't care that when she tried to pluck a piece of candy off the cake, she'd end up with frosting-covered hands.

"It's getting late. She needs to get a bath. Want to give Daddy his present?"

"Yeah, yeah."

"Let me clean your hands first."

I wore my #1 Dad hat as I read *The Jungle Book* to Jessie. Mary Ann said the sugar was going to keep her up, but she was out like a light a couple of pages into the Kipling classic.

"I hope you had a good birthday. We'll go out alone Saturday. Where do you want to go?"

"We don't have to."

"But we always go out and celebrate our birthdays."

"What's there to celebrate? Getting old?"

"You're not old, Frank."

"More than half my life is over."

"Half your life? You can be so dramatic."

"It's not drama, it's reality. If I'm lucky, I live to what, eighty-six, eighty-seven? It's half over, and that's not even discounting for what kind of life I'm going to have when I reach my eighties."

"That's ridiculous. There are plenty of older people living full lives. Look around you, for God's sake."

She was right. Down here, there were tons of people in their nineties that were more active than teenagers. "You're right, but it still doesn't change the math; half my life is over."

"If you look at it that way. But that's a depressing way to view it."

"There's no other way. It is what it is."

"Why not look at the gift of another forty-five years? I don't care what anyone says, forty, thirty, or even twenty years is a lot of time."

"I guess so."

"It is so. Look, we've known each other less than ten years. We have a lot of life ahead of us."

I said she was right but didn't really believe it. Maybe it was the scare I had with cancer and the constant nag in my mind that I was one of the people it was going to come back to. Forcing a mind shift, I said, "It'll be good to see Jessie grow up. Man, she was so happy that I was wearing the hat she gave me."

Mary Ann got up and sat in my lap. "I have another present for you. You want to start unwrapping?"

BEFORE JESSIE COULD EVEN CRAWL, I stopped leaving my gun out. I put my fingers on the firearm safe and the lid popped open. Picking up my Glock 30, I set it on the nightstand and went into the closet to grab my holster.

As I clipped on the holster, Jessie ran into the bedroom.

"Daddy, can I come to work?"

I bolted out and grabbed my gun.

"What's that, Daddy?"

I jammed it into its leather housing. "Something I need for work."

"What do you need it for?"

"Everybody at work has one."

"How come?"

"Just to . . . in case we need it."

"For what?"

She needed to know what a gun was at some point, but not today. "Oh, I almost forgot my hat. Do you see it?"

Jessie ran out. "Mommy! Daddy can't find the present!"

In another year, she wouldn't be so easy to distract. The Human Resources Department held a seminar dealing with the children of officers. I remember the speaker saying that kids under six would accept what you said and wouldn't recognize the danger a parent could face. The issue became more complicated as they matured; their exposure to crime and the role that law enforcement officers played raised real fears that had to be dealt with delicately.

It wasn't a conversation I was looking forward to, but I was glad I insisted that Mary Ann get a desk job. As for me, I wasn't patrolling the streets, but I wasn't working at Disney World either.

Shoving my wallet into a back pocket, my phone vibrated. It was a text from Derrick. He wanted to be sure I was coming in because he had uncovered information on a man that could be involved in Beth Wade's disappearance.

10

———

"Morning, Derrick."

"Morning. How was the birthday celebration?"

"Jessie made me a cake. She was so excited about it, I almost cried."

"She's so cute."

"You and Lynn thinking about having kids yet?"

"Thinking? She's pushing to have one now."

"You're not ready?"

"I was trying to follow the advice you gave me. You said to settle into the marriage, not to rush it."

I guess it was good guidance when I said it, but my position had shifted. "You guys are mature, and you've known each other a long time. You're married for a while, and if it's going good—"

"Yeah, it's going great."

"Go for it. You don't want to be like me; when Jessie turns ten and is playing soccer, I'll be the oldest father watching."

"That's why you have to take care of yourself."

I picked up the coffee he'd brought me. It was cold. "What time did you get here?"

"I guess I was a little anxious, couldn't sleep, and figured I'd come into the office."

"What did you find out?"

"I tracked down information on a guy named Roger Berry."

"Who?"

"He owns a contracting company and worked on a renovation on a hotel that Florida Peninsula had a claim on."

"A contractor?"

"Yep. And guess what happened?"

If he hadn't given me such a nice compliment earlier, I would have had to make a comment about the guessing games he loved to play. "No idea."

"Remember when the La Playa was under renovation, and then the hurricane hit?"

"Yeah, there was scaffolding around the hotel just before the storm."

"Because of the work being done, the La Playa was exposed, and water got into the building and caused all kinds of damage. The hotel wasn't able to open on time. They were shut for a couple of months longer than they had planned."

"I remember reading about it."

"The insurance claim was over a million dollars."

It was interesting, but what was he getting at? "And how is this contractor involved?"

"So, Florida Peninsula paid the claim to La Playa, but they sued the contractor for negligence based on a review by, guess who?"

I knew the answer to this one. "Beth Wade."

"Bingo. And guess what else?"

"Come on, guy. Just tell me, will you?"

"Sorry. The contractor is owned by Roger Berry, and he had a record for assault, but here is the best part; he was indicted in a murder-for-hire plot on an ex-partner."

"What happened?"

"He ended up pleading it down and served two years in Orlando."

"Jesus, this is big. Why didn't you tell me last night?"

"It was your birthday. I didn't want to interfere; you're always telling me about making sure I lead a balanced life."

I had to be careful with what I said to him.

"All right, we've got to get our priorities in order. Get a picture of Roger Berry and put it on the board. We have two guys that are work related. Both of them believe Wade screwed them out of money, in Berry's case, a ton of it. Though, relatively speaking, the money might mean more to Tony Anderson. And they both have records. Find out if Berry is still in business. If the suit put him out of business, that'd be a powerful motivator for revenge."

"We finally got the warrant for her phone records. I know it doesn't work like it does on TV, but these judges could do a lot better."

"The judges are pretty good down here. What needs speeding up are lab results."

"Yeah, definitely."

"I told Chester we need the casino videos ASAP. There's going to be hours of it. Let's see what we learn from it. If we see someone or something, we're on our way; if not, we'll establish that she was there and what time she arrived and left."

"If she left through the front door."

"I'm hoping we catch her leaving with someone."

"You think she's still alive?"

The phone rang, and as Derrick reached for it, I said, "I hate to say it, but I'm losing faith."

Derrick said, "It's Michael Whitaker."

I tried to recall if I knew what he did for a living. He was organized and never failed to follow up.

"Hello, Mr. Whitaker. How are you?"

"I'm fine, Detective Luca. I was calling to see what progress has been made in my father's case."

"Well, nothing has changed at this point. We're still waiting on an exhumation request."

"There's been no progress?"

"I'm sorry, but not yet."

"But you told my mother that you were confident you'd be able to bring this to a conclusion."

He was right. "I'm certain we will."

"Mother has waited thirty years, and her health isn't good. At this point in her life, just about the only thing she cares about is seeing that justice is done."

"I understand, and we're very close to providing that for her."

"How close? What is the time line?"

"It's difficult to say. It's out of my hands at this point. I submitted a request, and we'll have to see when it gets approved."

"So, it will be approved, and it's just a matter of time?"

"I believe so."

"Believe so or know so?"

"Exhumations are delicate and controversial. I wish I could provide more assurance, but there is nothing more I can say except that I'm committed to solving this case."

"That's what we've been hearing for thirty years. You shouldn't be making promises you can't keep, especially to someone like my mother."

He was right about the promises part, but I could solve this one. I knew it. "Thank you for calling. As soon as I have some news, I'll let your mother know."

I hung up and Derrick said, "He wouldn't let up?"

"No, but he's right. I wanted to tell him and his mother to call Chester. He's the one holding it up."

"He's not going to approve it, is he?"

"I doubt it."

"Why don't we do what you suggested with that kid in the Boyle case?"

"What are you talking about?"

"Remember, the kid who was a person of interest but had died? You didn't think it was him, and you wanted to avoid disturbing his parents, so you said to do the familial DNA testing."

How the hell did I forget that? Most of the effects of the chemo I was doused with had dissipated, but more often than was acceptable a hole in my memory would appear.

11

───────

IT WATCHED A KID PUT DOWN A NEW URN OF COFFEE. I HAD timed it perfectly. They always made fresh coffee in the cafeteria around 3:00 p.m., just when everyone started to drag. I pulled back the lever and inhaled as the coffee filled my #1 Dad mug.

"Excuse me, Detective Luca?"

I turned around. "Yes."

"This is for you."

He handed me an inch-thick manila envelope. "Thanks. You could have left it on my desk."

"The captain said to give it to you."

This newbie had to be careful not to get a paper cut from his pressed uniform. "As long as you put it in someone's in-box, you're covered." His name tag said Burlew, but the rest of him screamed rookie.

"Thank you, sir."

I broke the tape and took the contents out. It was two packets of documentation on the loans Beth Wade applied for. I started with the application she made to SunTrust Bank. She had asked for the loan on June 21, using the bank's internet loan portal. Less than three weeks before her disappearance, she wanted to borrow thirty thousand dollars.

She listed her income at sixty-five thousand dollars a year. Her husband was working as well, making me wonder, with the salary she made plus whatever he made, why they rented rather than owned a home. Was she gambling her money away?

I scanned the section where she stated what the money was going to be used for. Wade had listed simply that it was to pay for her mother's medical bills. Her mother seemed healthy. Was this a cover, or was there really a need for a treatment of some kind?

Grabbing the Wells Fargo documents, I flipped to see what she had listed as the reason. It was consistent. She was asking for a personal loan. You didn't go that route if you were buying a house, car, or starting a business.

Rather than call one of the stiffs in the Financial Crimes Unit, I Googled why most people applied for personal loans. Out of all the reasons, the only thing that made sense was to consolidate your debt. Rifling through the paperwork, I found Beth Wade's credit report.

She was carrying balances on her Visa and Mastercard credit cards that were both over ten thousand dollars. Was she looking to pay them off and substantially reduce the interest she was throwing away each month? If she used the thirty thousand to pay her debt off, she'd have about eight thousand left over. Was that for her mother or for gambling?

Derrick came in carrying his gun case. It was luggage-like and held five pistols. He was more of a firearms collector than I was.

I said, "How'd it go?"

"Aced it. I really like the new SIG Sauer. You should try it. They really improved the sight."

"Maybe next time. I'm good for another five months."

"I wish I could clean these guys now. I hate letting any residue harden."

"Do it tonight. It's not a problem."

Three of my guns needed thorough scrubbings and oiling. Two marksmanship certifications and months had passed since their last cleaning. Waiting any longer would be irresponsible. I knew two Jersey cops whose firearms had jammed, misfiring during an ambush. Fortunately, neither of them paid with their lives for being lazy.

It wasn't laziness. It was because of Jessie. There was no way I was going to hide in my closet and do a rush job on them. I needed her out of the house for a good hour before I'd start. The last time I cleaned them, she was napping but woke up and came into the office as I was dismantling my Glock.

"We got the loan documents. Wade was looking to borrow thirty thousand. She said it was for her mother's medical bills, but the credit report said she had over twenty grand on her credit cards."

"Twenty thousand? That's crazy. The interest has to be a couple of hundred a month."

"Debt controls you. Your choices are limited, and it should be avoided at all costs. I know life happens and sometimes you can't help it because of illness or maybe education, but most of the time, it's really simple; you don't have the money for something, don't get it."

"I know. My dad never used a credit card. My mom had one for emergencies, but they were old school."

"Did they have a mortgage?"

"A small one, but they paid it off early."

"Your parents are a rare breed."

"I thought he was cheap, growing up, but they retired at

sixty-two, and he bought a nice boat. It's used, but it's nice. He loves to fish, and they're happy."

"That's what counts, partner. Look, give Mrs. Wade a call. See if she has any medical issues or needs. Remember, she doesn't have to tell you. Ask her if there's any reason she would know that her daughter was looking for a loan."

"I'm on it. By the way, I checked on Berry's business, and it's still going."

"I want to talk to him. What I don't understand is how the heck did this guy, a convicted felon, land a job working on La Playa? That's a major league place."

"That don't matter, Frank. He served his time, and it's not like he's working with kids or in a security position. He's in construction."

"You're right. I guess I'm just frustrated. I talked to Chester, and he doesn't even want to talk about the exhumation. I'm going to pursue the familial DNA angle."

"It's really coming along. I was reading *American Police Beat* magazine last night. Do you get it?"

I shook my head.

"I like it. They had an article about searching the public databases, like Ancestry.com, for familial links to the DNA collected at a crime scene."

"I heard about that, but the sites don't want to cooperate anymore."

"Yeah, Ancestry.com and 23andMe supposedly got a lot of feedback and shut the door on us."

"I'm going to approach the kids, see if they'll give me DNA samples."

"Their father's dead; it shouldn't matter."

"I hope you're right, but I don't know if I'd even do it. Who wants to find out their father was a killer?"

"But if they believe he was innocent, it would clear him."

12

———

Derrick came in holding a shoebox. "They have the video."

I looked in the box; there were at least a twenty thumb drives. "Even if we divide it up, we're going to be at this for days."

"That's what I thought. At least they're labeled."

"We'll start with the entrance and parking lot surveillance, then go to the blackjack tables."

I pawed through the box. Most of them were tagged as videos of the gaming tables and slot machines. Three were labeled casino floor and another Zig Zag Bar.

I pulled out two drives, handing one to Derrick. "Take the entrance. I've got the parking lot."

"I'll grab a couple of coffees."

I popped the drive in and plugged 6:45 p.m., July 7 into the viewing program.

Coverage was limited. The camera only reached half of the lot's depth. Beth Wade's Mustang was parked much deeper in the lot. I played the video fast enough so I could see when anyone appeared, slowed it to see if it was Wade, then sped up again.

I kept my eyes on the monitor as Derrick handed me a cup. "The camera doesn't cover the entire lot. Wade's vehicle was parked out of view."

"We'll still see her entering."

"Yeah. Also, they gave us a feed that started in the middle of last month."

Sipping my coffee, I watched a steady stream of cars and an occasional bus enter the parking lot. The valet guys were parking half the vehicles that came up the driveway.

At 8:07 p.m. a white Mustang made a right into the parking lot. "I think it's her." I froze the frame as it passed and checked the rear plate. "Yeah, it's her."

I hit play and watched her make a left down the second aisle of cars before turning right toward the rear of the lot and out of view. I replayed the video. She was definitely alone. I let it play through until I saw her walk into view, stopping at the curb to let a bus pass. I hit pause and zoomed in.

Her shoulders weren't covered. It looked like the shirt her husband said she was wearing. I wasn't sure it was jeans, but whatever she was wearing hugged her curves. Her shoes were open-toed with a medium heel.

She stepped off the curb and crossed the street. There was nothing telling in the way she carried herself as she moved out of the camera's view.

I got out of my chair and came around Derrick's desk. "Go to eight oh five."

There was the spicy smell of his strong cologne. This Christmas I'd have to get him something a little subtler. We watched the doors slide back and forth as a handful of older women left. The video was high definition. We could use facial recognition software to get through all the footage, but the technology wasn't perfect, and I wanted to see things for myself.

A kid with tattooed arms came out and sat on a bench. The doors closed as he tapped out a cigarette.

As he lit his smoke, the casino's door slid open, and Beth Wade walked in.

I said, "She entered the casino at eleven minutes after eight."

"We have something to work with. She was definitely there."

"Check out the casino floor feeds. Follow her as best you can. See if she talks to anyone, where she goes. I'm keeping my eye on the entrance, see when she leaves."

I stood, rubbing my eyes. Two hours of staring at the screen and Beth hadn't exited. I'd fast-forwarded most of the time, and the stamp read fifteen minutes after ten. I knew gamblers could sit for hours playing, but I couldn't take the chance of hopping too far forward.

"You got anything?"

"I can't look at that red carpet much longer. This feed sucks. It's not the entire floor; it's the main passageways. I don't know why they even have this."

"Maybe to see if any players are working together. What about Wade?"

"She came into view twice. One time it looked like she was going to the bathroom, and another time toward the tables."

"Note the times, and switch to the blackjack tables."

Rubbing my neck, I sat back down and resumed the video. After ten minutes, Derrick said, "I got her. She's playing at a table with all men."

"She talking to any of them?"

"Looks like normal banter."

"She drinking?"

"There's nothing in front of her."

"How many chips she playing?"

"Oh, a cocktail waitress just came over. I can't believe they still wear those outfits. Looks like she ordered something."

"What about the chips?"

"Two red ones."

I got up to see for myself. "The reds are five dollars each. She's playing ten bucks a hand."

Wade was sitting in the last chair before the dealer had to play his cards. I knew that serious players wanted that seat, believing it gave them a measure of control. If they felt a picture card was due to come out, they'd hold off drawing a card to force the dealer to take it and bust.

"She has a nice couple of stacks of chips."

Wade put a green chip down. I said, "The greens are twenty-five bucks each."

"I don't think she was looking for a loan to pay Mom's medical bills. She's a gambler."

"They always believe they can win."

Wade slid another green chip into the circle.

"She's betting fifty bucks!"

"She's splitting her cards into two hands."

"You can do that?"

"Yes, most of the time people do it with two aces. Or with a pair of others, say nines, where they hope to get picture cards giving them nineteen, giving them a pretty good chance of winning two hands at once."

The dealer flopped over his cards and swept Wade's fifty bucks away.

"Not this time. She has a lot of chips; she should quit while she's ahead."

"Most gamblers believe they should press their luck when they're winning."

"I never really played cards, but my dad used to a little, and he always said to take some money off the table when you were winning."

"I'm with him. All or nothing isn't me."

Another dealer came up behind the table, and the woman dealing at Beth Wade's table raised her hands, clapped them, and stepped away. It was time to change dealers. Wade pushed a large stack of red chips forward.

"What is she, crazy?"

"She's not betting. She's exchanging them for greens, less to carry. She's moving on."

Wade did the same with her greens, getting a couple of blacks in return and left the table.

"Where's she going?"

"Probably to another table. She felt her luck was changing and that the new dealer wasn't going to help."

"She's heading to the bar."

"Look at the drive labeled Zig Zag. I want to go through the rest of the entrance."

13

———

The time stamp on the entrance footage read 1:45 A.M. and no sign of Wade leaving the casino. We needed to know how long she usually stayed.

Derrick said, "Some guy just sat down next to her."

I peered over Derrick's shoulder. The guy looked about fifty and had black hair and long sideburns. "You think Elvis and she know each other?"

"Looks like it, or she's one friendly lady."

The bartender set a fresh drink in front of Wade. "He's buying her a drink."

The man, who wasn't wearing a wedding band, clinked glasses with Wade and smiled.

"Find out who this guy is. Get a picture of him and ask the casino. The way he's talking to the bartender, he's a regular."

I stretched my back before sitting down. The video was playing for five minutes when Wade's drinking partner strolled out of the casino with a blond woman in a knee-high skirt and denim jacket.

"Elvis is leaving the building."

"She with him?"

"Nope, this guy gets around; he's with someone else." It was three minutes after two in the morning. I made a note to check the parking lot feed to make sure he left the grounds, but he didn't seem like he was someone we had to look into. For all we knew, the blond could have been his wife and had been playing the slots.

"Wade's on the move. She's heading to the gaming area."

"Let me know when you find her at a table."

There was no sign that Wade had left the casino. Had I missed her? The hotel claimed it had no record of her staying over. Did she slip away to a room with someone? If she did, it was likely a sexual encounter, as Wade didn't have a bag with her when she came in.

"She's standing behind a table watching people play. Maybe she's done for the night."

I looked at the video. There was an empty seat. "She's trying to get a feel for the table."

"A feel?"

"Yep. People who know how to play want to be sure they sit at a table with people who know the game. You don't want someone drawing a card when they shouldn't. Players really get pissed when that happens."

"But they have no idea what card is going to come up."

"To a large degree, but they try to increase their odds. If an ace hasn't come up in two rounds, they feel one is due. They're looking for a way to reduce the casino's built-in edge."

"What's the casino's advantage?"

"I think you can get it down to less than one percent if you play correctly. I remember one guy who played a lot; he would say certain bets were almost certain to lose."

"Makes sense to avoid sure losers."

"Yeah, but he was living in a rathole of a studio and drove a twenty-year-old car."

"She's sitting down."

"Looks like she knows the dealer and the guy next to her."

"Screenshot it, and get the casino to ID the dealer."

Derrick watched Wade play, and I went back to keeping an eye on the casino's doorway. The time stamp read 4:00 a.m., and there was no sign of her leaving. Derrick said, "Frank, check this out. It looks like the guy next to her put something in her drink."

I rolled my chair into the wall. "Let me see."

"See here, he's got his arm up, like he's trying to shield his hand. And look, right there, did he drop something in her glass?"

"Rewind it! Play it in slow motion."

I leaned into the monitor. "I'm not sure. It would have to be tiny and dissolve before she'd notice."

"There's some powerful crap out there. That date-rape drug GBH is a clear liquid, but I don't think this could be it. Maybe it could be Rohypnol without the blue dye. It dissolves fast, and no sign without the dye in it."

"This guy would have to have a set of balls to do this in public."

"It happens all the time in public. Maybe this guy has done it before. You don't need much; as little as one milligram can impair someone for eight to twelve hours."

"How do you know so much about this?"

"My second assignment in DC, I covered the nightclubs. We had a rash of incidents where older men would prey on twenty-year-old girls."

My thoughts went straight to Jessie. Just great. Something else to keep me up at night.

"Man, I'd like to set one of those guys straight. Man-to-man, not as a cop."

"People like them are deviants. They're mentally ill. No amount of prison time is going to straighten them out."

"Let's get back to business before I give myself a stroke."

"You want me to get the lab to see what they can get out of it?"

"You can try, but if the pixels aren't there, they're not going to be able to do anything with it. This ain't *CSI*, where you push a button and everything turns crystal clear."

My phone rang. "Detective Luca."

"Hi, uh, this is Tim Whiting. You wanted to talk to me?"

Bill Tate had fathered a son and daughter, each with different women. He was the guy we thought killed John Whitaker thirty years ago. It was his son calling.

"Yes, yes. Thanks for calling. I'm in the middle of something at the moment, but I'd like to speak to you about your father."

"My father?"

"Yes."

"He's been dead for over fifteen years."

"I'm aware of that. You see, his name came up in another case, and we're trying to clear him, but that would require an exhumation."

He gasped. "You want to dig his body up?"

"Not if we don't have to."

"Just what kind of case is this?"

"A homicide."

"Oh God. You think my biological father killed someone?"

"We're not certain of anything."

"Just what do want from me?"

"We'd like to obtain a sample of your DNA and run some

tests. That way it would avoid having to do an exhumation. It's not invasive, just a simple swab. Won't take more than two minutes. Is that something you're willing to do?"

"Look, you called me out of the blue about my father, who wasn't around in the first place and is now dead. You really expect me to just agree to this, one, two, three?"

"I understand that this is surprising. Why don't you think about it, and we'll talk another time?"

"Fine."

The line went dead.

"That was Tate's son. I don't know how much help we're going to get from him."

My desk phone rang again, and Derrick said, "Maybe he's calling back to say yes."

If he had called back and agreed, it still wouldn't have been as surprising as the call that came in.

14

———

IT WAS A WEIRD CALL BUT COULD END UP BEING THE BREAK we needed. The caller was concerned about remaining anonymous and wouldn't give me his name. I couldn't discount it, because he claimed to have information about what may have happened to Beth Wade.

I pressed him on what he had, but he said he didn't know for sure what had happened, but he was sure what he had to tell us was something we needed to know. Derrick didn't want me going alone, but the caller didn't want anyone else coming.

There was no shortage of psychics and nutjobs that had called in since the case had gone public. The difference was he worked at the casino and was a Seminole.

Derrick took his own car, parking in a lot on Immokalee and Collier Boulevard that housed New York, New York Pizza's second location. He kept watch as I walked in.

The empty restaurant was newer than the original location and had a different vibe to it. It was sleeker, on the contemporary side. The one consistent was the glorious smell of pizza.

My stomach growled. It didn't know it was just after 3:00 p.m.

My contact hadn't arrived yet. I slid into a booth facing the door and ordered a diet Coke.

As the server delivered the soda, a man in mirrored sunglasses, dungarees, and a beat-up cowboy hat entered.

As he surveyed the place, I noticed his ponytail. It had to be my guy. I gave him a thumbs-up and waved him over.

He nodded and burrowed himself into the booth's corner. "You got to keep this quiet."

"Absolutely. What's your name?"

"Look, I can't get mixed up in this. I just wanted to tell you something."

"I understand. Why don't you tell me what you know about Beth Wade, the missing woman?"

"I don't know her or anything, but everyone started to talk about her coming to the casino and disappearing."

"You work at the casino?"

"Yeah. Been there since it opened."

"What do you do there?"

"Look, this is all I'm going to say, that you should take a look at Magi Seke. They call him Michael at the casino."

"He works there?"

He nodded.

"Can you tell me why we should be interested in him?"

"He kidnapped a girl about five years ago."

"Are you certain about that?"

"Everybody knows it. He kept her locked up for close to five months."

"Where did this happen?"

"Miccosukee."

"On the Miccosukee Reservation?"

"Yeah, he kept her in a trailer there."

"What happened? The girl escaped?"

He shook his head. "Magi isn't right. He's disturbed, you know. Everybody knows it, and between the girl going missing and the way he was acting, the elders put it together and freed the girl."

The tribe handled its own law enforcement in Miccosukee. "Don't tell me he got away with it?"

"Magi is the son of Peyak Chetan."

"Who's that?"

"Chetan is a very powerful tribe leader. He was the chairman when it happened, and he kept everything quiet. That's when they moved him here. I'm telling you to take a good look at Magi Seke." He slid to the edge of the booth. "I got to get going."

As he rose, I said, "Thank you. I'm going to use the bathroom."

Before the door closed behind him, I called Derrick and told him to grab the plate number of the vehicle he was driving.

I hustled to my car, processing the possibility that a well-connected casino employee had something to do with Beth Wade's disappearance. They would need help. There were plenty of people watching camera feeds. I visualized the security office and the men staring at monitors.

Reaching for the Cherokee's door handle, I froze. One of the video cameras covered the doorway to the hotel. It was the only camera feed the Seminoles hadn't given us. I kicked the front tire before getting in my vehicle.

Logging into the DMV portal from my laptop, I plugged in the name of the man we had learned about.

I stared at the driver's license photo of Magi Seke. His black hair was parted in the middle, and his nose looked to have been broken. It was his averted eyes that filled me with mistrust.

The Native American was forty-two years old, five feet eleven inches, and a hundred and ninety pounds. He was large enough to subdue Beth Wade, even as feisty as she was known to be. I needed to interview him as soon as possible.

CHESTER WAS out doing an assembly at Palmetto Ridge High School. Of all the days to do public relations, he had to pick this one? Maybe I shouldn't have been so keen to get his approval.

I had been a third of the way up Immokalee, talking to the Indian at New York, New York Pizza. I should have just driven to the casino and dealt with the fallout later.

Who did they think they were messing with, a damn rookie? They're probably laughing at me, believing they got something over on me. I should have realized it earlier, and for that matter, how come Derrick didn't notice we were missing the hotel footage?

Derrick stepped into our office waving a file. "Lab grabbed a couple of nice photos of the guy sitting next to Wade."

"You need to send them to the casino, if we can trust those bastards to identify him."

"What the heck's going on?"

"They think they're cute. They didn't include the camera coverage of the entrance to the hotel."

"Could just be an oversight."

"They give us twenty-three drives, and they forget the one that covers the hotel's doorway?"

"I know, but there's no sense jumping to conclusions."

I was an Olympic gold medalist in that event. "If we find out Wade used it to exit, we'll know they're stonewalling us."

"Let me call the guy in the security office I sent the photos to. I'll ask him for it."

"You know, we should have known it was missing."

"I didn't even know they had a second entrance. I never went—"

"So, it's my fault they didn't give us the video?"

"No, that's not what I'm saying at all, Frank. It wasn't our fault they didn't give it to us. What's the big deal that it took us a day to realize it? They gave us hundreds of hours of it."

The big deal was I was supposed to pick up on shit like that right off the damn bat. "Call whoever you need to and get us that video."

15

AFTER CHESTER CAME BACK FROM ADDRESSING A HIGH school full of kids, he had a meeting with the board of commissioners who headed Collier's government. I wouldn't get to tell him what I discovered and have him make sure no one in the Seminole Tribe was going to run interference in my inquires.

The meeting was scheduled for ninety minutes. I decided to use the time usefully. I turned off Airport Pulling Road onto J and C Boulevard. The industrial area was busy. I passed a granite and marble business with scores of van-sized pieces of stone on display, then an orange self-storage building, making a turn into the parking lot for Baker's Towing.

I pulled up next to a pair of large, red vehicles that were used to tow disabled trucks. A handful of cars were parked alongside the white cinder-block building.

Three dispatchers wearing headsets manned desks. They barely looked at me until I held up my badge. One of them, with a Mennonite beard, got out of his seat. "What can I do for you?"

"I wanted to find out about one of your drivers, John Frelig."

"What'd he do?"

"I'm not sure he did anything, but his wife is missing."

"Really? He ain't said nothing." He turned to his coworkers. "John say anything about his wife going missing?"

They shook their heads.

"Who's in charge here?"

"Me, I'm Ray Baker. I own this place."

"Detective Luca." We shook hands. "How well do you know Mr. Frelig?"

"He's been driving for us for a couple years, maybe three or so."

"Any trouble with him?"

"Not that I know of. You think he's mixed up with his wife going missing?"

"We have no reason to believe so. I imagine you keep records of the calls you respond to."

"Yeah, sure we do."

"I'd like to take a look at what you have for Monday, July seventh."

"All right. We got the slips from when we get a call, or I can show the computer stuff. My sister puts it all in there for me, otherwise, without the computer, the state won't use us for the interstate."

"If it's not too much trouble, I'd like to see both."

"Sure."

He took a brown, accordion-styled file out of his bottom drawer. "This here's the slips for the month; the sections are the days." He dug into the tab marked seven. "Here's what we did that day."

There were twenty-two yellow slips of paper. This place

was doing a minimum of a five thousand dollars a day. Not a bad business, but the towing vehicles were expensive.

"Which ones were handled by Frelig?"

"These three."

I examined the work orders. One was for a tow off Collier Boulevard and another on Santa Barbara Boulevard. The one I was interested in was a call that came in for a car stranded on Oil Well Road. It was just fifteen minutes from the casino.

"John Frelig responded to all of these?"

"Yep, his territory."

"What times did these come in?"

"Well, we don't put the times on the order. I guess we should do that."

"You don't know anything about when they came in?"

"Well, they're numbered, so, this one here, on Collier, came in first, and the one on Oil Well was last."

"What shift was Frelig working that night?"

"Eight at night to six in the morning."

"It says jump start on the ticket."

"Yeah, guy waved him down, so there was no tow. Sometimes the drivers can get the car started if it's not an accident."

"You still charge, then?"

"Yeah, it's not as good as a tow, but there's the call, which is fifty bucks, plus twenty for the jump start."

"The tickets says NC. Did you waive it?"

He shook his head. "Uh, it was cash. But you know, we declare it, Officer."

The last thing I was worried about was a towing company skimming some cash to avoid taxes. What I was interested in was the coincidence that Wade's husband was in the vicinity where she was last seen.

"How large a territory is Frelig responsible for?"

"Up until midnight we got four trucks on duty. But after ten things really slow down, so we only have two. One guy, and it's been Hank for about a year now, covers everything west of Seventy-Five, and Frelig has everything east."

"That's a lot of ground to cover."

"Like I said, not much going on after ten. I'd cut it down to one if the county would let me. Can't make any money on the overnights."

"You use GPS to track your trucks?"

"We thought about getting it, but it's not worth the money."

"You notice anything different in Mr. Frelig's behavior the last week or so?"

"I don't really see him, except in the morning, sometimes. I get in when he gets off. Saw him yesterday, he seemed okay to me."

"He close to anyone who works here?"

"Most drivers bounce around a lot but not John, he's kind of a loner, a weird bird, you know. I mean, he's been working the graveyard shift the whole time he's been here. That'll burn out most people."

"Has he ever lost his temper?"

He shrugged. "We all do, every now and then."

"I'm only interested in Mr. Frelig. Now, if you know something, I'm going to find out eventually, so tell me."

"It was really nothing. Just one guy breaking another guy's balls. You know?"

"No, I don't know. Tell me."

"Well, Jimmy Peaks, he's on the six a.m. shift. Well, he's got one of those long pickups, with the double cab and all. It's a Tundra, and well, he kept parking it in a way that blocked in Johnny's car. And it would piss him off."

"When Frelig got off his shift he couldn't get his car out to go home?"

"No, everybody's got to leave their keys with us. We don't give 'em the keys to a truck without their keys. We need to have enough room if we have to store any trucks on the lot. We do work for Publix, and they contract with a mechanic out of Estero who uses our lot. Anyway, he'd get out after we moved Jimmy's car."

"And he didn't want to wait around?"

"Yeah, he got into it with Jimmy, and then Jimmy, well, he started to do it every day, and one day Johnny came in just before Jimmy got off and sucker punched him and kicked him in the ribs. Jimmy couldn't drive for a couple weeks 'cause of the bruised ribs and all."

"How long ago did this happen?"

"I think about six months ago."

16

───────

A boom of thunder sounded as I entered the sheriff's office. Chester had his readers on and had a foot resting on an open desk drawer.

"It's going to pour, but we need it. Never seen a summer like this. Hot as hell but hardly raining. What's it been? Ten days without afternoon rain?"

"The lake in the back of our house is so low, you'd think it was February."

"We'll probably get five inches to even things out. What was so urgent that you felt it necessary to call three times?"

"Sorry, sir. I knew you had an interest in the Beth Wade case, and I wanted to update you on it."

He put down the file he was reading. "All right."

"And we're going to need your help."

Peering over his glasses, he said, "What's going on, Luca?"

"We went through all of the video coverage of the casino's entrance. We have Wade arriving but have nothing showing she ever left. The hotel and casino are connected, and it's probable she used the hotel doorway when she left."

Lightning brightened the room as he said, "Then check the footage."

"The thing is, they never turned over that piece of surveillance."

"Are you implying the Seminoles are engaged in a cover-up?"

"It could be a simple oversight, but we received a call from someone who works at the casino, and he's a member of the tribe."

"What was the nature of the call?"

"He wanted to meet secretly, away from the casino. I had Detective Dickson trailing just in case it was a ruse, but he seemed legitimate, and what he told me is making me think the failure to turn over all the video may be deliberate."

Rain began to beat against the window.

"That's a serious charge, Frank. What did he say?"

"He told us that we should be looking at a certain individual, Magi Seke. It seems that he had kidnapped a girl a few years ago—"

Chester bolted upright. "Kidnapped? Where did this supposedly take place?"

"On the Miccosukee Reservation."

"But a crime like that falls under the Major Crimes Act. How could it not have been reported, triggering an investigated by the FBI?"

"Because the alleged perpetrator is the son of Peyak Chetan."

The creases in Chester's forehead deepened. "Chetan? He covered this up?"

"According to the witness."

"Are we sure this is reliable information? Who is this man?"

"He refused to give his identity, but Detective Dickson

took his plate number. DMV records confirmed he was Achak Alo. He lives on the Immokalee Reservation and is employed by the casino."

"What makes him believe Chetan's son is involved in Wade's disappearance?"

"Nothing specific, but he came to us, and Chetan's kid was working at the casino the night she went missing."

"If this is true, the repercussions, I can't even calculate them. It'll destroy the balance we worked so hard to achieve with the Seminoles. It'll reverberate through the entire state."

He forgot to mention it would jeopardize his reelection. "We've got to follow the evidence where it leads, sir. If it gets messy, so be it. We have a missing woman who we, frankly, thought was dead. But she may be in grave danger as we speak."

"We can't go off half cocked here."

"All I'm asking is that you get them to allow me to interview Chetan's son. Send a couple of officers to check around, see if there's any place he could be hiding Wade."

"A search? Just because we police the Immokalee Reservation doesn't mean we don't need a warrant."

"I understand it would amplify things. If you could get me a chance to speak with this Magi, we'll see how it develops and take it one step at a time."

"Fair enough. Give me a day, maximum."

THE SUN HAD EMERGED as Mary Ann said, "I guess you didn't like it."

Molto's black linguine, made from squid's ink, was a favorite of mine. "I'm going to ask her for the recipe."

"I heard it's a family secret."

"You know what I say about secrets."

"The only way two people can keep a secret is when one of them is dead."

"It's true. You want anything else?"

"No way. Get the bill. We'll take a walk."

I signed the credit card receipt and stuffed a couple of bills in with it.

"What are you doing?"

"Giving cash for the tip."

"Since when?"

"Derrick was telling me that when he waitered, they loved it when the tip was in cash."

"I can see why. Let's go."

We left Molto, the sun warming our backs as we walked east.

"Look at that new building." I pointed to a modern structure on Fifth Avenue. "I really like that. I bet the apartments are a couple of million or something."

"It's nice, but I couldn't imagine living there."

"Me neither, just saying I like the way it looks."

"Oh no, look at that graffiti."

The side of a building was marred with black and red stick figures. "You telling me this guy struck again? Chester created a task force to nail this guy."

"I know, but he's moving all over. A couple of days ago he made a mess of Vanderbilt Beach's parking garage."

"It's disgusting. Makes the place feel like some inner-city mess."

"Not good for tourism."

"I'm not for or against the cameras some cities are putting up, but if we had them, we would have probably nailed this guy already."

"I don't like the camera idea at all. It's creepy, Frank."

"You're right, I'm just saying from a law enforcement angle, it'd be another tool we'd have."

"It's a slippery slope. Look at what they're doing in China. A simple protest, and they track you down."

"I know. It's all about balance."

"I want to go into Blue Mercury. It just opened."

"Go ahead. I'll be outside."

Walking alongside the defaced building, I tried to determine where the punk who did this had come from. A low hedge rimmed a small parking lot that led to the structure's back entrance.

Surveying the area, a red object was suspended in one of the bushes. Approaching, I could see it was the cap from a can of spray paint. I searched the area, but there were no other traces the vandal had left behind.

I jogged back to the Cherokee and grabbed an evidence bag. It was a long shot, but I had to do something to stop this person from ruining my town.

17

MY SHIRT WAS STUCK TO MY BACK AS I WALKED THROUGH the parking lot. I bloused it, wondering how hot it was going to get as I went into my office.

"It's boiling out there already."

Derrick said, "There's a heat advisory. Lynn said it's going feel like a hundred and ten."

"Since when did these weather people start with all this 'feel like' stuff? They just want to talk everything up."

"You're right. Every time a storm is brewing, they start hyping it with x millions of people could be affected."

"I just wish the weather would go back to being two minutes of the news. I don't care what the weather is in any other place. If you're traveling or have family somewhere, just look it up."

"When they put us in charge, we'll fix that. Did you hear anything on Wade's phone records?"

"Not a word. It should have come right to us, but sometimes they send it downstairs."

"I'll check with them."

"Take this with you." I handed him the bag with the spray can top.

"What's this?"

"Last night we went to Molto on Fifth Avenue, and that kid doing all the graffiti hit another building. When Mary Ann stopped in a store, I searched the area and found it."

"Maybe they can pull a print or DNA off it."

"That's what I'm hoping."

Derrick left as I opened my email. Staring at thirty-nine that had come in overnight, I took a sip of the coffee my partner brought for me. There was nothing from the sheriff.

Chester was right. If the Seminoles were covering up for one of the elder's kids, the entire relationship with them was at stake. It was a matter of trust. If it had been broken, especially since it dealt with the safety and security of those frequenting the Immokalee casino, they would have shot themselves in the foot. Who would visit, knowing what had happened?

I didn't care either way about gambling myself, but I knew there were people who depended upon it for their livelihood and others who viewed it as entertainment. A feeling was coming over me, but I couldn't quite figure out what it meant.

After opening one email, I sat back in my chair. We had a couple of interesting leads to follow. It could be the most likely person in these types of cases, the husband. He'd struck his wife before, and he was in the area where she was last seen.

The work-related suspects were surprising, but there was no question there were viable. Wade had pissed off two men by reducing their sizable claims. If it wasn't passion, it was money that led to most murders.

Then there was the outlier suspect, the muscleman who

was having an affair with Wade. I wasn't discounting him as the possible killer, but at this time he was at the bottom of the list.

We needed to dig into all these men, but since she was last seen at the casino, any person connected to it required our immediate attention. I resolved to call Chester at noon to see where he was with the Seminole leadership and went back to my email.

Derrick bounded into the office waving a manila envelope. "We got Wade's phone records."

"About time."

He pulled a single sheet of paper out. "Let's see what calls we have."

"They give location data with it?"

"Yeah. Along with the name of the person on the other side of the call."

"Two calls to her husband. One at one oh five, and another at four fifteen."

"How long were the calls?"

"Quickies. Forty-nine seconds and a minute ten. Both of them were incoming calls."

"What else?"

"Holy shit. Renovation man Berry called her at five twenty-two."

I went to his desk. "She was on the phone with him for almost five minutes."

Looking at the list, I jabbed the paper. "She called Jerry Belcher from the casino at eight fourteen. It was a quick call."

"Did you see him enter?"

"No. And I don't think I would have missed someone with his build."

"Maybe it was to set up or confirm a get-together."

"When are we getting the hotel surveillance?"

"They said we'd have it before lunch."

"Okay. Find out what car that muscleman, Belcher, drives. There's a chance he came in the lot and met up with her."

Derrick tapped on his keyboard and I examined the list. There was a call to her friend Cybill Gates. Why hadn't she mentioned that when we met? Did it have anything to do with Belcher?

Besides the call to her employer, which we needed to understand the nature of, the balance of the list was self-explanatory, made to places like Nail Passion and Al's New York Deli.

"Belcher drives a 2016 Ford Explorer. A blue one."

I recalled a couple of them coming into the casino parking lot.

I PLUGGED in the thumb drive, and video of the hotel's doorway came to life. We had Wade inside the casino at least until twelve forty-nine. I hit triple fast-forward, stopping at a quarter to one in the morning.

There weren't many people coming or going. Other than someone going outside to smoke or a late arrival rolling an overnight bag, there was nothing of interest. I doubled the speed of the video, slowing it down whenever activity came into view.

At 2:47 a.m., a large man wearing a Boston Red Sox hat walked out of the hotel. He had his head down as he hurried toward the parking lot. As he disappeared from the camera's view, I wondered if it could have been Jerry Belcher, Wade's muscular lover.

The video rolled on, but there was nothing to see. My

watch sounded a pee-pee reminder. It was time to relieve the bladder the doctors made to replace my cancer-ridden one. My eyes were glued to the screen as I rose. I was just about to pause it when a couple headed to the doorway.

It was Beth Wade and a man who looked to be around fifty. They were laughing. It was three twelve in the morning. The couple stepped onto the sidewalk. They said something to each other and then separated. Beth veered left and the male right, crossing the street in front of the parking lot before moving out of the camera's range.

18

As I drove to the casino, I replayed my conversation with the sheriff. Something was off, but I couldn't put my finger on it. Was Chester holding something back? Why would he? He was a politician, which meant he'd bury something if he felt it would upset an ally. But at the end of the day he was a law enforcement officer. He would never let something as serious as a kidnapping go.

Chester showed some backbone in bucking their resistance to me interviewing a leader's son. I believed what he said about threatening to send the FBI in if we weren't allowed to speak with Magi Seke. But I knew it was the condition that I wouldn't ask about the older incident that sealed the agreement allowing me to talk with Magi.

What was the source of his obvious discomfort? Could the sheriff have revealed our source in exchange for permission to talk to Magi? Maybe that was it.

During our ten-minute talk, the sheriff made it clear how sensitive this was and the implications it carried with the Native American Indian community. Chester insinuated that the Seminole's leadership would organize rallies if they felt one of their own was being mistreated.

The house Magi Seke lived in was owned by his father. It was the only home in the horseshoe-shaped enclave that was maintained. The porch had a sag to it, but the lawn was cut, and unlike the other homes, it was freshly painted.

Approaching, I tried to gauge the space under the main level. Was there a crawl space? A place to tuck a prisoner or bury a body?

A breeze sent half a dozen porch chimes tinkling. The front door was open, as were several windows. It was mid-July. I didn't care how windy it got, but you had to grow up with no air-conditioning to live without it.

We saw each other through the screen door, but he made no effort to acknowledge me or get out of his recliner. I pushed the bell, which was barely audible over a TV game show.

"Come in."

The door squeaked as I opened it. A tabby cat rushed out and I stiffened, eliciting a chuckle from Magi. I surveyed the place as I introduced myself. The furnishings were a year or two from ratty. But someone kept the place clean.

There was another TV on in the house. It was coming from one of the rooms off a hallway to the right. Was there someone else in the house?

Magi wore a black leather vest over a bright red T-shirt. "Thank you for agreeing to speak with me."

He shrugged. "I was told I had to."

"Can you turn the TV down?"

He acted as if I never asked. Did he want it on to cover noise from a prisoner?

"What do you want?"

"You were working at the casino on the night of Monday, July seventh, correct?"

"I don't remember."

"You don't have to. The casino records and video surveillance place you there."

"So, why'd you ask?"

"What do you do there?"

"Maintenance, but you probably know that."

"And where do you do that?"

"Stuff breaks all over the place."

"Both the casino and hotel?"

"That's everywhere."

"What about the outside, the parking lot?"

He squinted. "Never, uh, not too much of the time."

I pulled out a photo of Beth Wade. "You know this woman?"

He took the picture, but it didn't appear that his eyes were looking at it. He silently handed it back.

"Do you know her?"

"Know her? What does that mean?"

Between the heat and the blaring TV, I was on the cusp of losing my patience. The last thing I needed were wiseass responses. Reminding myself that I was on an Indian reservation and technically a guest, I said, "Have you seen her at the casino?"

"She looks like a regular."

"So, you've seen her?"

"I could have."

"Did you ever speak to her?"

"Maybe a hello or something like that."

"Is that a yes?"

"Look, I don't have to tell you anything about nothing. You got no power here."

"I'm looking into the disappearance of this woman. She was last seen on casino property, and her vehicle was found in the parking lot. Now, you either cooperate, or we can find a way to invoke the Major Crimes Act, and you'll be talking to the FBI."

Anger flashed across his face. "I see that lady around, but that's all."

"You never spoke to her?"

"No."

This was a waste of time. I would need to shoot him up with Sodium Pentothal to get him to talk. We needed a connection between him and Wade, otherwise there was nothing concrete to build on. I ended the interview and looked into the kitchen on my way out, catching a glance at a heavily padlocked door.

Driving back, consumed with what was behind the door, my phone rang.

"Detective Luca."

"Did you hear a damn word of anything I said?"

It was the sheriff. "Yes, sir. What's the matter?"

"Don't play stupid with me, Luca."

"I'm sorry, sir, I really don't know what you're upset about."

"Did you threaten Magi Seke?"

"No sir."

"Did you tell him that we were going to turn this into a federal case and summon the FBI?"

"It wasn't like that, sir."

"What was it, then?"

"I, I was just trying to get him to talk. He wouldn't admit to the time of day, for God's sake."

"Didn't I specifically instruct you not to threaten anyone?"

"It wasn't a threat, sir. I said something along the lines that if it was a major crime then he'd have to talk to the FBI."

"Unless you have solid evidence to follow, I'm ordering you to stay away from Magi Seke. Is that clear?"

"Yes, sir."

I needed to know more about Magi without being insubordinate. There were ways to piece together his whereabouts that night through other employees and guests. We also had tons of video of the night, over three hundred hours, to scrutinize.

It was time to use facial recognition software to help us. We could build a database with images of every person of interest and check for interactions with Wade.

If we knew when the last time Wade had been there, we could expand the search for connections by looking at videos from that date.

19

THERE WAS A LONG LIST OF THINGS TO DO AND PEOPLE TO talk to. In most cases, we didn't have enough, or any, video to go by. In this investigation we had too much, but no footage of the hotel's corridors. We didn't know if she went to a room alone or with someone.

"Derrick, we've got to take a look at the casino's footage on the night of June thirtieth. Wade's husband said she went that night and used her credit card to buy gas at the Mobil station on Immokalee."

"I'll get it."

"Have the lab run it through the facial software. See if we can catch her with anyone we're looking at."

"If you want, I'll go out there myself and grab it."

"Sure. The sooner, the better."

"I'll be back in under an hour."

The first person I wanted to talk to after meeting with Magi Seke was Achak Alo, the Seminole who told me about him at New York, New York Pizza.

"Mr. Alo?"

"Who is this?"

"Detective Luca. We met a few days ago at the pizzeria."

"How did you find me?"

"Through Motor Vehicles. I have a couple of questions for you."

"I'm not talking to anyone anymore. You got me in trouble."

"Trouble? What do you mean by that?"

"They called me into the office. They were asking me about Magi and what I said to the police about him."

"How did they know we spoke?"

"Come on, man, don't give me that. I tried to help, and you ratted me out."

It had to be Chester who identified him. "No, I didn't tell anyone."

"Yeah, right. How else would they know?"

"Maybe somebody saw us and put it together."

"I was careful."

"What did you tell them when they questioned you?"

"I told them I didn't talk to nobody. I said it wasn't me."

"Good. Now, I need to understand—"

"I'm done helping."

He hung up. Chester had blown his cover, and a valuable source had been lost. I'd have to start fresh.

There was one more person to call before heading out to talk to Roger Berry. I dialed Cybill Gates to find out what she spoke to Wade about and why she didn't tell me they had a conversation the night she went missing. Gates didn't pick up. I left her a message.

The Vineyards was a gated community made up of a bunch of subdivisions that ran alongside Interstate 75. I'd seen the entrance but had never been inside the massive neighborhood straddling Vanderbilt Beach and Pine Ridge Roads.

I flashed my badge at the guard and took Vintage Colony Boulevard to an enclave of coach homes named Avellino Isles. A Ford pickup was parked in the driveway of the second-floor unit Roger Berry, the renovation contractor, was living in. Berry wasn't listed as the owner of the home.

Solidly built, with a widow's peak, Berry was guarded as he let me in. He had a bruise on his right cheek that was a day away from disappearing. Did Wade inflict it during her struggle to get away?

The floor plan was wide open, surprising me as they had been built in the nineties. There was no furniture in the area reserved for dining and just a couch, TV, and desk in the main room. Berry wasn't enjoying the long lake views from the lanai, unless he liked standing.

As we sat at a kitchen counter with crumbs on it, I said, "This is a nice place. Been here long?"

Turning his head, the top of a tattoo poked out of his T-shirt. "About a year. It's okay in here. A friend of mine was having trouble selling it, and I needed a place to stay after I had to sell my house."

"Divorce?"

"No." He shrugged. "I had to put some money back in the business."

"You do what you have to do."

"It's not easy. Everybody looks at the contractors down here and thinks we're making money hand over fist. That's bullshit. It's impossible to get good workers, and there's a ton of competition. Plus, shit is always happening."

I almost thanked him for the segue. "You worked on the La Playa renovation."

"Look, it's all a misunderstanding. I know I lost it with that woman, but that's all it was. I had nothing to do with her going missing."

How did he know she was missing? "You were upset that she knocked down your claim."

He threw up his hands. "I couldn't believe it. Like it was our fault a frigging hurricane came through."

"I understand they claimed you were negligent in not protecting the building."

"That was total bullshit. We did what we could. Who knew it was going to be a direct hit? Every day the forecast was changing. We couldn't get the materials anyway, and she knew it."

"Beth Wade?"

"Yeah, she knew damn well there was a run on supplies, and besides, the workers were heading out of town. Why was it my fault? What about the people who decided to do the job in the hurricane season? I tried to talk to her, but she didn't want to hear it."

"You have a record for assault and conspiracy to commit murder."

He put his forearms on the counter. "When I was younger, I lost my temper—like that." He snapped his fingers. "One time I got into it with some guy in a bar and went too far. But the murder thing was bullshit."

"Why don't you tell me about it."

"I don't want to talk about it. I served time for it, even though I shouldn't have."

"But you tried to have your partner killed."

"That's not what happened. It was very complicated. He wasn't carrying his weight, and I wanted to break the partnership up. But, of course, he wouldn't. I was busting my ass, and he was riding on my back. He didn't do shit to help me."

"So, instead of terminating the partnership you decided to terminate him?"

"No, no. That's not what happened."

"According to the charges that were filed, you tried to arrange a contract hit on him."

"I was just trying to scare him. That's all it was."

"You offered someone fifty thousand dollars to kill your partner."

"It was never going to happen. I never paid the guy a dime."

"That's because he got arrested the day before you were supposed to pay him."

"But—"

"Let's cut the crap here, okay? We know you withdrew ten thousand in cash two days before the hit man was arrested. We believe it was a down payment. If the assassin hadn't been arrested, you would have paid him, and your partner would have been murdered. He told us all about your plan."

"He was telling them stuff just to get a better deal for himself. I'm telling you, it was all bullshit."

"Everything is bullshit to you."

"Look, I did my time, so leave me alone about it."

"Where were you the night of Monday, July seventh?"

"I was home."

"Can anyone verify that?"

He shrugged. "I was alone."

"Why did you call Beth Wade the night she disappeared?"

"It was nothing. She told me to check in with her, you know, about the claim."

"Why would she tell you that?"

"Why? Because I was asking her to see what they could do. I told her this whole thing was going to put me out of business if I couldn't get the money."

"I see. Okay, that's all I have." Before I finished the sentence, he was out of his seat.

"Glad I could clear things up."

We were at the door, and I pulled a Colombo on him, pointing to his bruise. "How'd you get that shiner?"

"On the job."

"How?"

"Uh, ripping out a cabinet. Piece broke off and hit me."

To my ear, it sounded made up.

20

WE needed to know who the man walking out of the hotel with Wade was. There was nothing particularly suspicious about him, but he might be able to piece together what happened just before they exited.

The casino claimed they didn't know who he was. He didn't appear to be a Native American, but the stereotypical look had faded through the generations. It would be worth asking the lab to run him through facial recognition software.

Jotting myself a note, my desk phone rang.

"Detective Luca."

"Detective, this is Michael Whitaker."

Ugh. "Hello, Mr. Whitaker. What can I do for you?"

"I would like an update on my father's case."

"At the moment, I don't have anything I am able to share with you."

"Is that because it's confidential or because you've done nothing since our last conversation?"

"Actually, I have worked on the case."

"That's reassuring to hear. When can we expect a resolution?"

"I know this may sound harsh, but let me remind you that your father's murder is a thirty-year-old case."

"You think my mother and I don't realize that? We've been living with this nightmare for three decades. Just how long do you think my mother is going to be with us?"

How long would any of us be around? "We're doing our best, Mr. Whitaker."

"Well, after thirty years, you'd have to agree that doesn't seem good enough. Wouldn't you?"

I wanted to tell him I wasn't the detective who handled the case in the first place and that he was lucky I was working on it, but that'd feel good for about three seconds. "Believe me, if anyone understands your frustration, I do. There's nothing more to say other than I am waiting on responses from two quarters and will update you as things develop. Have a good day, Mr. Whitaker."

I hung up before he had a chance to say anything. Is that how it was going to be for me at the end of my life? Instead of enjoying myself as my money ran out, would I be trying to button up the open items in my life before checking out? Was there really any satisfaction to knowing who caused so much sorrow in your life?

There had to be six or seven situations where someone we knew was terminally ill, and all they wanted was to make it to see their child married or to welcome a grandchild into the world. It seemed like a worthy goal from my perspective and a source of joy, but what was that person really feeling? It had to be a sadness of incredible magnitude.

Here it was, your grandchild was born, but you knew you wouldn't be around for the first birthday or to see her ride a tricycle. With my concerns about the cancer coming back and missing out on all things Jessie, I couldn't imagine what they were experiencing.

Like everyone else, I wanted to go fast. A massive heart attack or something immediate and without pain. It seemed an easier way to exit, though I knew if they told me I had a half an hour before my departure, I'd die of fright in the first five minutes.

I needed to get outside in the sun and out of the cloud I had disappeared in. Pushing back my chair, the phone rang again.

"Detective Luca."

"Uh, this is Tim Whiting."

You know how I feel about coincidences, but this was nothing of the sort. This was something akin to a higher power intervening. Possibly the force of the old woman's karma coming. There was no other way to explain it.

"Hello, Mr. Whiting. Did you have an opportunity to consider my request?"

"Yes, I'll do it."

I pumped a fist in the air. "That's welcome news. We appreciate your cooperation."

"I'm not sure why I'm doing this, but something is nagging at me to do it."

In my line of work, evil seemed to be a couple of steps ahead. It was nice to see good intervening for a change.

"It's the right thing to do, sir. What would be a convenient time and location to collect the DNA sample?"

"You said it would be quick, right?"

"Yes, less than two minutes."

"Uhm, maybe tomorrow or next week."

"If you're free now. I can meet you anyplace."

Otherworldly power or not, I couldn't take a chance he would have a change of heart.

"I just got home, but I'm going to be leaving in an hour."

"I'm leaving now. See you in twenty minutes, maximum. Thanks again."

AN HOUR later I was in front of my monitor. If I did nothing else, knowing the lab had the Whitaker case DNA made it a productive day.

21

———

I WENT DOWN THE STAIRS TWO AT A TIME. USING FACIAL recognition software, the lab had come up with a couple of hits on the man leaving the hotel with Beth Wade. Whoever he was, we needed to talk to him, as he may have been the last person to see her alive.

After signing in, I was buzzed in. When the door swung open, I was greeted by Peter Sample and the faint smell of bleach. Sample was a digital forensic examiner, a position that didn't exist a couple of years ago.

"Detective Luca, it's good to see you again."

"Likewise. Thanks for calling me on this."

"I hope it helps."

"Me too. There's a chance she may still be alive."

"Poor woman. Come with me."

I followed his white coat into a darkened room. Sixty-inch monitors hung on three walls.

"We made a copy of the videos, and I put markers on each appearance by a person of interest."

"How exactly does this work?"

"The software uses biometrics to map a person's facial

features. It stores it mathematically and compares it to every face, looking for matches. Since the casino is looking for card counters and cheaters, the video is hi-def, and we can work with it."

"Amazing. Are you able to run the video at a higher speed when using the software?"

"No. We run it at normal speed, but we can run it twenty-four seven. And we have four copies of the software."

"Incredible time-saver, if it's accurate."

"That's why we don't push the speed. They'll probably figure a way to do that soon, but it was originally used for live feeds. A couple of retailers use it to confirm identities when making a payment."

"They're going to make me obsolete."

"That makes two of us. You ready?"

"Let's do it."

"Here's the image stored in the database."

The left screen displayed a close-up of the man seen exiting the hotel with Beth Wade.

"This is the first hit. It's time stamped eight forty-two p.m. on July seventh.

The center monitor had an image of the mystery man walking toward the men's room. He had a glass in his hand.

"That's him."

"He went in and out of the bathroom before disappearing off the feed. This was the next match."

I stepped toward the right-hand screen. The man was playing blackjack. To his right sat Beth Wade. She was playing the last hand before the dealer.

I stepped toward the monitor. "How could that be?"

"What do you mean?"

"We never saw this footage, and it's from 11:09 p.m."

"It's the week before."

"Oh, right. We need to get an ID on this guy. What else you got?"

"Looks like he was playing the slots earlier that day."

Mr. Nameless was standing in front of a slot machine. "What's he using, a credit card to play?"

"No, he must be a regular. He's inserting his card, like a rewards program, to track his activity to get comps."

"We got him. They have a Player's Club for their regulars. If that's what it is, we can cross-check it against their database."

"That'll do it."

"Clip me a photo of this with the time stamp. We'll get the casino to tell us who he is."

I SWUNG off Orange Blossom Road into the parking lot for First Baptist Academy. It was a massive complex with a large, sprawling building and ball fields. The church-run school provided education for kids of all ages, starting with pre-K up to high school.

Picking out Jessie's first school was not only a pain in the ass, it was expensive. Sending a kid to a nursery school for a couple of days a week was more than I paid to go to John Jay College. I knew college tuition was out of control, with schools using parents' fear for their kid's future to extract obscene amounts of money out of them, but I had no idea what it cost for a child to socialize and play with crayons.

Like every parent, I wanted the best for Jessie and was originally on board with enrolling her in a prekindergarten program. Mary Ann said it was the money, but I began to get uncomfortable when the process felt too sales oriented.

I circled past a colorful playground to the administrative

entrance and parked. Mary Ann was talking with a woman in the covered area by the doors. She gave me a big smile as I approached.

"Frank, this is Melinda. She has a little boy who's Jessica's age."

"Nice to meet you."

We shook hands. "You're going to love it here. Sally, she's seven now; she went to pre-K here and never left."

"That's good to hear."

She said, "Let's get going or we'll be late, and they don't like it when you're late."

Was this nursery school or boot camp?

We were shown into a room where six other parents were. I whispered to Mary Ann, "We're doing this as a group?"

"Yes, I told you the spots fill up right away."

We sat through a thirty-minute slide show before going on a tour of two classrooms and a playground they said was only for the nursery school.

Information packets in hand, Mary Ann and I headed to her car.

"Nice place, isn't it?"

I shrugged.

"What's the matter?"

"It feels too big. Look at this place; it's gigantic."

"I know, but they keep the pre-K in a separate wing."

"Jessie's not used to places like this."

"She'll adjust."

"I don't know if it's safe."

"What are you talking about?"

"There's no security, and you have older kids running all over this place."

"You heard what she said. The faculty-to-student ratio is five to one, and the building is locked."

"I don't know. It's expensive. They want five thousand dollars for three half days a week?"

"That's what all these schools charge."

"That don't make it right. Plus, this place is Baptist. We're Catholic."

"They're both Christian."

"I don't want to confuse her."

She rolled her eyes. "I got to get back. We'll talk about it tonight."

I pecked her cheek and went to the Cherokee. I opened the door to let some of the heat out. Just as I was getting in, my phone rang. It was Derrick.

A body had been found. It was a female, thought to be somewhere between thirty and forty. I was hoping it wasn't Beth Wade, but whether it was or not was beside the point; it was bad news. I typed a text to Mary Ann: pre-K would have to wait; we had a corpse on our hands.

I hit send, put the strobes on, and raced out of the parking lot.

22

———

Strobe lights on, a patrol car was parked in front of a small sign that read Gargiulo Produce. Waving to a uniformed officer, I turned off Immokalee Road onto a sand and gravel path that served as the farm's back entrance.

My rearview mirror reflected the dust storm I was kicking up as I made my way toward a pair of police cars parked in a V formation. I slowed to avoid choking the handful of people gathered near the vehicles.

I signed in and ducked under the yellow crime scene tape. A ruddy-faced officer who looked as if he hadn't had his first shave greeted me. "Detective Luca?"

"Yes."

He stuck out a hand. "Officer Forman. I've heard a lot about you."

"Hopefully, some of it was good."

"Oh yeah. You're kind of a legend. I want to join homicide one of these days."

"Were you the first on the scene?"

"Yes, sir. I was patrolling just outside of Ave Maria when I heard the call from dispatch."

"Did you or anyone touch anything?"

"No, sir. My main instructor was in homicide for thirty years, and he drilled it into us."

He would be the first rookie who resisted the urge to get too close and contaminate the crime scene. "Keep up the good work, Officer Forman. Who reported it?"

"That guy over there with the straw hat." He pointed at a short man standing between two officers. "His name is Ruffo Rodriguez."

"Okay. Now, where's the body?"

"Right this way, sir. I gotta say, it's pretty nasty."

"If you want to work in homicide, you better get used to it."

I wanted to tell the kid that when you saw a body, you had to think of the how and why questions and not the who. Keeping your mind focused on trying to figure out how the crime occurred was the only way to keep your sanity. If you focused on who they were as a person, the fact they may have kids or a partner, you'd get depressed.

"Yes, sir."

I stumbled on a rock as we crossed a field that had just been plowed. I wiped my finger across the top of my lips as I surveyed the area. There wasn't a toothpick-sized slice of shade in sight.

"It's just past the edge of the field, by that tank."

The rusty, round tank looked like it was used to store irrigation water. Crime scene tape was tied to one of its legs, stretching twenty yards to a stake in the ground.

"You put the tape up?"

"Yes, sir."

I scooted under it, and a step later a canal, half filled with water, came into view. Between the Native American population and the rebels living in the area, the length of the hair on the body floating in the water could have belonged to a male or female.

But I knew the corpse was female and probably Beth Wade. The clothing seemed to match. The rope around her midsection looked like it was tied to a weight at the bottom of the canal. Most people didn't realize that the gases from decomposition would force the body to surface despite being weighed down.

As I stepped to the water's edge, my stomach lurched. The corpse's face was bloated and had been ravaged by birds and insects. I swallowed and took another look around. The road I parked on was fifty yards away. Whoever killed her would have had to carry or drag her across the field, most likely at night to avoid detection.

Wade weighed a hundred and twenty to thirty, if I recalled. A heavy, bulky load for one person. Were there two people involved, or was it the bodybuilder, Jerry Belcher?

A mangy row of scrub pines and bushes separated the canal from another field. Was there an access road closer to the canal? If there was, whoever carried the body would have to cross through the vegetation, likely leaving fibers behind.

Walking around the tank, I noticed Gianelli trudging across the field. Cameras were dangling off both his shoulders. Scattered near the water storage unit were hoses, a pump, a generator, and a handful of gas tanks. None of them looked like they had been recently used.

"Hey, Frank. What are you doing way out here?"

"Same as you, my friend. We go where the bodies are."

"It's been quiet. They got me snapping burglary, vandalism shots: you name it."

"How about that kid doing the graffiti?"

"Yeah, but the shots are nothing more than what's been in the paper. What do we have here?"

"Female, midthirties, in the canal. After you do your thing with the corpse, I'd appreciate it if you took a bunch of landscape shots. Make it three-sixty; I'm wondering about the killer's egress."

"No problem."

"Where's Bilotti?"

"The doc was right behind me." He looked over his shoulder. "He's right behind the crime scene vans."

A trail of dust dissipated as the procession of vehicles slowed to a stop. The clicks from Gianelli's camera faded as I made my way to greet the medical examiner.

"How are you, Doc?"

"Good, Frank. How's the family?"

"All good. What did you have to drink last night?"

"A Saxum, it was amazing. You drink anything interesting?"

"Oh man, I love that wine. Hey, we had the amarone you gave me. It was really good; Mary Ann liked it too."

"Which one was that?"

"Uh, it had a black and silver label with an old stadium on it."

"Right, it's called Arena."

"That's it."

"If you ever see Quintarelli, grab a bottle. It's expensive but worth it."

"Better than the Bertani we had at Reilly's retirement party?"

"Absolutely. I noticed the sign Gargiulo. Do you know they have a winery out in Napa?"

"Really?"

"It's right in the Oakville district."

"Wow. Look, I'm pretty certain the body is a missing woman named Beth Wade. Her mother is a friend of Chester's wife. He had me looking into her disappearance."

"Sorry to hear that. Where is the body?"

"In an irrigation ditch on the other side of the field. It looks like whoever dumped her tried to weigh her down."

"Let me get my waders on."

"Go ahead, I'm going to have a look on the other side of the hedge line."

I pulled out of the driveway and made a right, heading west. Just past the hedge line was a deeply rutted path. My shoulder bounced off the window as I made my way along the road. I stopped opposite the water tank and got out.

The irrigation ditch was on the other side of the vegetation about thirty feet away. Though it was much closer, the greenery was thick. Even though there was a full moon the night of Wade's disappearance, you still couldn't see the canal. You had to know it was there.

Bilotti would confirm if she was killed here or not, but it was my belief she was murdered elsewhere and dumped here. Driving around with a dead body would make the coldest of killers anxious as he searched for a discreet spot. I walked deeper into the property. About twenty yards away, the greenery thinned.

It was an easier area to cross, but why would he backtrack once through? Why not just put the body in the water once he got to the other side? Wade wasn't a big woman, but it would still be easier to drag her than carry her. Either way, I was going to get forensics to comb over the hedge line to see what they could pick up.

I got back in the Cherokee convinced the killer knew the

area. Was he someone who worked in agriculture or a Seminole?

Driving toward Naples, I fought back against a depressing feeling. There was no chance of riding to the rescue to save Wade. She was dead. It was no longer a missing persons inquiry; it was a murder case.

23

Derrick gave me a thumbs-up when he came in. "They got a print off the spray can cap you found."

"Good. Now, we got to hope they get a match."

"The lab said they can't promise when, but they'll run it against the database."

"Hopefully, it'll be before he strikes again. Did you see what he did to Freedom Park?"

"I saw it on the news last night. It's disgusting. I'd like to get a bunch of first responders together and have each one of them kick him in the ass."

"If it's a he."

"Sooner or later we'll grab the bastard. I don't want this place to look like Detroit."

"They say the Motor City is on the way back."

"That's what they want you to believe. We went up there to see Mary Ann's aunt last year, and let me tell you, it's a disaster."

"Oh. I know they say that guy from Quicken Loans was putting a lot of money in the city."

"Yeah, he built a headquarters for his business and a couple of other things, but they're a long way off. Look, did you ask them where they were with looking for Magi on older footage?"

"Sample said they were a quarter of the way through, but nothing yet."

"We may have to go further back. Widen the search to find anything."

"Sure. Just tell me where you want to start, and I'll get the footage."

"I was thinking about going back three weeks to a month. If Wade went gambling at least once a week, it'd give us four shots at establishing a connection."

The phone rang. Derrick reached for it, saying, "All right, I'll get it going and tell the lab to search the most current footage and work their way backward."

He flashed me a thumbs-up. "That was Sample. They got a hit on Magi talking to Wade."

"I'm going to see Chester."

I WAS SHOWN into the sheriff's office. He was wearing a frown and a red tie. "Take a seat, Frank."

"Thank you for making time, sir."

"I trust you know we're walking in a minefield. At night, no less."

"I realize the political implications, but I feel that we've got to follow this lead. It's clear that Magi knew Wade."

"What exactly did the video show? And I don't want any embellishing, Luca."

Embellishing? Did I have a history of that? And we were back to Luca instead of Frank. "Just a week before Wade disappeared, she was at the casino bar, a place called the Zig

Zag. Magi Seke was walking by and spotted her. It was clear it was not their first encounter."

"And you know this how?"

"Body language, sir. She put on a big smile when he approached her, and they talked for a solid ten minutes."

"Okay, so it appears as if they knew each other. He works at the casino, and she is a regular there. It seems normal that they would know each other."

"This man held a woman captive. I have to disagree with you, sir. It's anything but normal; it's a connection begging to be explored."

"This was a week before, correct?"

"Yes. He also denied knowing her. When I showed him a picture, he made like he didn't know her. That's a direct contradiction to the way he reacted when he noticed her at the bar in the surveillance video."

"And there is no other way to ascertain if he was involved in her murder?"

"Detective Dickson has spoken to people who know Magi, but they're all closemouthed."

"What about the fellow who put you on his trail?"

I wanted to say that he was pissed because you opened your mouth. "I think they got to him. He doesn't want to talk to us anymore."

"Who got to him? The tribal leadership?"

"It appears so. Word leaked out that he was the one who brought Magi to our attention."

"I'll reach out to Chetan again and set up an interview for you."

"Thank you, sir. If it's all right with you, I'd like to bring him down here. I believe we have the authority."

"That would be a mistake. We do the policing for them,

but they'd invoke their rights, and we don't have nearly enough to declare it a major crime."

Not yet, was my preferred response, but instead I said, "It's your decision, sir."

———

DERRICK SAID, "What did the sheriff say?"

"He's going to make a call and set up another interview."

"Is he going to let you bring him in?"

"No. I knew he wouldn't, but let me tell you something about dealing with Chester." I closed the door. "He's a politician first and a cop second. I'm not saying he's a bad leader, but Chester's too cautious. Sometimes you have to ruffle feathers, but he's always worried about how it's going to play, rather than the results."

"Nothing could be worse than the police commissioner in DC. To him it was all politics. He'd bend like a slinky anytime a group didn't like this or that. It was nuts, especially when the morgue is full and people are afraid to walk the streets. It's the nation's capital, for God sake. At least Chester can say he keeps Collier safe."

"What I wanted you to understand is that you have to stretch when you work with him. Always ask for more than you want. I know that's a good strategy in most dealings, but with him it's essential. You got that?"

"Sure. But you're not going anywhere, are you?"

"Not yet."

"What's that supposed to mean?"

"Nothing. Just that I'm not getting any younger, and with Jessie, well, I've got to think more about the future."

"You thinking of moving upstairs?"

"I really don't know what I'm thinking. Look, now that this is a homicide, we need to put a murder book together."

"I already started one. The interviews are right here." He tapped a pile of documents with a forefinger. "And I asked Gianelli to forward me a set of photos."

The department was in good hands. Another year or two of me teaching him the ropes, and who knows? Maybe I would take a desk job.

24

———————

We had an identity on the man exiting the hotel with Beth Wade. He was forty-six-year-old Ben Rowan. He ran an import firm that specialized in knickknacks and promotional tchotchke, mostly from Asia. Rowan lived in Summer Wind, a community along Pine Ridge Road.

Every time I drove past that neighborhood it would remind me of the Sinatra song. I had been in there once on a domestic violence call. From what I knew, it was all rental apartments in there. There were some amenities, but if Rowan had a business making money, he might have been blowing it at the casino.

I stared at his driver's license, which pegged him at six foot, but it was his eyes that caught my attention. They weren't quite right. His left eye was slightly off-center. He had the kind of smile that was generally forced for these types of photos. With a receding hairline, he seemed like an ordinary middle-aged male. I was eager to talk to him.

Rowan's business was located in a strip center on Golden Gate Boulevard. The green-roofed building had an assortment of unrelated businesses. I cut the engine and headed toward a storefront with a red, white, and blue sign that read The Promo Pros.

A bell chimed when I opened the door and walked in. The counter separating the public and worker spaces was filled with giveaway items emblazoned with various company names. A young girl was on the phone and smiled at me. She was the only person in the bullpen area fronting three offices behind it.

A large printer was slowly spitting out a colorful banner. The girl was writing while she spoke, and I gravitated to a display that held a dozen beverage insulators. It was hot in Florida, but they were another needless gadget to stick your name on. Another rack had a manicure set, candles, and oven mitts, all bearing logos.

"Welcome to Promo Pros. How can I assist you today?"

"I'd like to speak to Ben Rowan."

"Oh, I'm sorry, he's not in today. Can I help you with something?"

"No. Will he be in tomorrow?"

"I hope so. He hurt his back and went to the doctor."

"I see. When did he do that?

"They say about ten days ago. I just started last week."

"Ouch. Well, I hope he feels better."

Climbing back into the Cherokee, the thought he might have wrenched his back carrying Wade floated through my mind. When I got back to the office, I'd call his house. If he was there, I'd run over.

As I THREW my jacket on a chair, Derrick said, "Sheriff wants to see you."

"He set up the Magi interview?"

"He didn't say. I asked if I could help him, but he said when you got back he wanted to see you."

I picked up my jacket and headed to the stairwell. Chester was a politician, but he generally delivered bad news in person. Was that why he wanted to see me? What would I do if he said we couldn't speak with Magi? I had no plan B. Like most Native American tribes, the Seminoles stuck together and protected their own.

The idea of enticing someone, maybe with money or a trade for dropping a charge, flooded my mind as I arrived at Chester's office. His secretary opened the door and the sheriff said, "Come on in, Frank."

"Thank you, sir."

"What is the latest on the Wade case?"

"We're working several threads. We identified the man who exited the hotel with Wade. In fact, I was trying to see him when you called. I'll catch up with him later."

"How is the work-related line going?"

"We're going to bring in both men soon, but I'm afraid that angle means this is no longer a missing persons case but a homicide."

"Her mother is on the verge of a nervous breakdown."

"It's heartbreaking for any parent."

"Take care of your girl, Frank."

"I plan to, sir."

"You still feel it's necessary to interview Chetan's son?"

"Absolutely. It's the only lead we have that has a person of interest with a kidnapping in their background."

"Possible kidnapping. Remember, nothing was proven."

"But—"

"No buts, Luca. That's the type of accusation that has me

concerned in the first place. Don't forget that they don't have to talk to us."

"I know, sir. I'll be careful. There's nothing to worry about."

He snorted. "Nothing to worry about? Do you realize what a public relations nightmare this can turn into? If it appears we are targeting a minority, we'll have all the activists from New York and beyond down here."

"I appreciate the position this puts the department in, but we have a valid line of inquiry to follow. We can make the case why we're interested in Magi Seke to anyone who will listen."

"That's the problem right there. No one will listen, they'll just go off half cocked, making accusations and calling us racist."

"That's ridiculous."

"I know it, but they'll cite the fact that Collier is over eighty-eight percent white, and minorities are underrepresented."

"Hold on, sir. That may be true, but we can't allow that to affect an investigation. I know some people don't believe it, but to me, justice is color blind. We can't be intimidated away from following a viable lead."

"I don't want you acting like a cowboy—strike that. As I already stated, this is delicate, and I expect you to be sensitive in your probe. Don't push it, and for God's sake don't make any unfounded accusations. Do you understand?"

"Absolutely, sir."

I took the stairs slowly. We had a murdered woman and a possible serial kidnapper to deal with. I knew that was as serious as it gets, but I couldn't shake the dread that the sheriff was on the verge of letting politics dictate the department's activities. It wasn't perfect by any means, but I considered Collier County and its sheriff's department a bastion of fairness. If that wall cracked, or God forbid, fell, I was going to retire and become a watchdog for Jessie.

25

IT WASN'T SURPRISING THAT THE SEMINOLES REQUESTED THE interview take place in a casino office. The building's location on reservation property offered Magi a measure of safety.

What was unexpected were the trio of lawyers in the room. Introductions were made. Sitting to Magi's left was an outside lawyer, Tom Brogan, a well-known criminal lawyer. To his right was someone I didn't know, Robert Best. His business card stated he was an Indian Affairs lawyer out of Miami. Seated next to Best was Yako Huma, a tribe member and attorney.

Was it my karma? I loosened my tie. I was outnumbered, and even for me, the room was too warm. Magi flinched when I tossed my notebook onto the table. I pulled out a chair and said, "I appreciate the opportunity to speak with Mr. Seke this afternoon. It's good that he has representation. However, for the sake of expediency and order, I'd like there to be one spokesperson, when necessary."

A quick huddle ensued. I took a closer look around the

room. In the left-hand corner it appeared that a camera was trained on me.

As I surveyed the rest of the room, the whispering ended. Brogan said, "I'll handle any objections, clarifications, rebuttals, or commentary."

His being a criminal attorney made me wonder if they knew something I didn't.

"Good. Shall we get started? Mr. Seke, you're employed by the Immokalee casino as a maintenance worker. Correct?"

"Yeah, that's right."

"And in that capacity, you are free to roam the casino and its attached hotel, right?"

Brogan put his hand on Seke's forearm and said, "Roam? Rephrase the question, Detective."

"Your work duties require you to have access to the entire casino and related hotel. Correct?"

"Yeah."

"Were you working Monday night, July seventh?"

"I already told you I was."

I slipped a picture of Beth Wade out of my notebook and slid it across the table. "Do you know this woman?"

Seke didn't pick it up. "I don't know. Like I said last time, I work there and see a lot of customers."

"You may have seen her but don't know her?"

Brogan said, "Hold on. Your question is much too vague. Clarify what you mean by know her. Are you asking if my client is familiar with her or is a friend of hers?"

"Fair enough. The woman in the picture is Beth Wade. Have you ever spoken to her?"

"I don't know, maybe a hello or something."

"Have you ever had a conversation with her? Something more than just an exchange of greetings?"

He shook his head.

"Is that a no? You haven't had a talk with Ms. Wade?"

"I didn't."

"Have you ever had a drink with her?"

"No."

"Were you ever in any part of the hotel with her?"

"No."

"I understand you had some trouble a couple of years ago."

Brogan said, "Is there a question in there?"

"Approximately five years ago, on the Miccosukee Reservation, weren't you accused of holding a woman captive in a trailer?"

Brogan's face whitened. He turned to his client, who said, "That was bullshit. I wasn't doing nothing. She wanted to be there. She could've left anytime she wanted."

"Then why was the trailer locked from the outside?"

"To keep her safe. She was scared. A lot of people were after her."

"Who or what was she scared of?"

"There were these men trying to get her. I seen them myself."

"And you locked her up to protect her?"

Brogan stuck an arm in front of Magi. "My client has already stated that the woman was there voluntarily."

"Is that so?"

"Yeah, I was only trying to keep her safe."

"Then why did your father, Chetan, a Seminole leader, intervene?"

Brogan said, "Don't answer. You cannot speak for anyone else. That would be speculative hearsay."

"As punishment for, as you say, protecting this woman, you were banished from the Miccosukee Reservation and forced to live in Immokalee. Is that right?"

Magi shrugged.

"How did you meet the woman that was staying in your trailer?"

"At a bar."

"What bar was that?"

"The Cypress Lounge."

"And where is that located?"

"At the Miccosukee Casino."

"Is that where you worked before being sent to work here?"

"Yeah."

I flipped to the back of my notebook and took another photo out. Brogan leaned forward as I slid it to Seke.

"Is that you standing by the bar with a woman?"

His eyes darted away from the picture. "Yeah."

"Can you tell me who the woman you are talking with is?"

"I don't know, some girl."

"That girl is Beth Wade. The woman you claimed not to have spoken with."

Brogan said, "Hold on, now, Detective. There isn't proof my client engaged in a conversation with the woman. She could have simply asked him where the woman's restroom was."

"We have video footage of your client approaching and speaking with Ms. Wade for fifteen minutes. Unless the bathroom was one in Las Vegas, there was something else going on here. My job is to find out what. Please answer the question, Mr. Seke."

"I don't know. We were just talking."

"About what?"

Brogan said, "Detective, it was a private conversation, which is not a crime."

"Were you enticing Ms. Wade so you could protect her like you did the woman in Miccosukee?"

"I didn't do nothing."

"Did you meet Ms. Wade outside of the casino?"

"No."

"Did you kidnap Ms. Wade?"

"No, I didn't. I swear."

"Did you harm or kill Ms. Wade?"

"No."

Brogan stood up. "My client has answered all of your questions. This interview is now over."

How would the Seminoles react now that they knew we had established that Seke knew Wade? Would they protect Seke from further questioning?

I found it curious that none of the lawyers intervened when I referenced the Miccosukee incident. Was that a tactical move, a nonverbal admission that something had occurred in case Seke was involved in Wade's disappearance?

We needed something tangible to expand the Seke inquiry. We needed an insider leaking something or a piece of evidence pointing toward Seke to keep Chester off my back.

26

IT WAS THE FIRST AUTOPSY I MISSED. THERE WERE PLENTY OF reasons to avoid attending the slicing and dicing of Beth Wade's body; the problem was, none of them were any good.

I just didn't want to be there. I couldn't understand why I felt that way, I just did. Mary Ann tried to draw it out of me, and I was truthful, to a degree. She was good with the armchair stuff, so much so that I almost tabled the idea of going to see Dr. Bruno, who'd helped me with my fear of becoming a father.

Mary Ann said she noticed I was becoming more negative, and she was concerned that I might fall into depression. She thought my refusal to attend an autopsy might be an instinctual way of protecting myself. It was as good an explanation as any head doctor could come up with. But it was wrong.

I wasn't depressed or on my way there. The only way I can explain it was the feeling that life was moving fast; whatever time I had was not only shrinking, but I was spending most of it dealing with twisted people and criminal behavior.

The other thing I was close to acknowledging was something Mary Ann had nailed two years ago: I was engaged in transference. It wasn't direct, but anytime a crime involved a female, I'd find myself thinking about how to protect Jessie from a similar fate.

It was normal, I told myself. What parent wouldn't have such thoughts? With me, though, I noticed it wouldn't pass. It would linger and I'd dwell on it. At first, I rationalized it was because of the additional baggage of being a homicide detective, but now, on my way to Dr. Bilotti's office, I knew it wasn't completely true.

I was hoping to get some clarity from the autopsy. Her soggy pocketbook, stripped of any cash or credit cards, hadn't provided any information other than a confirmation it was Wade. I couldn't discount robbery, but it didn't feel like that was what happened. Both Derrick and I tended to believe Wade's murder was either opportunistic or an attempt to throw off an investigation.

Bilotti's medical examiner's office was adorned with aerial shots of vineyards and family photos. It was an oasis of sorts. I couldn't help but wonder if it helped Bilotti deal with the realities of his job. Maybe there was more to learn from him than wine and biology.

Headphones on, Bilotti was behind his desk, tapping on his keyboard. I'd always figured he was listening to vocal notes he made as he performed an autopsy, but he looked so serene, I wondered if he was listening to classical music.

He took his headset off. "How are you doing, Frank?"

"Good, Doc."

"You sure?"

"Yeah, why?"

"You didn't attend the Wade autopsy."

"I know, sorry. I had a doctor's appointment, you know, for my bladder, and I missed the last two. Mary Ann was on my back, and I figured with all your experience, you could handle it without me."

"How did it go?"

"Everything is good. I have some pinching from the scar tissue, but the new plumbing is holding up."

"Good. Now to more important things; you drink anything good lately?"

"Nothing to compare with the bottle of Spanish wine you gave me."

"That was a Tempranillo. Good ones are tough to come by, but it's getting easier, and there are a lot of them in the thirty-dollar range."

"I have to check them out."

"You should check out some of the Rossos coming out of the Mt. Etna area. The soil there is volcanic rock, which results in small berries with intense color and flavors that are unique."

"I'm getting thirsty. What grapes do they grow?"

"The red wines are made with Nerello Mascalese."

"Never heard of it."

"Check those wines out. You're going to enjoy them."

"I won't remember the grape, but I'll remember it's a red from Mt. Etna."

"Good. Let's get to it, then. I'm teaching a class at Gulf Coast this afternoon."

"Sorry. What can you tell me from the autopsy?"

"The cause of death is suffocation."

"With a ligature?"

"No. By hand. The killer pinched her nose and covered her mouth. The victim had a severe laceration at the left-center base of her skull. She suffered a substantial cerebral hematoma that stunned or caused a loss of consciousness, which probably provided the attacker an opportunity to suffocate her without a big struggle. We could find no evidence of any skin under her fingernails; however, they were recently clipped. Whether the killer did it or not you'll have to determine."

"How short were her nails?"

"Extremely short. Now, she was in the water for several days, and we're unable to determine if it was done immediately prior to her being submerged."

Checking how Wade kept her nails was not a problem, but the idea we had a deliberate murderer on our hands was. I never worked a homicide case where a killer was knowledgeable and cool enough to consider DNA being left under their victim's fingernails. Maybe it was the simple fact that he recently watched a TV episode that had a reference to fingernail DNA.

"She was moved, right?"

"Definitely. No water in the lungs. The victim was dead when she entered the water."

"Time of death?"

"I wish I could be more specific, but I believe it is in the range of eight to twelve days."

That meant she was either killed the night she was last seen or had been held somewhere before being murdered.

"Okay. What about any evidence of sexual activity?"

"It does not appear recent activity, but it is not definitive. Given the decomposition and scavenging."

My stomach lurched at the thought of parasites attacking this poor woman's private parts.

"Any other wounds?"

"Bruising on the wrists that was probably the result of being restrained."

"Male hands?"

"Not possible to distinguish."

"What about anything she might have ate or drank?"

"Stomach contents indicate a meal, meat based, possibly a burger, six to eight hours before death."

If she was held captive, would a killer feed her before murdering her? Or had she set him off? Wade was a fighter. She could have attacked him in an attempt to break free and he retaliated.

"How long before the tox reports?"

"These days, anywhere from a week to two."

"How do you think this went down?"

"This is a tough one. The skull wound could have been caused by someone forcing her head onto a hard object or by a direct strike from behind. That the victim was placed in water and had her nails cut indicates someone familiar with forensics."

"If she was struck from the rear, what kind of weapon was used?"

"Again, difficult to ascertain. It was blunt, though, perhaps something like an iron bar."

"From her physical condition, could you speculate on whether she was held captive for any period?"

"Not really. She had food in her stomach. Let's see what the toxicology report evidences. There's a possibility an indication of malnutrition will be found."

27

————

This was my second trip to the home of Ben Rowan, the gambler and Promo Pros owner. It turned out they didn't have a house phone, which wasn't unusual, but no one was home when I went by the first time, and he wasn't at work.

Rowan didn't answer his cell phone either. While it was true that with all the robocalls, most people wouldn't answer a call from a number they didn't recognize, most of us would listen to the voice message left by a caller.

Why hadn't Rowan returned a call from a detective? Did he think it was a scam? It was a possible reaction, but the idea he had run began to creep into my thoughts.

His back was so bad that he couldn't work, yet his not being home bothered me. I swung off Pine Ridge into Summer Wind. Rowan lived in the last yellow building on the left. Someone walked past a front window, easing my mind.

The buildings were old but recently painted, albeit in a lemon color. A woman, on the cusp of obesity, said, "Yes, what is it?"

I held out my badge. "Detective Luca, Collier County Sheriff's Office."

"The sheriff's office?"

"Yes, ma'am. Are you Mrs. Rowan?"

She whispered, "Yes."

"Is your husband home?"

"Ben?"

Did she have more than one? "Yes, Ben Rowan."

"He's away, on a business trip."

"Is that so? When did he leave town?"

"Uh, a week ago."

"Where did he travel to?"

"To China. To visit his suppliers."

"How often does he travel for business?"

"A couple of times a year, you know, to see customers, go to trade shows, and every year or so he goes to Asia to look for new products."

"Was this a last-minute trip?"

"I don't think so."

"You don't know for sure?"

"I'm sorry, I've been running back and forth, taking care of my mom. She's been in and out of hospitals, battling cancer. I even forgot my sister's birthday last week."

"I'm sorry to hear. When is your husband due back?"

"Uh, what date is today?"

"July seventeenth."

"Oh, he's back the twentieth."

"I understand your husband likes to gamble."

Her shoulders sagged. "Is that what this is about?"

"How often does he frequent the Immokalee casino?"

"Too much, if you ask me. At least once a week if not twice."

"He plays blackjack?"

"That, and for some reason, I guess it's the gambler in

him, he plays the slots. He tells me he's going to win the jackpot one day."

"He goes in the evening?"

"Yes. A couple of years ago he was sneaking away during the day, but I threatened to leave if he didn't get help."

"And he did?"

"Yes, he went to group therapy at the David Lawrence Center. It helped."

"How much does he wager?"

"He tells me five dollars a hand. I know he's lying, but it's nothing more than ten or twenty. After we lost the house, I took over the finances. He gets two hundred a week for expenses. If he wants to go without lunch to gamble, that's his choice to make."

Two hundred a week was a lot of money to lose each week. "His business going okay?"

"Yeah, pretty good. The trade war with China's made him look into other places he could get products from, like Vietnam."

"Did he talk about anyone he met at the casino?"

"Sometimes he would, especially if they won big."

"He ever mention a woman named Beth Wade, who also was a regular at the casino?"

"Beth Wade?"

"Yes, she played blackjack as well."

"No, I don't think so. Why?"

"Nothing, just thought I'd ask. Tell Mr. Rowan I'll see him when he returns."

I sat in the Cherokee replaying the chat with Mrs. Rowan. She never invited me in, which seemed unusual, but she was alone, and it was the right call; imitating a law enforcement officer was an old ploy deviants used. I had to make sure Jessie understood that she shouldn't take a badge or identification at face value. It was perfectly fine to ask the presenter to wait while you called to verify its authenticity.

Rowan was overseas. Convenient or coincidence?

Pulling my cell phone out, I made a call.

"Promo Pros. How may I help you?"

"This is Detective Luca. I came in yesterday looking for Ben Rowan."

"Yes. I remember. You're the one who looks like George Clooney."

"You told me that Ben Rowan had hurt his back and was at the doctor's."

"Yeah, well, that's what he told us to say anytime he wasn't in."

"But I'm a police officer."

"I know, but that's what he told us to say. I heard the woman I replaced was fired because she told somebody something different, like he was at a casino."

***

THE TALK-RADIO STATION I was listening to on the way home had a motivational speaker on. He sounded like he could improve anyone's life. I wondered if the advice he dished out so easily was something he followed himself. Either way, it was uplifting to listen to and made me realize I had to do better in the "being grateful" department.

Mary Ann and Jessie were out on a playdate. Changing into shorts and a T-shirt, I decided to take the speaker's advice. He said that we have to celebrate our small wins. I went to the closet and pulled a bottle of wine from the Rhone Valley and popped the cork.

I poured a glass and went outside, settling in a chaise. Sniffing the wine, I tried to identify what I was smelling. I took a sip and rolled it around in my mouth. It was all dark fruit. Maybe blackberries and plums, or was it blueberries? I took another sip and heard Jessie calling for me.

I took another taste and was about to get up when the slider opened, and my two reasons for living came over.

"Daddy, Daddy, Cindy got a dollhouse. Can I get one?"

"Really? Was it nice?"

"Her daddy made it."

Five-thumb Luca would have to buy one. "Mommy and Daddy will take you the store to see what they have, okay?"

"When? When can we go?"

Mary Ann said, "If we have time tomorrow, we'll go before Daddy gets home. If not, we can go with Daddy on Saturday."

"Okay, tomorrow. Do they have one like Cindy's?"

"Maybe. We'll see. Go check the tomato plant, okay? See if it grew."

Jessie ran to the corner of the lanai, and Mary Ann took a sip of my wine. "Wine on a Thursday?"

"Just celebrating a little."

"You caught the Wade killer?"

"No. But we got the guy doing the graffiti."

"You did? Don't tell me it was from that cap you found on Fifth Avenue."

"Yep. Crazy thing is, they found a match for the fingerprint in the database. The guy had a prior for smoking marijuana in public."

"He was arrested for smoking pot?"

"Nine years ago. It's funny, marijuana is about to be legal everywhere, and it's what led to catching this guy."

I raised my glass. "Here's to databases. Salute."

28

BEN ROWAN HAD A CHECKERED PAST, BUT IT WAS ALL
financially related: a handful of suits, a pair of bankruptcies,
and a credit score that mirrored a blood-pressure reading.
Mrs. Rowan might be in line for sainthood.

It was probable that most of his problems stemmed from
his gambling addiction. He didn't have any brushes with the
law aside from being involved in a road rage incident.
According to the report filed by the Tampa police, Rowan had
been assaulted by another driver.

Closing out the inquiry screen, I said, "There's nothing
criminal on Rowan. He's a mess financially, but there's not
much else."

Derrick said, "You always say it's usually greed that's
behind a homicide."

"True, but Wade didn't have much. How would Rowan
have benefited from her death?"

"Maybe he was desperate. She could have had a good
night."

"We can look a little further into that, but from what I saw
she wasn't exactly killing it that night."

"He could have been borrowing from the wrong people, and they wanted their money. He could have been threatened if he didn't pay and looked at Wade to buy time."

"Unless we can find evidence of a meaningful debt, it wouldn't make sense. Poke around some on it, but the priority right now is to see if you can find anyone that can get us to crack the Seminole silence."

"I like the sound of that: Seminole silence. It sounds like a movie."

"Check with the substation up there. See if they have any informants we might be able to lean on. Get ahold of Crowley. He owes me a favor."

"I'm on it."

"All right, I'm going to see Hercules."

***

BELCHER WASN'T in the gym. One of his lifting buddies, who brought to mind the Incredible Hulk, said he might be having lunch. He suggested I look a couple of doors down from LA Fitness. Sure enough, Belcher was sitting outside the Fit Fuel Café talking to a normal-sized man with a beard.

I approached, and his companion saw me and said goodbye. I pegged him as Belcher's steroid supplier. It was more proof the criminal set had a sixth sense that enabled them to detect a police officer from a distance.

Belcher was sucking on a straw from one of two jumbo-sized containers in front of him, one a beige sludge, the other lime green. I pulled out a chair and said, "That's a hell of a lunch. What's it taste like?"

"You get used to it. It's not bad."

"They sell that here?"

"No, I mix 'em up at home."

The straw he was using was as wide as the water pipes under a sink. "What do you put in it?"

"Ah, a lot of stuff, mostly proteins, amino acids, that sort of thing."

I was certain his cocktail included a couple doses of the latest growth hormone. His arms were so bulky I wondered how he could turn the steering wheel to make a U-turn. I also pondered if the steroids impacted his sexual activity. When I researched its effects, I knew it screwed with moods and could result in anger-filled rages, but it also said it could improve erectile performance.

He could have been more horny than normal, and if Wade refused to satisfy his urge, the rejection may have led him to become violent.

"Makes you feel good?"

"Oh yeah, makes me feel alive."

Belcher had veins in places I'd never seen on my body. "Unlike your girlfriend Beth Wade."

"It was terrible what happened to her."

"When was the last time you spoke with her?"

"Oh, I don't know. A while ago."

"Let me refresh your memory. You spoke on the phone Monday night, July seventh, the last time she was seen alive."

"Really? It was that same day?"

"Why did you call her that night?"

"Just to say hello, see how she was doing."

"And how was she?"

"She seemed fine."

"Did she tell you where she was?"

"Yeah, she said something about the casino."

Something? "What else?"

"Nothing, really. To tell you the truth, I was looking for a little company, if you know what I mean."

"I have no idea what you mean. Why don't you explain it?"

He frowned. "I was looking to hook up with her."

"Have a sexual encounter with Beth Wade?"

"Yeah."

"The last time we spoke, you indicated that you didn't see her much anymore."

"That's right. I hardly saw her. You know, when I'm training heavy, I shut everything out. I need to focus."

"Aren't you competing soon?"

"Yeah, four days away. I'm pumped. Can't wait. I'll tell you, I'm in about the best shape of my career. And it's because I'm focused like never before."

"You shut everything out?"

"Yeah, it's the gym, then recovery, and back in the gym."

"But you called Ms. Wade to hook up."

"I, I was, look, all this stimulation and this"—he lifted a bottle up—"gets me riled up. I need a release."

"Did you go to the casino to meet her the night of July seventh?"

"She wanted me to come there."

"Did you go?"

"I thought about going but didn't."

"And why was that?"

"I didn't feel like driving up there. It would take too long. I'm in training. I got to be focused on that."

"You didn't have the time, is that it?"

"Yeah, exactly."

"But you had the time to call her, try to set up some sort of date and have relations with her. Wouldn't that take time?"

"Yeah, but I don't like going to the casino. Hey, man, from outside you can smell the smoke. They don't have a real separate section for the smokers. It's bullshit. You know, I can't be breathing that crap in, especially close to a competition."

"You're right about the smoke, but we have video of your truck coming into the casino's parking lot."

"My truck?"

"Yes, sir."

"It wasn't me, man."

We had a truck whose make, model, and color matched his. The problem was that Florida only required rear license plates, and the footage only captured the front of the vehicle as it entered the driveway. When the pickup left the property, it used an exit which caught only a side view of the vehicle. We didn't know if it really was Belcher or not and had been trying to get proof that he was out that night.

What was interesting was his response. He didn't say it wasn't his truck but that it wasn't him driving it.

29

THE CARLISLE'S LOBBY, A CIRCULAR, TRIPLE-STORIED SPACE, was cheerful and sunny. The woman's disposition at reception matched perfectly. I hated to spoil her party by showing her my badge. It wasn't any of her business why I was there nor worth my time explaining it.

"She was in the gym when her son came in a few minutes ago. It's down the corridor to the right."

It was one of the things that made Southwest Florida different from New Jersey. Up there, weather aside, as most people aged, they decreased their activity. Down here, people in their eighties and nineties still exercised. And I don't mean walking in a restaurant.

One of our neighbors is ninety-five years old, but every morning he's out pushing his walker around the block. I remember going over to him when I saw him struggling.

"You need a hand?"

"No."

"Maybe you should take it easy."

"I'm not ready to RIP."

"I, I, didn't mean anything, certainly not rest in peace."

"It's not rest in peace. It's rust in place."

"You're right. Go for it."

The long hallway was filled with residents and family members all standing next to the wall. The line of people was at a standstill. I scooted around them, spying the reason for the holdup: the dining room.

I checked my watch. It was fifteen after eleven. The sign on the door stated that the dining room opened at a quarter to twelve.

There was music coming from a room at the end of the hall. I walked past the gym and peeked through the door. It wasn't entertainment for the residents. It was a large ensemble playing a song I recognized as a Sinatra tune. I wanted to hang around and listen, but I was on the clock.

As soon as I walked in, Michael Whitaker headed over. His mother was sitting in a wheelchair moving a plastic bowling pin from one side of table to the other.

"Detective Luca, it's good to see you."

"How is she doing?"

"She's tough, but these TIAs are taking a toll on her."

"Sorry to hear that. Are those small strokes?"

"Yes, ministrokes. She lost some mobility in her left side. That's what the occupational therapy is for."

"She looks good, though."

"Yeah, but she's fading, and the thing that worries me is she seems to be giving up."

"I'm sorry. That must be hard."

"You have no idea. It looks like Mom is almost done. Why don't you wait in the living area off the lobby?"

He was right. I had no clue what he and millions of others were going through. Getting old sucked, but it was miles better than the alternative. He wouldn't want to trade his parents' longevity with mine.

I sat in a club chair by a grand piano. There was a small bar across the room. It was empty now, but I knew that wouldn't last. Naples was a town where everyone loved their cocktails.

Michael Whitaker pushed his mother into the room, and I stood as he wheeled her over.

"Mrs. Whitaker, it's nice to see you again."

She extended a liver-spotted hand. She was thin, but her gray eyes were clear, and she pulled her shoulders back just before we shook hands.

"And you, Detective. I hope you're going to keep your promise."

"I think I have."

I settled into my chair, and her son sat next to me. "So what do you have to tell us?"

"I believe we know who murdered your husband, ma'am."

"Believe? That sounds like what they've been telling me for thirty years."

"I understand your frustration. I'm not sure your son told you of the difficulties we were having in regard to an exhumation of the man we believe killed your husband."

"So, it was Frank Tate after all."

"We think so. We used a DNA technique to conclude that the DNA discovered on your husband's body was his."

"Technique?"

"Yes, ma'am. It's called familial DNA matching."

Her son said, "How accurate is this?"

"Oftentimes we collect DNA at a crime scene and run it through a database but do not get a match. If a person hasn't been arrested for a felony, we won't have their DNA on file. In this case, his son agreed to give us a sample of his DNA, and that is how we know it was Frank Tate."

"You didn't answer on the accuracy."

"Nothing is one hundred percent, but I am confident it was Frank Tate. He knew your husband, had a long record, and we have as much of a match as possible with his son's sample."

"Frank Tate. We had him over for dinner dozens of times. We lent him money . . ." She sniffed back some snot. "It's unbelievable."

"I'm sorry, ma'am."

"Don't be. I'm grateful to know who did it. I owe you a debt of gratitude."

"It's my job, ma'am."

"I'm sure you have more than enough to do without looking into on old case."

"I'm glad we were able to resolve this for you."

<hr>

I WAS BACK in the St. Croix Apartment complex. It was convenient that Beth Wade's husband worked nights, enabling me to see him during the day. I smelled cigarette smoke as soon as he opened the door. With his wife dead, he was moving on, smoking inside the home.

Frelig looked tired, which was natural after working the overnight shift, but there was a weary look to him. He wasn't getting much sleep. The question was whether it was because of the loss he suffered or the worrying that he'd be exposed as his wife's killer?

He picked up a mug that was sitting on the glass kitchen table. "You want a coffee?"

"No, thanks."

Frelig popped a pod into a machine, and the smell made me reconsider my answer. He emptied four packs of sugar into his cup. He wasn't going to lose his flab by doing that.

"Do you have any leads that you're following?"

"Several, but I'm not at liberty to discuss an open investigation."

"Are you close to finding who did it?"

"Like I said, I can't talk about it. Have you thought of anyone who might have done it?"

He sipped his coffee. "I still think it was someone at the casino. She was having a good night, and people, they're always watching, you know what I mean?"

"You think she was murdered over money?"

"Yeah, somebody wanted the money she won. I mean, like, what else could it be?"

I was tempted to tell him that the far majority of time it was the husband who killed his wife, especially those who got into physical altercations with their spouses.

"Though robberies sometimes turn into homicides, I'm not certain that is what we have here."

He ran a hand across the stubble on his chin. "People do all kinds of things for money."

"No doubt. I wanted to ask you about the night of July seventh, after you last saw your wife."

"I went to work and didn't get home till, like, six thirty the next morning."

"Okay. What was work like that night?"

"What do you mean?"

"What did you do all those hours?"

"It was a normal night, nothing unusual."

"Was it busy?"

"No, I think I only had, like, one tow that night."

"You actually had three calls, according to the records Ray Baker showed me."

He leaned forward. "You went to my job? You're going to get me fired, man."

"You have nothing to worry about if you didn't do anything wrong."

"What's that supposed to mean?"

"Exactly what I said. You don't have to be concerned about your job if you weren't involved in your wife's murder."

"Well, I wasn't. I had nothing to do with it. She was my wife, for God's sake."

"Let's stick with what you did that night. The tickets say you responded to three motorists, right?"

"If that's what the records say, it's probably right."

"Two of those calls came through a Baker's dispatcher. The third one, you claimed that someone flagged you down."

"Yeah, that's right. This guy was waving as I was cruising on Immokalee."

"Whereabouts?"

He hesitated. "Uh, sorry, had to think about it. It was by Oil Well Road."

"What kind of a car was it?"

"I'm pretty sure it was a BMW, an older one. The guy needed a jump. You know batteries don't last down here; the heat kills them."

"He was stuck there, and you just happened to drive by and jump-started his car?"

"Yeah, happens all the time."

"Does it really? I find that strange. Everybody has a cell phone, and they use it to call someone when they need help."

"Yeah, the guy said he called his brother and was waiting for him when I came along."

"What side of the road was he on?"

"He was headed toward Naples."

"What color was the car?"

"Uh, white."

"What did the guy look like?"

"You think I made this up or something?"

"What did the driver look like?"

"He was just a regular guy."

"What was he wearing?"

"Jeans and a T-shirt."

"What kind of vehicle was it?"

"I said it was a Beemer."

"And it was stuck all the way east, by Oil Well Road?"

"Yeah, that's right."

"You told the office that this guy paid in cash."

"I remember that."

"Isn't that unusual?"

"No, most of the times it's a credit card, but people still use real money."

"You know, where this car supposedly was is only about fifteen minutes from the casino."

"If you say so."

"Is that a coincidence?"

"What?"

"Your wife was last seen a couple of minutes from where you claimed to be."

He shrugged. "So?"

"Here's what I think. I believe you made up the story about the stranded driver flagging you down. You needed a cover to be close to the casino, and you thought this was a perfect way to do it."

"So, you think I killed Beth? You're crazy, man. I didn't do nothing."

30

Derrick caught me in the hallway. "Casey said that none of the patrol cars saw a car stranded in the area Frelig claimed."

"He's climbing the suspect ladder, two rungs at a time."

"What do you want to do?"

"I'd rather not ask the media for help, but it'll be the quickest way to find out if his car story is true."

"It's desolate out there, especially at night, but there's always someone coming or going to work. Maybe we'll get lucky."

"It'll be Frelig who's the fortunate one."

"I'll draft something up for them to use and run it by you."

"Thanks. Don't mention the vehicle type. I don't want any prompting going on."

"No problem."

"All right, let me get on my way to see Gates."

I EASED the Cherokee over the spiked rail that prevented anyone from leaving the lot and pulled as close to the terminal as possible. A kid in a yellow shirt trotted over.

"I'm sorry, sir. You can't park there."

I showed him my badge. "I'll just be a few minutes, if that's all right?"

"Sure, no problem at all."

The temperature inside had to be a good twenty degrees cooler. Counters stretched from one end of the building to the other. Hertz had the largest presence. Not surprising, since they'd moved their headquarters down here a couple of years ago.

As I headed for the yellow counter, I wondered what this place would look like in ten years. With the increased usage of Uber, Lyft, and who knew who else, demand for rental cars had to be declining.

Behind one of five stations, Cybill Gates was glued to her monitor. She was wearing a black and yellow Hertz shirt. As I approached, an employee shouted, "Cyb, Jerry's on line two."

She looked up, spotted me, and paused before saying, "Tell him I'll call him back later."

Waving, I tried to compute the odds that there was another Jerry in Cybill's life.

"Do you have a minute?"

She scrunched her pixie nose. "They don't like it when we leave the counter."

"Tell them you're taking your break early. I'll be outside."

The sliders opened, and I was engulfed in heat. It took the chill out of me. I never understood why they kept the AC so low. Electricity was much cheaper down here, but in my view, it was still a waste of money.

Gates's thin legs looked like poles sticking out of her black skirt. "I only have ten minutes."

"That's fine."

"Did you find out who killed Beth?"

"Not yet, but I can't talk about an ongoing investigation."

"What did you want to talk to me about, then?"

"When we met at your home, you never mentioned that you spoke with Beth the night she went missing."

"I called her?"

"Yes. We have the phone records."

"And I didn't say anything about it?"

"No. Why was that?"

"Because you never asked me about it."

"You needed a detective to ask you about a call you made to a woman who went missing a couple of hours later? Don't you think it would be natural to mention it? Even in passing, like, she's missing? I just spoke with her."

"I guess so."

"What did you talk about?"

"Oh, just this and that."

Was this woman kidding me? "You're going to have to do better than that. What was the conversation about?"

"I just called her to see how she was doing. She hadn't been to the gym in a couple of days, and I was concerned. That's all."

"And what did she say?"

"Not much, just that she had been busy and was at the casino. She said she went there because she had a fight with her husband."

"Beth Wade told you she fought with John Frelig the day she disappeared?"

"Yeah, that's what she told me."

"Was it an argument or a fight?"

"I'm pretty sure she said fight."

"Did she say it was physical?"

"From what I know, most of the time it was."

"Just to be certain, the night of July seventh, Wade told you she went to the casino because of a fight with her husband?"

"Yep."

"You said you weren't close with her but yet you called her?"

"Just because we weren't close doesn't mean I didn't care about her. We were gym buddies. When she didn't come in for a couple of days, I got concerned."

"What time do you go to the gym?"

"Most of the time around nine in the morning."

"And Beth would come at the same time?"

"Yep."

"If she wasn't there that morning, why did you wait until nighttime to call her?"

"I don't know. It's when I remembered, you know, thinking of the next day and all."

"Do you know why her mother gave me your name as a friend if you weren't close?"

She shrugged. "How would I know? Beth never mentioned any other friends. Maybe I was the only one she had. I really got to get back inside."

"I have one more question. You just received a call from a Jerry. Would that be Jerry Belcher?"

"Uh, no. I mean, I don't think so. It was probably Jerry Delta that called. I got to go."

As Gates headed to the car rental center, I turned to go to my car. Staring me in the face was a sign that read Delta Airlines.

What was Gates hiding? She claimed not to like muscle-men, but there seemed to be something going on between Belcher and her. Why hadn't she revealed the call earlier? If what she said about a fight was true, we'd have to look at whether Frelig was incensed enough to kill her. Their marriage was rocky, and Wade could have told him she was leaving him, setting him off.

On the other side of it, would the fight and the frustration of her marriage make Wade feel so lonely that she'd let her defenses down and get involved with the wrong man?

31

———

Driving to our next appointment, I had mixed feelings about the Preschool for the Arts. The concept of focusing on the creative side of things made sense. It was prekindergarten, after all, and from everything I read, if you encouraged a child to be creative, they'd handle academics better as they aged.

What I didn't like was the exclusive feel. It was a bit too snobbish for me. And the school's facilities were located in a Jewish center. Like my feelings about the Presbyterian preschool, I wanted it nondenominational. If there was a religion attached to it, I wanted it to be Catholic.

The other thing was its cost. It was expensive.

Following Mary Ann north on Route 41, my phone rang. It was Bilotti.

"Hey, Doc, how's it going?"

"Good, can you talk for a minute?"

"Sure. Actually, I'm on my way to see another preschool for Jessie. Boy, are we in the wrong business."

"It was nothing like that when we raised our kids. We sent

them to a couple of camps and play groups before they went to kindergarten."

"I'd like to do that, but at this point we need Mary Ann to work."

"I understand. Good luck with it."

"Thanks. What's up?"

"We just received the toxicology report on Wade."

"Anything on it?"

"Nothing besides a blood level alcohol of oh point eight."

"She was drunk."

"Legally, for the purposes of operating a motor vehicle, she was. However, that doesn't mean she was unable to function."

"Watching the footage of her at the end of the night, she didn't appear to be out of it."

"Other than that, there was nothing of note."

"Her nutritional values were all okay?"

"Yes, nothing outside of the normal ranges. I'll forward a copy of the report for the murder book."

"Okay, Doc. I appreciate it."

"My pleasure, Frank. Oh, I'm going to send you an email for a hot little winery in Paso Robles. You're going to love their wines. They're California Rhone Rangers. Get on their mailing list. They're about to do another release."

"Expensive?"

"Fifty to sixty dollars a bottle, but worth every penny."

"That's steep, but I can swing a bottle or two."

"You won't regret it."

"Thanks."

What Bilotti told me did nothing for the case. When was I going to get a break? I thought about her blood alcohol levels. The casino was all too willing to give its customers free drinks. They disguised it as a perk, but the reality was, they knew that drinking impaired your ability to reason and led to risky behavior.

We didn't know what her history with drinking was. Could she handle her booze, and that was why she didn't appear to be bombed? Or was it possible she had a drink or two after leaving the casino?

If so, the question was, with who and where?

I made a left onto Ninety-Fourth Street and parked next to Mary Ann. This school's name was fun and different. I said to Mary Ann, "I get a kick out of the school's name."

"It's cute. I'm glad you like it."

Before I set foot in Little People's School, in Naples, it had two things going for it. Most importantly, they invited police officers and firefighters to school to teach children how to be safe, and it was conveniently located. The school was across the street from Whole Foods and Mercato. We could grab groceries or a bite to eat when we picked Jessie up.

Actually, it also had another check mark in the pro column; it was cheaper than the other schools.

We were greeted by a pleasant woman who taught the children, not a sales-oriented administrator. They had camera surveillance, and the lobby area was locked from the outside but also secure from the areas where the kids were.

As we neared the end of our tour, I hoped that nothing would pop up that would turn me off the place. We retreated to a shared office. It was the first place where they actually asked about our daughter. It was refreshing.

I expected that she would close by saying that Little People's School seemed like the perfect fit, and she didn't disappoint. It didn't alter my opinion of the place.

"What do you think? Because I really like this place for Jessie."

"It's nice, but there doesn't seem to be a lot of time for learning."

"They do the alphabet and how to say words the right way."

"But that's about it."

"She's only three. They have plenty of interaction time, and it's her first structured environment."

"You're right. It will probably be a good transition for her."

"Yeah, and the location is great. I say let's do it."

"Let's sleep on it."

"But we saw a bunch of other schools, and this place just feels right for Jessie. Look, we know our kid better than anybody, and for me, this is for her."

"I'm not saying no, Frank. We're not going to sign up this second. Let's think a little more about this choice. There's no sense in rushing it."

"But you like it, no?"

"Yes, I like it. All I am saying is to slow it down."

"Sure thing. I'll see you later." I kissed her cheek and climbed into the Cherokee, feeling good.

Stopped at the light on the Vanderbilt Beach intersection, I shifted from preschool to the Wade case. Had Wade left the casino parking lot with someone else, had a drink or two, and met her killer?

No one said she was streetwise, but she was no kid and wouldn't get into someone else's car at that hour unless she knew them. You certainly wouldn't have a drink with someone who abducted you. But who would be hanging out in the part of the lot where cameras couldn't reach?

32

Derrick came in shaking his head. "The lab said there's nothing they can do with the video of the Explorer. They said there was no way to enhance it, even to see if it's a male or female driving. The light is too bad. No way to tell if it belonged to that muscleman, Belcher."

"Damn it."

"I can't believe it. I was certain they'd be able to do something."

"If the pixels aren't there to begin with, there's nothing anyone can do."

"If this was *CSI* they could."

"You got that right. These TV shows make everything look easy. Those damn directors should work a real case with us."

"It'd be too boring, buddy."

"Amen."

"Oh, I called Wade's mother and her husband about her drinking. They said she liked her vodka but never got sloppy."

"So, she had a capacity to handle her booze. There are plenty of people who can function with alcohol blood levels that would floor others."

"You don't think she met up with someone and had a drink after leaving the casino?"

"Oh, she encountered someone, but it wasn't for a drink."

"What do you want to do next?"

"I'm hoping someone steps up in the Seminole community or they make a mistake and need a get-out-of-jail card. Let's see what happens, but for the moment, we have Belcher, Frelig, and Rowan, and Berry, and Anderson who think Wade screwed them over."

"You know, on Belcher, it might be a good idea to ask the lab to run the facial recognition software to see if he was at the casino."

Why hadn't I thought of that? "We have someone with a build like his leaving, so yeah, get that going. It's a great idea."

"Thanks."

"On Frelig, we're waiting on the cell phone warrant, and we need Rowan to get his ass back in the States. That leaves us with Berry and Anderson."

"They both have records and have been violent."

"And it's about money, money, money. Greed and passion, neck and neck as homicide motivators."

"Nothing's changed in a couple of thousand years."

The phone rang as I said, "We're hardwired as a species."

Derrick said, "It's Mrs. Wade. She wants to speak to you."

"Hello, Mrs. Wade. It's Detective Luca. What can I do for you?"

"I just had a very disturbing call."

I immediately thought pranksters, but then she continued.

"A man. I'm pretty sure he was disguising his voice. He said he wanted the money that Beth owed him."

I jumped up. "What did he say, exactly?"

"He started off with, just because your kid is gone, it don't mean her debt is gone. He said he expected me to pay the money that he lent her."

"How much did he say she owed him?"

"Twenty-five thousand. I just can't believe she would borrow money from a creep like that. Why didn't she come to me?"

"What did you tell him?"

"That I didn't know what he was talking about, and he said don't play dumb with me. I said, I wasn't lying about it and that I didn't have that kind of money anyway."

"What did he say to that?"

"He said he didn't care and that I had to find the money."

"Did he make any threats?"

"What do you mean? The entire call was a threat."

"I was trying to see if he mentioned anything specific."

"No, just that he wanted the money. How do I know she even borrowed any money from him?"

I wanted to say that with her daughter's gambling problem, it was probable that she borrowed from an unsavory source, but instead I said, "Your daughter had applied for a personal loan. Remember?"

"Yes, but what does that have to do with this creepy call?"

"It's evidence she needed money."

"Everybody needs money."

It was obvious she didn't want to think of her daughter dealing with people who loan sharked, and there was no point in piling anything onto a grieving mother. "While I don't think you are in any danger, I'm going to have a patrol car sit on your block as a precaution. Additionally, I'd like you to grant us permission to access your phone records. Though the caller probably used a burner—"

"A what?"

"Burner is slang for a phone that can't be traced. It's preloaded with talk time, and when you're done you either add more time on it or toss it, like criminals do."

"Oh, I see."

"I'd like to see if we can trace the caller. Is that okay?"

"Yes. I don't want him bothering me again."

"I'd like you to be extra careful. Don't answer the door if you don't recognize who it is, and keep your outdoor lights on. Both front and back. If you hear or see something at your house or anywhere, call 911 first, then me."

"Okay. This is scary."

"Don't worry. These are common-sense suggestions. Now, if he or anyone calls again, let me know immediately."

"I will. Do you really believe there's nothing to worry about?"

I'd rather answer a question about the meaning of life. "Yes, there'll be a car on your street within the hour. Don't open the door for strangers and keep your lights on. You'll be fine."

"Okay, I will. Thank you."

Hanging up, I said, "Ask Casey to park a patrol car on Mrs. Wade's street. She received a call from someone looking to collect on a debt her daughter owed."

"Holy shit! It could be that they pressed her daughter for payment and it got out of control. She died, intentionally or not, and now they're going after the mother. How much we talking about?"

"She said it was twenty-five thousand."

Derrick got up. "People have been killed over a lot less."

"It's depressing."

"I'll go see Casey."

"When you get back, have the suits upstairs draft a letter of authorization for Mrs. Wade to sign. We need to see if we can trace the call."

33

———

IT WAS NINE FIFTEEN, AND TOW-TRUCK FRELIG WOULD probably be sleeping. It was childish, but it felt like the perfect time to call. The phone only rang once before it was answered. Had I dialed the wrong number? The voice was female.

"Hello?"

"This is Detective Luca with the Collier County Sheriff's Office. Is John Frelig available?"

"He's sleeping."

"Please wake him up."

"Really?"

"Yes, really."

She dropped the phone, and I heard her call his name. A minute later, Frelig picked up the phone.

"I was sleeping, man. What do you want?"

"Did you have an argument with Beth Wade on July seventh, the last time she was seen alive?"

"What?"

"You heard me. Did you argue with your wife the last time she went to the casino?"

"Who told you that?"

"Never mind who told us; answer the question."

"Yeah, we argued a little."

"Why didn't you say something to me?"

"We argued a lot; it was no big deal."

"What was the nature of the fight?"

He sighed. "It was the gambling, her constant gambling."

"Was she addicted?"

"If she wasn't, she was close. But you couldn't tell her that. She was putting us in a fucking hole with the losses."

"You said she was having a good night at the casino. That she was winning."

"She said she was. She'd win every now and then, but never enough to cover the losses, and I was goddamn sick of it. You know, she made good money at her job, but she pissed it all away."

"Do you know if she borrowed money from the wrong people?"

"No, but it wouldn't be a shock. She left me with, like, twenty grand in credit card debt."

Even though Wade was dead, if he was on the credit card account he'd have to pay. It seemed unfair in a case like this, but I understood why the rule existed. "Can you think of anyone she would have gone to that could be considered an unconventional source of money?"

"Not really."

"It looks like you've moved on."

"What's that mean?"

"You have a lady friend over."

"It's none of your business. My wife is dead, but you know that, don't you?"

Sure, I knew it, but I wanted, no, make that needed to know who did it.

I leaned back and closed my eyes. Everything in a homicide detective's training made a husband the main suspect. Frelig was no different, but I felt sorry for him. Being married to someone with an addiction or obsession was extremely challenging and colored the way you thought and rationalized.

It was no excuse to kill someone. If he was overwhelmed, he could have left her. Frelig and she not only fought, it got so bad the police were called. He was in the area with a story we were trying to authenticate.

With a new woman warming his bed, it was clear whatever feelings he once had, they were gone. It was true his wife was dead, but even the coldest of us walking the planet wouldn't sleep with another woman, especially in the bed you shared with your wife, a week after she was found dead.

We had no footage of Frelig in the casino or entering the parking lot with a Baker's tow truck. That wasn't particularly unusual. That kind of vehicle would attract attention and be remembered.

Had Frelig used another car, a friend's, or was it his new lady friend's vehicle? Had he parked the tow truck in a concealed area and walked to the casino, cutting through the preserve? He knew her car.

If the damn casino would have installed cameras that covered their entire property, we'd have solved this already. It made me angry, but the reality was most businesses didn't cover their entire parking lots. With the price of electronics coming down, I was certain a situation like this wouldn't happen ten years out.

My mind strayed to the real possibility that satellites would capture all movement in the open. Then the phone rang.

"Homicide. Detective Luca."

"Uh, hi, my name is Lauren Strom. I was Beth Wade's neighbor about ten years ago."

"What can I do for you, Ms. Strom?"

"Well, I was away in Australia, visiting my daughter, and I just got back and heard the news about Beth."

"Yes?"

"It might be nothing, but I just kept thinking, then telling myself it didn't mean anything, but then, I said it couldn't hurt to let the police know, in case they didn't."

"Do you have something to tell me?"

"It's about her first husband, Scott Dorsey. He's not a nice man, and considering what happened to Beth, you should take a close look at him."

"Not being a pleasant person doesn't mean they're a murderer, ma'am."

"I'm not a child, Detective, and I don't appreciate being talked to as one."

Fair enough. "I'm sorry. It wasn't meant as an insult. Is there something in particular about Mr. Dorsey that concerns you?"

"There certainly is, because I don't know many men with two ex-wives that were both murdered."

I found myself looking at the receiver. I'd heard of a couple of cases like that but had never been involved in one.

"You're saying that her first husband, Scott Dorsey, had another ex that ended up murdered?"

"That's right."

"When was the other woman murdered?"

"About six years ago."

"How long after their divorce?"

"Geez, let me think, probably about four years or so. It's tough to say. They were separated for a while, but four years seems about right."

"What was the wife's name?"

"Angela."

"And this happened in what town?"

"In Estero, we've lived a couple of doors away from him for ten years now."

"Okay. Thank you for calling me with this."

"You think I'm crazy, don't you?"

"No, ma'am."

"You should look into Scott. He's not stable. He got away with murder once, and I don't want him to get away with killing Beth."

"What do you mean he got away with murder?"

"He was a suspect, but they let him go. I don't know why, but he did it. I guess they couldn't prove it or something."

"I'm going to look into this. I promise you."

34

———

The traffic on Golden Gate thickened when the road narrowed. If someone who didn't live here looked at the sky, they'd never be able to predict the weather. As I traveled east, large, dark gray clouds looked ready to battle with the blue sky to the west. I had no facts to back it up, but there was more sun the closer you were to the water.

I crawled along as a couple of raindrops bounced on the windshield. I had one more light to go through. My phone rang. It was Derrick.

"You got a second, Frank?"

"Yeah, stuck in traffic, but I'm just about there. What's up?"

"Guess who just got booked?"

I loved Derrick, I really did, but his guessing games were driving me mad. Was he going to bring a Slinky in next? "Clint Eastwood."

"Sorry. Tony Anderson."

"The guy with the homeowners insurance claim Wade denied?"

"One and the same. Guess what he was—"

"Just tell me, I'm pulling into the parking lot."

"Another assault. This time it's a bad one. The victim is in the ICU."

"Get as much info as you can about it."

"Done. Good luck."

The sun came out as I parked in front of Promo Pros. I held the door for a customer who was leaving with two shopping bags.

Rowan was adjusting a large printer. He was wearing a black back-support band over a white, long-sleeved shirt and beige chinos. Before I got to the counter, a twenty-year-old kid hustled to the other side.

"Welcome to Promo Pros. How can I assist you today?"

"I'd like to talk to Mr. Rowan."

At the sound of his name, Rowan looked over. His face dropped. He knew exactly who I was.

"I'll be right there, Johnny."

He punched a couple of numbers into the machine's keypad, and it started to pump out copies of something with a lot of orange on it.

"Why don't you come on back to my office?"

I followed him to a cubbyhole, whose walls were adorned with banners he'd made for clients and photos of him with groups of Asians.

Rowan's receding hair was darker than his DMV photo. "How was your trip?"

"Good but tiring. The Chinese want to bring you to every factory, and the dinners and drinking I could do without. Plus my back has been acting up."

It was hard not to stare at his eyes to figure out what was wrong. "Sounds like a fun trip the first couple of times, and then it's boring."

"Exactly."

"You go to the Immokalee casino often?"

"Uh, not that much."

"Enough to be in the Player's Club."

"I guess."

"You were there on the night of July seventh."

"I don't remember exactly."

"You were. We have you on the casino's cameras."

He shifted in his chair. "I guess so, then. What's the problem?"

"The name Beth Wade mean anything to you?"

He tilted his head. "Beth Wade? Sounds a little familiar. There's a girl who plays blackjack; her name's Beth, but I don't know her last name."

I took a photo out of my Moleskin. "This her?"

His left eye flicked between being centered and to the left. "Yeah, that's her. She's a good little player."

I didn't know what the "little" reference meant. Was he referring to the size of her bets? If so, that meant he was laying down larger bets. "How well do you know her?"

"Not well. I mean, she was at the casino a lot, and we both liked to play blackjack."

Liked? He referred to her in the past tense. "What can you tell me about her?"

"Honestly, she was kind of a flirt."

Again, was. Not is. "Can you elaborate on that?"

"Well, it's not nice to talk about someone who's no longer with us."

"You're aware that Ms. Wade was murdered?"

He shook his head.

"You were out of the country when her body was found. How would you know that?"

He pulled out his cell phone. "I got the *Naples Daily News* app and saw it."

"We believe you are the last person to see her alive."

The color drained from his face. "Me?"

"We have video showing you and her leaving the hotel's casino early in the morning of the eighth. What were the two of you doing before you exited?"

"Nothing. I mean, we were gambling at the same table for a while, and then on my way out I saw her by the lounge talking to some guy."

"Describe him."

"I didn't get a good look at him, but I think he might have been one of those Seminole Indian guys."

"You think he worked at the casino?"

"He could have."

"You saw her talking to this guy as you were leaving?"

"Yes. That's right."

"So, how did you end up leaving at the same time as her?"

"Well, like I said, I saw her, and I said I was leaving. The next thing I know, she says to hold on, she was leaving too."

"Did the fellow she was talking to say or do anything?"

"He looked mad."

"In what way?"

"I don't know; he just did. Anyway, she said he was a creep."

"Beth Wade made a comment to you that the man she was talking to was a creep?"

He nodded. "Yep, he seemed like one too."

"Did she mention anything else about him?"

"No, that's all she said. She was happy to get away from him."

"You left the hotel together and separated in the parking lot?"

"Yes."

"Did you see her again?"

"No."

He looked to be telling the truth. I had watched his white Passat leave the parking lot. The lab was able to blow up a couple of photos that indicated no one was in the passenger seat.

"Did you notice anyone else in the parking lot?"

"I wasn't paying much attention; I was looking at my messages. There could have been."

"I'd like for you to look at some pictures, and see if you can identify the man she was talking to."

"Okay, but I didn't get that good a look at him."

"Thanks for your time. I'll be in touch."

I stepped outside. The sky was as blue as it gets, and the sun was shining. If Rowan could identify Magi Seke as the man Wade was talking to, it would make the Seminole a prime suspect. Wade would never be interested in a guy like Rowan. He was too old farty for her.

They were gambling friends. When Rowan said goodbye, Wade used the opportunity to get away from whomever she was talking to. That man got insulted and may have went after her. I had to find out who this person was.

OUR APPEAL for anyone who had seen a stranded car in the Oil Well and Immokalee Road area yielded no results. Forty-three calls had come in, covering sightings of deer, trucks, and three about a strange man roaming around, but no one came forward to verify Frelig's story.

It was almost like they had read or saw a newscast with a different request. It wasn't that unusual. We knew the crackpots and people genuinely wanting to be helpful would call, but it was strange that not one saw or pretended to see a car stuck by the side of the road.

Though I considered her husband a valid suspect, I was leery of using the absence of confirmation too heavily. It just wasn't hard evidence. I tended to believe Frelig had fabricated the story, but if I kept warning Derrick to stick to the evidence, I'd have to occasionally do so myself.

It was time to request a warrant for Frelig's cell phone. I was interested in whether the towers his cell bounced off of were closer to the casino than the location he claimed the stalled car was.

If we could reasonably prove he was near the casino, he'd have a lot of explaining to do. I didn't believe he was smart enough to shut off or take the battery out of his phone, but with the information that TV shows and the web offered, it couldn't be discounted.

Information in any form was useful. The fact was, even if Frelig helped someone that was stuck, it didn't mean he hadn't gone to the casino afterward.

I logged into the warrant portal and framed my request. Given that Frelig was the husband and the couple had a record of domestic violence offenses made me confident my petition would be granted.

35

"How'd it go with Rowan?"

"He said Wade was talking to a male at the end of the night, right before he left. According to him, she wanted to get away from the guy, calling him creepy, and when Rowan came by, she went with him as cover."

"Could it be Seke?"

"That's what I was thinking. Rowan said he looked Indian, whatever that means."

"I don't remember seeing her talking to anyone around that hour."

"I know, but it could have been in a hallway or somewhere without surveillance. We need to go over the footage again. It won't take us long. We're talking about the period, say, twenty minutes before she exits the hotel."

"You think this guy grabbed her?"

"That's the thought. But we should be able to see if he leaves within a minute or two of her, otherwise she'd be gone."

"Or she sat in her car, checking her phone for a couple of minutes."

"Let's stop speculating and check the video."

"I have the Anderson story."

"Hold it. Let's get past this. Where are the drives?"

"In the credenza. I'll get them."

"Did you send a request to the Lee sheriff for the case file on Wade's ex-husband's first wife?"

"I'm sorry, man. I was wrapped up with—"

"Don't beat yourself up; just do it now."

I RUBBED MY TEMPLES. "You have any Advil?"

"Yep." Derrick opened a drawer and tossed me a bottle.

We had spent two hours looking at video and couldn't find Wade talking with anyone before she left.

"Thanks." I spilled two capsules out and swallowed them without water.

"I don't know how you do that."

"You should have seen the crap I had to take for my bladder cancer. You get used to it. This is nothing."

He shook his head. "Since we couldn't find the mystery man leaving, it probably wasn't the killer."

"Maybe, but if it was an insider, they could have left through another entrance."

"There's that, or Rowan was bullshitting us."

"I want to show Rowan a picture of Seke. See what he says."

"And a layout of the place. See where he says he saw them."

"I was going to." That was entirely true. The map was a better idea than me asking Rowan to describe it to me.

"Just making sure. You want to hear about Anderson now?"

"I'm all ears."

"Two years ago, Anderson bought a barbecue from Fergusons. Something broke, and when he was told that it wasn't under warranty any longer, he went crazy. He demanded they fix it and said that the salesman who sold it to him said he had a five-year guarantee. He sees the guy working with a couple on the showroom floor and interrupts them. The guy says he's busy, and Anderson picks up a faucet and starts beating the guy with it."

"Anderson is a lunatic."

"No doubt. A couple of other salesmen intervene, but the guy's head is cracked open and he's unconscious. We sent a couple of cars down, and an ambulance took the poor bastard to the hospital."

"What's his condition?"

"Critical and in ICU."

I shook my head. "Over a frigging barbecue?"

"Do you want to talk to him?"

"Let's wait till they charge him. Maybe we can find some way to dangle a deal in front of him to get him to talk about Wade."

"Makes sense. Oh, this came in while you were out."

He handed me a sheet with a Verizon logo. It was Mrs. Wade's phone record from the day she received the call about her daughter's debt.

There were only five calls listed, but the one I was interested in had Prepaid Unit in the account holder column.

"Another strikeout." I handed it back. "File it in the murder book. I'm going to call her."

"Mrs. Wade? This is Detective Luca."

"Oh, hello. I didn't recognize the number, and I thought maybe . . ."

"How are you doing, ma'am?"

"As best I can."

I couldn't imagine what this poor woman was going through. Her daughter was an adult, but losing a child was something nearly impossible to get over. "Try and hang in there. I know it's tough, but it will get a little easier."

"I hope so."

"We were unable to identify the caller through Verizon's records. The call was made using a disposable, prepaid phone."

"Oh. Nothing seems to be going in my favor these days."

"Have you received any calls or contact of any kind concerning the alleged debt your daughter had?"

"No. I would have called you."

"Good. Nothing remotely suspicious?"

"No. But I haven't been feeling like going out lately."

"I understand. Did you think some more about who it possibly could have been?"

"I did. I racked my brain, but no one came to mind."

"Well, keep thinking about it. You never know when something will pop into your head. It will probably be in the middle of the night."

"I'm up most of the night anyway."

"Try and get some rest, ma'am. As far as this caller is concerned, we're going to keep a car outside your home, just in case."

"Please thank the sheriff for me. It helps make me feel safe."

"You are, ma'am. Have a good evening."

Derrick said, "How was she?"

"The only word is sad. I feel for the woman. What pain she must be in, and then she gets this whacko calling her for money."

"I'm glad she didn't just pay him."

"She's not the type to get scammed."

"Is that what you think this is?"

"Not really, but it could be. There's no shortage of scumbags combing through the obituaries looking for someone to take advantage of."

"I don't know how these bastards sleep at night."

"I hate to tell you, but it's probably a lot better than we do."

"I sleep pretty good, man."

"That makes one of us. Just to be sure, go see Casey, and let him know the patrol car stays until we tell him to pull it. He's a good guy, but if he gives us any bullshit, we'll tell him she's Chester's friend."

36

———

My email pinged. Something came in from the Lee County Sheriff's Office. It was Scott Dorsey's file. I opened it. Beth Wade's first husband had a couple of brushes with the law. The file had three tabs to it.

I hit the homicide one and began reading.

On March 23, 2014, Angela Dorsey's body was discovered by her sister, who had gone to get her for a shopping outing. The cause of death jumped off the page: suffocation. The front door was unlocked, which led the police to believe she knew her killer.

Scott Dorsey's first wife had recently begun a relationship with a Rodney Long. Mr. Long had a drug-related record and was the first person questioned. Though neighbors reported the couple fought, Mr. Long had a solid alibi.

It was the victim's phone records that led police to her ex-husband. He had begun calling his ex-wife around the time she started dating Mr. Long. Interviews revealed that Mr. Dorsey was a possessive and jealous man. His DNA was also found in her home.

I read the police interview of Scott Dorsey. He denied any

knowledge of his ex-wife's murder and said that he was home watching a James Bond movie during the period the killing took place. He claimed that his calls were related to checking in on her as she had broken a couple of ribs in a fall taking down her Christmas decorations.

When he was asked about the fact his DNA was detected at the crime scene, he offered a plausible reason. Three days before her murder, he had stopped at her house to give her some documents he had of hers. Angela's mother was terminally ill at the time, and she had begun to prepare for her death. She realized that cemetery documents where her father had been interned were with Scott and asked for them.

No one followed up with how he knew she had been injured. Though the police were unable to verify his alibi, they turned their focus on a gang that was doing home invasions in the area. As they canvassed the neighborhood, a woman who lived at the beginning of the victim's street told police that she had seen a car matching the one owned by Scott Dorsey the night of the murder.

They brought him back in but were unable to corroborate the information placing Scott Dorsey near the scene. No charges were filed against him or anyone else. It was now a cold case, another unsolved homicide stacked onto the pile.

Paging through the other tabs, it was clear Dorsey had anger issues as well. There were three public fights, each with men who had been talking to his wife, and a road rage incident.

I closed my eyes and leaned back, thinking over what I read. He couldn't have planned the mother's illness to go to her house, but he could have seized on her demise for a reason to go to her house, knowing he'd drop his DNA. Or the simple, personal interaction with her could have led to an internal rage.

Maybe the subject of her new boyfriend came up. Or the boyfriend could have stopped by or called when Scott was there. No one looked at that possibility. They should have tied Scott's visit to a time and then cross-checked her phone records and asked Mr. Long about it. But they hadn't.

It wasn't my case nor even in my county, but what I considered a valid thread to follow was left unexplored. That bothered me.

The other point gnawing at me was the similarities in how the women were killed. While it was the third leading method in committing a homicide, it was a distant third. Suffocation represented only 3 percent of all murders, thirty times less than using a gun and eight times less likely than a stabbing.

I didn't need a bookie to tell me what the odds were of a man, a jealous one at that, who would have two exes murdered through suffocation. They were longer than finding a good Chinese restaurant in Naples.

On the other hand, killing two former lovers, years apart, would evidence a patience rarely seen. My experience with jealousy, which was passion related, was extensive. In some twisted minds they would be unable to handle a transgression, real or imagined. Their rage would build until erupting in a criminal act.

There was a certain patience, a stalking quality that was common in half the cases I'd worked. But waiting years after separating was something I hadn't encountered. Had there been some act or event that triggered Scott Dorsey's need for revenge? How many men were roaming out there hunting down their ex-lovers?

He was someone I needed to talk to. I wanted to show Rowan a picture of Seke first. But if he said it was the man Wade was talking to, I'd lose my reason to talk to Dorsey. He wasn't my business if there was no connection to Wade, but I was making it mine either way.

Before I went to Rowan, I just had to get some intel on Dorsey. I dialed a number.

"Hello, Mrs. Wade. It's Detective Luca."

"Did something happen?"

"No. There's nothing to worry about. I had a question about Beth's first husband."

"Scott?"

"Yes. What can you tell me about him?"

"He's a phony. When they were dating, he was Mr. Charming. He'd even bring flowers for me, but after they got married, his true colors began to show."

"What do you mean by that?"

"Scott was obsessed with anything Beth did and especially who she did it with."

"You mean he was jealous?"

"Absolutely. He was very controlling."

"Did he get physically abusive with your daughter?"

She sighed. "Yes. I wanted to choke him, the little coward. I told Beth to leave him, and eventually she did."

"Had Beth mentioned anything about talking to or seeing him recently to you?"

"They got to a point about a year after the divorce was final where they began being civil to each other. Scott was upset when she filed, and he begged her to come back, but it was too late. But they had settled into some kind of friendship. I called him when she went missing, just in case he had contact with her."

"Had he?"

"No. Said he hadn't talked with her in a couple of weeks. I called him to let him know what had happened."

It was rare that a parent would ever actually say the words

killed or murdered. "Do you think he could have played a role in your daughter's murder?"

"I, I never thought of him being the one. I don't know; it seems disconnected. It's been such a long while since they were together. But he was obsessed with her."

"I understand."

"Do you have a reason to suspect him?"

I didn't want to tell her about what I'd learned. "Not exactly. I'm looking at everything and everyone. I want to bring her killer to justice."

37

———————

A UPS GUY CAME INTO PROMO PROS CARRYING A LARGE box. He said hello to one of the employees and dropped the box on the counter. There was Chinese lettering on the label, and the box was marked Made in China.

A kid working the printer took the box and opened it by his workstation. He took out an umbrella, a Frisbee, a small cooler, and a framed photo as Rowan made his way toward me.

"Mr. Rowan, the new samples came in."

"Who told you to open it? Put everything back, and leave it in the storeroom."

"Uh, sure."

He waved me in. I followed him to his office, where there was a new sign behind his desk.

"I like that." It read Without Promotions, Something Terrible Happens . . . Nothing!

"Most people don't realize that if they don't promote their business, no one will know about it. Everybody is focused on the web these days. They think Facebook is the only place they need to advertise. Guess what? They're fooling themselves." He picked up a pen with the Promo Pros name on it. "Something as simple and cheap as a pen is effective. It seems old school, but it sits on a desk, in front of you, all day long."

He was the furthest thing from a Madison Avenue advertising person, but he did have a point. "That makes a lot of sense."

"I think so. Everybody wants something new. I go to China like everyone else, looking for ideas and tchotchke for companies to give away or get their name on. The problem is, there's a limit to things if you have a budget, like most people."

"You find anything new this trip?"

"Nothing but an umbrella that has a piece that drops down around half of it. It'll keep you drier and is a great place to slap a logo."

"Good luck with it."

"Thanks. You came about the photos?"

I pulled out a map of the area where the hotel and casino came together. "Can you tell me where you saw Beth Wade and the man talking."

Rowan took the schematic and turned it around. "Right around here."

He pointed to an area that had limited camera coverage. "You're sure?"

He nodded. "Pretty much."

I circled the area and exchanged the map for a photo of Magi Seke. "Is this the man you saw with her?"

His left eye vacillated as he looked at the image. "I think so."

"How positive are you?"

"I don't know, about seventy percent."

"How about this one?" I slid a picture of an officer in the robbery division.

Rowan put the pictures side by side. "This is tough. It could have been either of them."

The two men had similar builds and hair color, but other than that, they didn't look alike.

"Try again, please."

After another ten seconds, Rowan slid both images across his desk. "I'm sorry, but that's the best I can do."

I thanked him for his time and left. Driving east on Golden Gate, I thought about the visit. I tried to put a positive spin on him, saying he was 70 percent sure it was Seke, but by the time I took the ramp for the interstate I realized I was kidding myself.

The fact he said it could be either man amounted to nothing. Even if we found out it was Seke, we couldn't bring Rowan in to testify he saw him with her. Any defense attorney would tear his testimony to shreds.

As was customary, I placed a courtesy call to the Lee County Sheriff's Office. As I exited onto to Corkscrew Road, I knew Chester would never consent to another interview with Seke on the basis of what Rowan said. As I headed west, it was clear that we needed more, much more.

Turning off Three Oaks Parkway, I entered a large community known as The Brooks. The guard gave me directions, and I wound my way to Magnolia Boulevard. Scott Dorsey lived at the end, in one of two houses in a cul-de-sac. Nice, except it backed up to Three Oaks, where cars were going by at sixty miles an hour.

Dorsey's one-story home was brown with matching barrel roof tiles. I never saw a home where everything was the same color. It was about twenty years old and Mediterranean in style.

I dodged a sprinkler and jogged up the driveway. The door swung open as I approached. Dorsey was wearing a long-sleeved, blue shirt and pressed jeans. Either he was trying to make an impression or was one of those guys who had everything hung up in their garage. He was wearing cologne that reminded me of what Derrick wore.

I introduced myself, and he invited me in. The home was neat, and he kept the temperature even higher than I did.

We sat around a country French kitchen table. It was the same color as the cabinets and countertops. He was consistent, if boring, and never asked me if I wanted something to drink. He was a neat freak.

"I wanted to ask you a couple of questions about your ex-wife, Beth Wade."

"I went to the funeral. It was upsetting."

"Do you have any ideas on who might have killed her?"

"How would I know? We've been divorced for years."

"Didn't you keep in contact with her?"

"No, why would I?"

"Her mother said you kept in touch with her."

"It was only every now and then."

"When was the last time you saw her in person?"

"I don't know, a while ago."

He was being evasive. "I need a more definite time period."

He shrugged. "Maybe a month or so before she was, you know . . ."

Was that a hint of a smirk? "Where did you see her?"

"At the casino."

"You saw her at the Immokalee casino?"

"Yeah."

"You knew she liked to play blackjack?"

"Who do you think taught her how to play?"

"You go there often?"

"No. I rarely go."

"Were you there the night of July seventh?"

"No. If I feel like gambling, me and some friends get a card game together."

"Beth went there a lot, and I understand she was a good player."

"Like I said, I taught her. It was one of the few things she listened to me on."

"She was a bit of a rebel?"

"I'd say more like independent than a rebel. She had some fight in her, I'll tell you." He smiled.

Controlling men liked going after strong women; they'd try to break them, getting some kind of twisted high out of it.

"You've been involved in a couple of domestic violence calls. From both wives."

He shrugged. "Nothing I'm proud of. They started it, but I should have walked away."

Blaming two women unable to answer for themselves was not a winning tactic in my book. "What do you think of the fact that both of your ex-wives have been murdered?"

He looked me straight in the eye. "How do you think it feels?"

"I'm asking the questions around here. You're a gambler; you know the chances that having both wives murdered is one in a zillion."

"So is getting hit by lightning twice, yet it happens all the time."

It wasn't all the time; it was rarely, but he had to minimize his situation. "People tell me you're the jealous type."

"Who's people?"

"Witnesses who knew you and your wives."

"Witnesses? What are you trying to do, tie me to Beth's, uh, situation?"

I'd been a homicide detective for over fifteen years and never heard anyone refer to a killing as a situation.

Though I'd imagine no man or woman would be happy to see their former partner with another love interest, I asked, "You didn't like it when your exes dated other men, did you?"

His eyes narrowed. "We were divorced."

"Let me ask you about John Frelig. What can you tell me about him?"

"He was a tow truck driver."

"What is that supposed to mean?"

"Nothing."

"There were a couple of domestic violence calls that we responded to involving both of them. They were pretty ugly."

"She told me about it."

He didn't comment on Frelig raising his hands to a woman because he was a sleazebag who did the same thing.

"You don't like Frelig, do you?"

"There's nothing to like."

"Tell me about Rodney Long."

He shifted in his chair. "What about him?"

"How did you feel about him dating your ex?"

"Man, that was a long time ago." He stood. "I got to get going."

38

Cutting the crust off Jessie's toast, I said, "Why don't you try eating it? All the big girls eat the crust."

"Not me, Daddy. I don't like it."

Mary Ann said, "Don't force her, Frank."

"I'm not forcing. Her tastes may have changed. That's all."

"Don't forget to sign the Little People's School papers. I want to drop them off today. They'll need a deposit."

"I did already. They're by your pocketbook." I put the toast on Jessie's plate. "Here you go, sunshine."

"Thanks. I'm going to put the deposit on the Visa card. They don't charge extra for using a credit card, and we get the points."

"Sounds good."

"What do you have going on today?"

My cell buzzed. "Still trying to make something break on the Wade case."

"Morning, Derrick, what's going on?"

"Looks like somebody wants to talk."

"Who and what?"

"A Seminole named Bolo Lora was arrested last night. He had a meth lab outside of Immokalee, and guess who he claims to know about?"

"Magi Seke."

"Bingo."

"Where is he?"

"They have him in a holding cell at the substation."

"Did he have an arraignment hearing?"

"No, they knew we were interested in him and held off."

"Was he cooking when they picked him up?"

"No, they were watching the trailer for over a month. There hadn't been any activity since the big sweep in May."

"They said he's ready to talk about Magi?"

"He said he has some information."

"I assume he's got a record."

"Oh, yeah. All drug related."

"I hope he's not playing us. The word was out we were looking for info on Seke."

"We'll see. You coming in first?"

"Nah, I'll go straight there. I want to talk to this Bolo character."

"In that case, I have some other news."

"About?"

"Take a guess."

"I gotta get going, man. Just tell me."

"Lynn's pregnant. I wanted to tell you in person, but I'm busting here."

"Wow! Congratulations. We're so happy for you. How far along is she?"

"She's about twelve weeks now."

"Fantastic."

Mary Ann said, "What's going on?"

"Lynn's pregnant."

"How wonderful. I'll call her later."

THE COLLIER COUNTY SHERIFF'S Office had a facility in Immokalee known as District 8. It was on First Street, by the Immokalee jail. There was much more crime in Immokalee than in Naples, and the residents were poor. I shook off the sadness that had settled on me and pushed open the door to the station.

I read through the file of evidence. Bolo Lora had been suspected of cooking batches of methamphetamine on the Miccosukee Reservation and transporting it to sell in Immokalee. It was nasty stuff that was ruining lives by the tens of thousands. A mule had been caught on Alligator Alley with two garbage bags full and identified Bolo as the head of the operation.

Word must have gotten back to Bolo, as he seemed to have ceased operations and disappeared until he surfaced at a trailer under surveillance. The drug unit had the runner they'd caught and a local user who bought off Bolo.

The interview room was smaller than our master closet and hot. Bolo Lora was in street clothes, a gray T-shirt with an eagle image and jeans. I backed up my chair, away from the smell of sweat and alcohol.

"I'm Detective Luca with the sheriff's office."

He kept rubbing the back of his hand. Bolo's long and unkempt hair swayed as he nodded. He spoke in a gravelly voice. "You my ticket out of this shithole?"

The condition of his teeth told me something about his lifestyle.

"Running a meth factory? I'm not sure anybody could help you."

"But I got info on that squirrel Magi."

"Tell me what you have, and I'll see what I can do."

A drip of sweat rolled off his chin. "I gotta know what kinda deal I'm cutting before I talk."

"Look, you're not making any deals here. You give me what you know, and we'll go from there."

"But they said—"

I loosened my tie. "Start talking."

"He's the son, you know, of Chetan, and that's why he gets away with it."

"What does he get away with?"

"All kinds of shit. I mean, I was up in Miccosukee when that whole thing with the girl hit. They covered it all up, man. And you know, the girl's daddy, well, he got a cushy job at the Hard Rock casino in Miami."

Who were these people who would trade what happened to their daughter for financial gain? The only trade I would make involved a bullet.

"We know all about that particular incident."

"Then why didn't you do anything about it? I'm no saint, man, but that's some bullshit there."

It was a good question. If you really got down to it, the reason was politics. "We're interested in Magi Seke, so if you have something new to tell me, now is the time. Otherwise, I'm going to head back home to my house, where it's nice and cool."

I put a hand on my can of pepper spray as Bolo's face reddened. "What do you want?"

"The woman who went missing at the casino. What did you hear about that?"

"I told 'em. I think Magi had something to do with it."

"I didn't come out here for you to tell me what you think

about anything. Now, tell me what you know and why, or I'm out of here."

"Hold on, man."

"Hold on? Let me tell you something. I know judges, and these days they're coming down real hard on people like you. Multiple offenders aren't getting any slack anymore. Those days are over. You're in a world of trouble. Now, start yapping before I leave you here to rot."

"I seen Magi where the body was found."

"Where was that?"

"Gargiulo's. He was coming out the driveway."

"How did you know it was him?"

"His car. He's got one of them cars or like a crossover-type one. It looks like it came outta the old days. You know what I mean?"

"No."

"The front is big like cars from the fifties, that the kids used to cruise around in."

I didn't know cars other than ones I either thought were sharp or ugly. This one didn't appeal to me. "A Chrysler PT Cruiser?"

"Yeah, I think that's it."

I wanted to pull some images on my phone, but the jail's Wi-Fi was terrible. "How do you know it was his?"

"Nobody got those around here, and his is yellow."

I tried to recall if a car like that was by Seke's home when I first interviewed him.

"Even if it was him, he could have been working there or lost his way."

"Oh, it was him all right, and he works at the casino."

"What else do you know?"

"Oh, come on, man. What I gave you is everything, man."

39

———————

As soon as I stepped in the office, I dropped a bag on my desk and put my arms around Derrick. "Congrats, my friend. You guys are in for the ride of your life."

"I can't believe it's really happening. It's a little scary."

"I know what you mean. When we found out Mary Ann was pregnant, I was, like, happy and terrified at the same time."

"Really? That's kind of like how I feel."

"It'll get better. Wait until you can feel the baby move around; you'll get so excited that you'll never look back."

"Can't wait."

I grabbed the bag and pulled out a bottle of champagne. "Congratulations."

"Thanks, it's not necessary, but I appreciate it."

"Just make sure Lynn doesn't drink it while she's carrying."

"You kidding? She's been avoiding half the stuff she used to eat."

"I know what you mean. Mary Ann was the same way. I'm not against all of the precautions, but if everything was bad for you, how the hell did we turn out okay, especially with all the smoking going on then?"

"Can't imagine kids being stuck in a car with the windows closed and the parents puffing away."

"What were they thinking?"

"What happened with the snitch?"

"He said he saw Magi Seke coming out of the Gargiulo driveway, where Wade's body was dumped."

"If that's true, sounds like Seke is our guy. How sure can we be?"

"He claimed to know it was Seke because of the car. Seke apparently drives a yellow PT Cruiser and say it's the only one around."

"I can run a DMV report for yellow Chryslers and sort it by zip code."

"Exactly what I was thinking."

"Great minds think alike."

"You got it, Mr. Daddy-to-be. Look, I don't know if it was a dream or not, but I was in bed last night thinking about the case. So, do me a favor and check with Frelig's friends and neighbors; see if anyone lent him their car."

"Dream or not, it's something I was—"

I balled up the bottle's paper bag and tossed it at him. "You were thinking of?"

"You know what they say about great minds."

"As someone with one, I do."

"Let me get moving. What are your plans?"

"Right now, I'm going to have the lab run the facial recognition software on Dorsey. He said he wasn't there, and I can't go through all that again; my eyes will fall out."

WAS it really possible to have so many suspects? Try as I could, the motivations for each of them were all strong enough to be believable. Except for Magi Seke. We could not find any evidence he had a relationship with Wade, unless it was in his head. At this point in the investigation, a motivating factor could not be established, so I classified Seke as someone with mental health issues.

Anderson and Berry were in the "driven by money and revenge" camp, and Dorsey, Frelig, and probably Belcher were love interests in the "passion and revenge" camp, though the weightlifter could've been driven into a rage from steroids.

On the way in, a thunderstorm had swept through the area, causing half a dozen auto accidents. I could only imagine the traffic backups. It was a good thing I didn't have to drive out to the Immokalee jail.

It felt like cheating; I didn't have to get in my car to go see Tony Anderson. He was being held in the Naples jail, a part of the sheriff's office where I worked. Collier County had a large complex at the intersection of Route 41 and Airport Pulling Road.

Not only was the sheriff's office there, but conveniently, the courthouse was a short walk across Harrison Road. As someone who spent way too many hours in courtrooms, half of it wasted as defense lawyers slowed or maneuvered to buy time, I was grateful it was close. The county had most of its administrative offices there as well, including the agency that fueled all governments, the tax collector.

The jail here was small. Most of its occupants leaned toward white-collar crime and domestic violence. It also had a large drunk tank for the continual stream of booze hounds that permeated the area.

I buttoned my jacket as I waited for Anderson to be

brought in. Keeping the AC at a low temperature kept the smell of humanity from seeping into other parts of the building. The locks on the door whirred, and a second later Anderson shuffled into the room.

The shackling was part safety protocol and part dehumanizing. He was wearing a bright orange jumpsuit and a frown. At least it hid the hair on his body.

"You can take the cuffs off."

The corrections officer looked at me like I'd asked to date his daughter. Anderson held his arms up, and the guard unlocked his hands but not his legs. I thanked the officer and told Anderson to sit.

As he dragged the chair out, he said, "This about Beth Wade?"

"Yes. She was found murdered. Dumped in a canal near Immokalee."

"I saw it on the news."

"You got yourself in deep trouble with this one. I spoke to the DA about your case, and they're definitely going to file for attempted murder. In the first degree."

"That's bullshit."

"You think so? According to the lawyers, your actions qualify as premeditated. You called Fergusons, and when the answer wasn't good enough for you, you got in your car and drove down there. Then you attacked the poor guy."

"They can't do that."

"Oh, yes they can. You know what the penalty for attempted murder in Florida is? Life in prison with zero possibility of parole, if you're lucky. If not, it's the death penalty."

"There's no way that's gonna happen. I didn't do it on purpose; it just happened."

"And that's if he survives, and it's sketchy that he's going to. He dies, and you'll be right behind him."

Anderson leaned on the table. "He's not going to pull through?"

"Doesn't look like it. If he does, chances are he'll be a vegetable."

Anderson slouched. "It was an accident. My lawyer said it'd be some kind of an assault. I know I'll do some time, but nothing like you're trying to scare me with."

"Look, you want some help? Maybe there's something we can do for each other, but stop with the accident stuff or I'll walk out of here."

"How can you help me?"

"I can't promise a miracle, but if you cooperate, you don't have to worry about them killing you."

"They ain't gonna kill me. What do you mean by cooperate? How?"

"Tell me what happened with Beth Wade."

"I got nothing to say. My lawyer said not to talk to anyone."

Anderson was hiding something. He clammed up when Wade was brought up. I didn't like him, but what didn't square was the fact he was reckless. He'd lose whatever self-control he had in a flash. Someone like that usually would leave a trace of their involvement.

There was nothing about Anderson that told me he was meticulous. His house was upside down, and his personal appearance and his explosions of rage were the polar opposites of a detailed planner. Still, there was something just below the surface with Anderson that needed airing.

I had an idea that could provide clarity.

40

———

"Hey, Robbie, how is it going?"

"Good, Frank. What can I do for you?"

"Tony Anderson. He's sitting next door on an assault charge, and as you know, we have an interest in him. From the file, it didn't look like you went for a search warrant."

"Didn't feel like we needed it. The crime happened in a public place and it's on camera. We don't need to piece together a case. This guy's lawyer is going to force him to accept a plea."

"Look, I appreciated the courtesy you extended, I really do, but I gotta ask for another favor."

"What's that?"

"Anytime I bring up the Wade case with him, he shuts down. There's something there. I can feel it. It's like the back of my head is hooked up to electricity or something."

"And?"

"I need you to go for a warrant to search his property. See what turns up. We're at a dead end at this point, and I need something to sink my teeth into."

"I don't know, Frank. We're about to give it to the prosecutors."

"I'll draft it for you and add what we have on the Wade
case."

"I'm already up to my ass in paperwork—"

"Thanks, man. I really appreciate it."

"Whoa!"

Starting for the door, I said over my shoulder, "I'll have
the request to you within the hour."

I ran down the stairs and wanted to lock our office door.
Derrick said, "How did you make out with Roblinski?"

I smiled. "Kind of talked him into it. He wants me to draft
the request."

"Perfect. I called the DMV. We should have the report on
yellow Chryslers before you're done with the Anderson
search docs."

***

"I'M GOING to have to get a couple of six-packs for
Roblinski. He said he was going to sign it and walk it over to
the suits."

"Good. I'll split the cost with you."

"Don't worry about it. He and I go way back. I used up a
favor, but a case of Molson will ease his pain."

He laughed. "Sounds good. We got the DMV report."

"Is it long?"

"More than I expected. Why would you want a yellow
car?"

"Sorted by zip?"

"Yep."

He handed me the list. I scanned the details. Magi Seke's
car was the fourth one down. "At this point, I don't care

about anything other than Immokalee and maybe, just maybe, anything in a zip for East Naples."

"Makes sense."

"Look, even though this is rookie work, I'll run these down myself. I'd like you to finish up with anyone Frelig could have borrowed a car from."

"It's been tough getting in touch with all the neighbors. Most of them are working full time."

I raised my eyebrows.

"I know. I don't know what tough is. It's not hard. I was just doing a little complaining."

I threw out one of my favorite Lucaisms. "You know what I say: Don't complain unless you can offer a solution to the problem."

"You're right."

I was, but the problem was, like most people, I had diffi-culties adhering to it. I grabbed my sports jacket. "Let me know if you come up with anything. Otherwise, I'll see you later."

The PT Cruiser registered to Magi Seke was a 2010, the last year the crossover was made. In Immokalee's zip code, there were four other vehicles like his. I didn't know how many Cruisers Chrysler made, but it was never a big seller.

As I headed east, I rolled around why there was such a high concentration of them in Immokalee. It had a hatchback that was good for carrying things, and a lot of people worked in agriculture out there. I didn't think that was it, as pickup trucks would better serve that use.

Passing the intersection for Oil Well Road, my mind shifted to Frelig. This was the area he claimed to have been flagged down by a stranded driver. No one had come forward to confirm his statement. I tried to envision how he'd juggled the use of another car. We knew he was out this way. He would have had to stash a car he borrowed, using it to go the balance of the distance to the casino.

That would mean a friend or neighbor wouldn't need their car for a longer period. As if a higher power was intervening, my cell vibrated. Was it Derrick with news on Frelig?

I pulled my phone out, hopeful the universe was answering my plea for a break in the case. I tossed the phone on the passenger seat. The screen had read Private Number. It was nothing but a spam call.

Pulling in front of the first address on the DMV list, I knew why Immokalee had so many PT Cruisers. The reason was purely economic. The vehicle was no longer produced because there was no demand. They hadn't made them in nine years, and those still on the road were old and cheap.

Gravel crunched under my shoes as the realization that the color yellow probably qualified for a further discount. The place was more bungalow than house. A paintbrush hadn't been near its walls in twenty years.

Two stairs led to a porch with a rocking chair and a ratty couch. I knocked on the screen door. The Cruiser was registered to a thirty-seven-year-old male named Bob Walu, but a woman came to the door.

Brown skinned with hair parted into a braided pigtail, she had her mouth closed. I couldn't tell if he she had any teeth.

I held my badge up. "Detective Luca, from the sheriff's office. Is Mr. Walu home?"

She shook her head.

"Do you know when he'll be back?"

Another negative shake of her head.

"I'm looking for his car, the yellow one."

She pointed inside the home. "Out back.

"Can I take a look in the yard?"

"Okay."

Hand on my holster, I walked along the side of the house and peeked around the corner. Two cars were on blocks, one of them the yellow Cruiser, the other a Volkswagen. A thick film of grime covered both vehicles. Neither had been on the road in months.

I HEARD the propellers before I saw the crop plane coming in for a landing. The next house was across the street from Immokalee Regional Airport. I drove right past the home. The PT Cruiser in the driveway was a convertible.

Turning around, I headed toward a neighborhood named Davenport on a strip of road that served as Immokalee's main drag. There was no shortage of people sitting in front of stores, many of them vacant.

I also came up empty. The Cruiser in the driveway of the Titus Lane house had been customized with red flames and expensive rims. It looked like it belonged in the TV show *Happy Days*.

The last vehicle to check out was registered to a nearby address in an area called Sanders Pines. It looked like a nice middle-class neighborhood. The homes were on the small size but maintained. I turned onto Eden Street. A landscaping crew was spread out cutting several lawns on the block.

A yellow PT Cruiser was parked in the driveway near the end of the street. The plate matched the one registered to a Seminole male named Vine Strongheart. I parked and peeked inside the vehicle. The driver's seat was wrapped with a beaded cover, and a feathered ornament hung from the rearview mirror.

I rang the bell. There was no answer. Poking my head around the side of the home, a woman with hair down to her ass came out of the house next door. As she headed to her car, she said, "Vine's not around. He and Cherry left yesterday for the NCAI conference."

"Oh, thanks. What does NCAI stand for?"

"National Congress of American Indians."

"Oh, right." I never heard of the organization. "Where's the meeting being held?"

"Montana."

"How long do they last?"

"Not sure, maybe a week."

I said thanks and jumped back in the Cherokee for the half-hour ride back to the office.

41

HANGING UP THE PHONE AFTER TALKING TO THE LAB, I WENT to see for myself. They had a facial recognition hit on the casino footage: Dorsey, whose exes had a habit of dying, had been at the casino on June 30. It was the last time Wade was there before the day she went missing.

Peter Sample greeted me. "How are you, Frank?"

"Doing good. Hey, congratulate Derrick when you see him; his wife is pregnant."

"Nice. That was quick."

"Maybe. Show me what you got."

I followed Sample into a viewing room. "Here's the earliest we have, from what you sent us anyway."

A freeze-frame of Scott Dorsey coming through the casino's doors appeared. The time stamp read 8:49, June 30, 2019.

"Let it run, please."

Dorsey melded into a sea of people.

"We picked him up here."

The middle screen jumped to life. Dorsey was moving toward a blackjack table. He stood behind the seated players for a couple of hands and moved to a second table where he watched but did not play. After just two hands, he turned and walked away, disappearing from the camera's view.

"He makes another appearance at the bar."

Footage of Dorsey walking into the Zig Zag Lounge came alive. He headed straight to the bar where there was a woman with her back to the camera. I didn't need to see the face to know who she was: Beth Wade.

Dorsey took a seat next to her and ordered a drink. When the drink came, he clinked glasses with Wade, who was engaged in a conversation with a man to her right. Dorsey took a couple of sips and then nudged Wade. When she didn't acknowledge him, Dorsey elbowed her again.

This time an animated Wade turned toward him. Though there was no audio, it was clear she was yelling at him. The bartender came over, raising his hands.

Wade stood up and shook her head. She turned as if to walk away but grabbed her drink, tossing the contents at Dorsey. Her ex-husband's jaw dropped, and I felt a smile breaking out as he brushed off his shirt.

"I had the same reaction. She got him good."

I got rid of my smile and nodded. "Anything more with him?"

"Just of him leaving."

"Roll that for me."

Head down, Dorsey hurried out of the main entrance. A second camera picked up the back of him as he crossed the street into the parking lot. Dorsey disappeared from view, walking to the rear of the lot.

"Anymore of him?"

"No, that's all the software picked up."

"Can you copy the bar scene for me?"

"Sure. I can email it to you."

"Perfect."

I GRABBED a salad and a wrap from Jason's and ate it at my desk. I kept rolling around what Bolo Lora, the meth snitch, had told us about seeing Seke's car. The location and timing of the sighting, if not fabricated, seriously implicated the Seminole in Wade's murder.

It was clear he knew her. He was working the night she went missing. No matter how it was dressed up, there was a history of him acting improperly with women. Adding his appearance at the remote location where the body was discovered made it difficult, if not impossible, to explain away.

Unless the meth dealer was lying. He had plenty of motivation to concoct a story about Seke. But did he? Even if he did make it all up, that didn't absolve Seke. There was more than enough coincidence and path crossing to keep him high on the suspect ladder. If we could place him where the body was dumped, we'd be on our way to a solve.

I stuffed the last of my chicken wrap in my mouth and got an idea. Why not subject the snitch to a lie detector test? His public defender would object, but we weren't going to use it against him in court.

We might be able to dangle a carrot of some kind to get him to agree. If he was telling the truth, we'd need him to testify, and that would only serve to increase his value to us. I wasn't in favor of cutting meth dealers any breaks, but right now I had a killer to catch. If he could help us, we'd make a deal with him.

After we put Seke behind bars for good, I'd keep my eye on Bolo, and as soon as he resorted to his old ways, I'd make sure we locked his ass up forever.

I was leaving a message for Bolo's lawyer when Derrick came in shaking his head.

"What's the matter?"

"Can't find a soul who would've lent a car to the hubby, Frelig."

"You think somebody is covering for him?"

"Could be, but I made it clear that lying was obstruction of justice."

"You should know by now that doesn't resonate with half the population."

"You're right."

"Who is his closest friend?"

"I couldn't find one. Everybody kept saying he sticks to himself."

"Did you check with the other drivers at Baker's Towing? Maybe he's got a buddy there."

"One of the first places I checked."

"There's a chance he used a rental car. It's dangerous, but we all make mistakes."

"We'd need a warrant to check the car companies."

"Yeah, but I have an idea."

I looked up a number and punched it into the phone.

"Thank you for calling Hertz. This is Brian; how may I help you today?"

"Cybill Gates, please."

"Hold on, sir."

"Hello, this is Cybill Gates."

"Ms. Gates, this is Detective Luca."

"Oh, hi."

"I need a favor. We're trying to ascertain whether a certain individual rented a vehicle from you."

"That's confidential information, sir."

"I understand, but this is about catching your friend Beth

Wade's murderer. Time is of the essence. We need to apprehend him before he kills again."

"I know but—"

"It's just one person, and we're only interested in a single day in question. Can't you help us, please?"

"Who is it?"

"John Frelig."

She gasped. "That's her husband."

"That's correct."

"What date?"

"July seventh."

"I'll see what I can do."

42

———

"Hurry up, Frank. We can't be late."

"I'm coming."

I hadn't been this conflicted since moving out of the house I shared with my ex-wife.

"What's the matter, Daddy?"

"Nothing, pumpkin."

"But you're not happy."

"Daddy's happy. I'm a teeny, tiny bit sad that you're going to school because I don't want to share my Jessie with anybody."

She hugged my legs. "Oh, don't worry, Daddy. I'll be back. Right, Mommy?"

"Of course, honey. Then we'll have lunch, all of us."

"Even Daddy?"

"Yep."

"Yeah, Daddy's coming to lunch. Where are we going?"

"Any place you want, but Joe's Diner is close to the school."

THE PARKING LOT WAS JAMMED. I wanted to turn around, but I followed the procession down a lane lined with red cones and parked.

Mary Ann said, "We're here."

Jessie was quiet. I turned around. She was scared. "It's going to be fun, pumpkin. You'll make some new friends and be back so fast you won't believe it. Mommy and Daddy are just going to be across the street to go shopping, and we'll be waiting for you."

"Daddy's right. Come on. I think they're going to be finger painting today."

"Really?"

"Yep. Let's go."

We both held hands with Jessie and walked her toward a teacher holding a bunch of purple and blue flags.

"Who's this?"

Mary Ann knelt beside Jessie, whose lip was quivering. "Tell her your name."

I wanted to scoop her up and run back to the car. Then I heard her whisper, "Jessica. My daddy and mommy are police people." Before letting go of her hand, I surveyed the adults scattered over the property.

"Wow. Good to meet you, Jessica."

The teacher let Jessie pick a flag. It was a purple one, and then she wrote on a plastic bracelet of the same color and put in on her wrist. She said, "Are you ready to have fun today, Jessica?"

When she nodded, my heart fluttered. I grabbed Mary Ann's hand as we watched Jessie get led into the Little People's School. My wife tugged my hand. "Come on, let's go to Whole Foods while we can."

I wanted to go to a window and watch my little girl. Leaving her home with a nanny was difficult at first, but it was our house with one adult. Here she was in a foreign environment with thirty other kids and a handful of adults. I needed to see what was going on and wished I'd put a camera somewhere.

Recalling an episode of *Black Mirror*, where technology allowed parents to see what their children saw and to protect them from even the slightest threats, like a barking dog, made me reconsider. It didn't pan out well in the show and was a reminder to be careful what we wished for.

"She's going to be fine; we need to get moving."

I knew she was right, but it didn't make me feel better. "I'm in the mood for some pasta tonight, maybe with broccoli rabe. Let's get one of those grain breads too."

"I could have predicted that you'd need comfort food." She wrapped her arm around me and kissed my cheek. "I wish we had more time. We could sneak home, and you know . . . maybe tonight."

"Promises, promises."

IT WAS A WASTE OF TIME, but I decided to take 41 north into Lee County. I'd never seen much of the massive community, and this was an opportunity to do that as I did my job. I craned my neck passing Jessie's school. Was my decision just a twisted way to keep an eye on her school?

I ran through yesterday morning again. Dropping Jessie off for orientation was an experience that would linger for a lifetime. The very idea that a nursery school would have an orientation had turned me off. But it was something I couldn't miss. I wanted her to attend that school, so I grudgingly agreed to go.

It turned out that I had been wrong; the school was not

only smart but sensitive. They knew it was a good idea, not just for the kids but also for their parents. When she starting going on a daily basis in two weeks, we'd all feel better about it.

I smiled when I looked at the finger painting sitting on the passenger seat. Trying to decide what wall I'd tack it on, I approached Coconut Point Mall. I made a right onto Coconut Road, leading me to The Brooks main gate.

The guard handed me a map of the area with a highlighted route to Scott Dorsey's home. The handout mentioned that the community was spread out over twenty-five hundred acres, much of it preserved as open space.

I passed several gated neighborhoods featuring ritzy homes I pegged at well over a million. There was a nice mix of price points and types of housing and plenty of people taking walks and riding bicycles.

Deciding that it seemed like a nice place to live, I turned onto Dorsey's street and pulled the sun visor down. I checked his grass. It was no greener than the neighbor's, yet the sprinklers were on again.

I waited, and as a stream of water rotated, made a dash for the door. Dorsey didn't know I was coming but was still dressed like he was going somewhere. It was long sleeves again. It was the end of July. Maybe he was on blood thinners. Or was it a tattoo he was hiding?

He put a smile on. "Detective, uh, sorry, I forgot your name."

I was sure he hadn't. "Luca, Frank Luca."

"What can I do for you?"

"You want to do this out here?"

"Come on in." I followed him down the hallway. He used his foot to push aside a gaggle of hose connected to a vacuum. "Was just about to do some cleaning."

"This won't take long."

We took the same seated position as the last time. I took my Moleskine and phone out and placed them on the table.

"When we talked last, you said you didn't like to gamble."

"That's right, I don't."

"You said you didn't go to the Immokalee casino either."

"I hardly ever go."

"When was the last time you were there?"

"Oh, I don't know. It's been a while."

"A week?"

"No, much longer than that."

"A month, a couple of months?"

"Something like that."

"Let me show you something." I grabbed my phone and played the first clip. I held it so he could see it. "That's you entering the casino, isn't it?"

"I guess so."

"It's not a guess; that's you. There is no question. You know what date that is?"

He shrugged.

"June thirtieth."

"So?"

"You said you never go there, hadn't been there in months."

"I never said that. I said I hardly ever go there, and if I did, so what? It's none of your business."

"That's where you're wrong, Mr. Dorsey. It is my business." I played the second clip. "That's you taking a seat next to your ex-wife." I paused the video. "How come you never told me you saw her just a week before she disappeared?"

"It was a coincidence running into her there."

"Oh, I don't think so. I think you knew she'd be there, and you were obsessed with her."

"No, that's crazy. Things were over between us for a long time."

"What did you talk about?"

"Nothing, really, just this and that."

"What was it that set her off? The this or the that?" I played the balance of the clip, and Dorsey shrank into his chair.

"What did you say to her?"

"Something about her loser husband. It was nothing. I was, like, shocked at her reaction. It was so overdone. She ruined my damn shirt. I still can't get the stain out."

"Why did you follow Beth Wade to the casino that night?"

He stood up. "First off, I didn't follow her there. I went to play cards, that's all."

"We couldn't find any evidence you laid down a single bet that night."

"That's because I had to leave when she threw her drink on me."

"Why'd you go to the bar, when you can get free drinks when you're playing?"

He shrugged. "I saw her there and wanted to say hello."

"By insulting her husband?"

"Look, I don't know what you're after, but I didn't do anything to her."

"I find it curious that a week after you had a fight with her, in a place you say you never go, that she went missing. Don't you?"

"I'd like you to leave now, Detective. You've taken enough of my day with your witch hunt."

43

I'D BEEN IN COURT FOR THREE HOURS LISTENING TO ONE bullshit motion after another. The defense attorney, Dennis Feinberg, was an old hand at delay tactics. I actually liked the guy outside of the courtroom, but on the job, I wanted to jump up and scream to have him disbarred.

After a couple of drinks at a retirement party he told me something that stuck with me. I had been busting his balls about his stalling tactics, even nicknaming him Dennis the Delayer.

He looked me straight in the eye and said, "You laugh, but delaying is the best friend a defense lawyer has. Each day that passes is a plus. You never know what witness is going to get sick or die or what evidence gets lost, and best of all, memories erode. Slowing down the game is what it's all about."

To a large degree, he was right. He knew once it was in the hands of a prosecutor, most investigations ground to a halt. The majority of police departments had too much crime and not enough manpower to stay with a case as it went to trial. If a case ran into trouble, the prosecutors would reach out to us, but by then we were at a disadvantage and often couldn't save the case.

However, there was a contingent of us that kept in close contact as a courtroom case unfolded. I didn't want my efforts to go to waste and at the hint of trouble would bust my ass to close whatever opening the defendant's mouthpiece created.

As I walked across the street to our building, I hoped there was something that would make the day productive. I grabbed a coffee from the cafeteria and went to my office.

Derrick said, "Man, you were gone long. How'd it go?"

"Feinberg was himself, burning the clock with all kinds of nonsense. At one point, I thought O'Leary was going to sanction him."

"He's the worst lawyer."

"Not if you're on the other side of the table."

"I guess so. Look, Verizon sent over Muscleman Belcher's records. I just printed them and was about to go through them."

"We should have had them weeks ago. Why Judge Clement rejected the first warrant is a mystery. He spoke to Wade the day she went missing, for God's sake."

"We have 'em now."

"Let me see." He handed me three sheets of warm paper. The only information I was interested in was the location of the call Belcher had with Wade and where the cell phone was the rest of the night of July 7.

Moving my finger down the list, I located the call at 8:14 p.m. The three cell phone towers that handled the call were along the Immokalee corridor. He was in a car when the call was made, and he was heading east.

I checked the next location his phone pinged a tower on. "Holy shit. He turned his phone off after speaking to Wade."

"What?"

"After Belcher spoke to her, there's no activity. The only explanation is he turned his phone off to avoid detection."

"This is huge."

I looked over the list again to be sure. "I double-checked. If this report is accurate, after speaking with Wade at 8:14, the phone was off until 7:08 a.m. on the eighth."

"He spoke to her, set up a meeting of some kind, and went dark."

"He knew we'd check the location of his phone."

"But he could have just left it home. It would have given him some support on his alibi."

"True, but we're too attached to our phones. He probably thought about leaving it behind but worried if something happened he'd need it."

"He could've gotten a prepaid."

I got up and started pacing. "That's what he should have done, but maybe the crap he's putting in his body affected his judgment."

"What do you want to do? Bring him in?"

"I have to think this through. What's bothering me is the motivation. My line of thought was she rejected him, and he was pumped up on steroids and lost it. The time line here doesn't fit a rage."

"He could have made a date to see her, went out there and then . . . nah, that doesn't work if it's a steroid rage thing."

"What other scenarios would set him off, premeditated or not?"

"Maybe something happened at the gym."

"I don't know. We need to understand what steroids can do to you." I headed to the door. "I'm going to see what Bilotti knows about them."

Dr. Bilotti was on the phone. I really liked his vineyard pictures, but my favorite was a photo of him and his wife at Antinori's new winery in Tuscany. They were in a glass room that hung over a cellar full of barrels of wine. It was modern looking. Bilotti said it was so innovative that it was in an architectural magazine.

I wanted to go there one day, but it would probably have to wait until Jessie was out of college. By that time, it'd need a renovation. Bilotti hung up. "How are you, Frank?

"Good, you?"

"I'm all right. Look, I was just about to leave for the day. We're taking a ride to Marco."

"No problem. I have a quick question."

"Sure. What's going on?"

"I'm pretty certain a person of interest is on steroids. He's a bodybuilder. I know a little about what they call roid rage and want to understand what it's really about."

"I'm no expert in the area, but I've had a dozen cases over the years."

"Tell me what you know."

"The use of anabolic steroids is dangerous on many levels. Essentially, someone is placing extra testosterone into their body. This makes it easier and quicker to build muscle, and initially, it can have a positive impact on their mind-set. However, almost invariably it turns negative, and it is common for a user to experience dramatic mood swings."

"How long does it take for the negative effects to show?"

"That would depend on the type and dosage being used. It's safe to say eventually a user will become more aggressive, hostile, even exhibiting classic signs of mental illness, like schizophrenia. Taking these types of steroids also leads to higher rates of suicide than in the general population."

"The term roid rage seems to me that it's like an episode where someone loses control. Can someone go into a rage, say, at eight at night and commit a violent act six hours later?"

"It's certainly possible. Manic episodes have been known to last days."

"Days? Oh my God. I can't imagine that."

"Unfortunately, it happens."

"That's sad." I stood. "Thanks, Doc. Have a good time tonight."

I thought over what Bilotti had said while taking the stairs back up. The possibility that Belcher had been in a steroid-induced mania and lost contact with reality was plausible. The bodybuilder had spoken with Wade and was traveling east when he did. Then his phone went dark.

Coming out of the stairwell, I pulled out my cell and punched a number in. "Doc? Just one more question."

"Go ahead, Frank."

"When someone is having a manic period, can they act rationally at times?"

"Being in a manic state leads to unpredictable behavior. Though most of it is irrational, they can experience periods of lucidity."

44

Derrick put the call on hold. "Frank, it's Roblinski."

I picked up the line. "Hey, Robbie, what's going on?"

"We're at the Anderson residence. You better get down here."

I stood. "What did you find?"

"It'd be better if you saw it yourself."

"Don't touch anything. I'm on my way."

I hung up and said, "Let's get going. Robbie said they found something. It's gotta be related to Wade."

The front of Anderson's house, in the Golden Gate section of Naples, was crowded with police cars. We checked in with the officer at the door. Roblinski was in the kitchen.

"What did you find?"

"Follow me."

We went down a narrow hall that had spiderweb cracks along its walls. We came to a doorway, and Roblinski stepped aside saying, "Check this out."

I stood inside the doorframe and flicked the lights on. Derrick, looking over my shoulder, said, "What the hell?"

One wall was plastered with three images: one of Beth

Wade, another of a State Farm storefront, and the last of Wade's employer, Accurate Insurance. Each of the photos had a red X drawn over them, but Wade's photo also had a couple of circles on it.

They were crudely drawn, but there was no mistaking it was a target.

Roblinski said, "Take a look in the box."

"Let's put gloves on."

We knelt by a cardboard box to the left of a desk. Derrick said, "What is it?"

I carefully pawed through the wires and fingered a length of pipe before standing.

"Bomb-making materials. Anderson was building a bomb."

"Holy crap."

I took a step toward the photos. "Who was he going to blow up?"

Derrick said, "Probably one of the businesses. I'll bet he was targeting her company."

"Could be, but I think he'd go after State Farm for even hiring Accurate."

I pulled open a drawer. A notebook with a lime-green cover called to me. Lifting it out, I paged through, stopping where Anderson had scrawled something in pen. I held it out for Derrick. "Check this out."

He read it out loud: "Wade should be dead, dead, dead."

"The question is whether somebody got to her before he did."

I thumbed a couple of pages ahead to other notations in the same handwriting and read out loud. "Berry said she lives off Immokalee near Walmart. Works out of her house most days. Drives a white Mustang."

"Anderson and Berry know each other."

"They're in this together?"

I handed him the notebook. "That's what it seems like."

"This feels like an assassination. Anderson and Berry were working together to kill her."

As I started rummaging through the other drawers, I said, "Look through the rest of the book. See if there's anything else."

I pulled out a shoebox filled with photos. Every one of them had Magic -Marker lines through the faces of the people in them. I wondered which one was the salesman at Fergusons.

A thick blue folder marked Claim contained the documentation for his homeowner's claim. Like a seven-year-old, Anderson had scribbled over the State Farm name on each piece of their letterhead. Was there even a head doctor in the county that could help this guy with his anger issues?

The chain of custody would be complicated if I removed anything from the home. The notebook was something I wanted, but instead I took pictures of the incriminating pages and the bomb-making supplies.

Derrick and I joined the search of the premises. The big question, other than if the place would fall down before we were done, was whether we would find a gun.

Like the second time you visit some places, the pimples began to show. In this case the damage suffered here made it look more like terminal acne. The floor in places was uneven, with visible cracks in the tile. I had to tug on a closet door so hard I thought it would come off before it opened.

The balance of the search didn't turn up anything to support the commission of a crime, but we had enough. It was time to go, but I didn't feel good about the discovery. Rather than the pump I'd get with a big moment in a case, sadness came over me.

When I put the key in the ignition, Derrick said, "You feeling all right?"

"Yeah, I'm okay. It just bothers me to see something like that."

"You mean the bomb and all?"

"Not exactly. Listen, there's a life lesson right here."

"About getting violent?"

"No. Anderson was upset that his home was nearly inhabitable, but his dispute should have been brought to court. That's the obvious thing here."

"Absolutely."

"But it really didn't matter who was at fault, the insurance company or the contractor. You see, the problem was Anderson's inability to put the situation in the rearview mirror. Instead, he obsessed over it, letting his emotions dictate a response. Sometimes you just got to turn the page, no matter how you've been wronged."

DERRICK TACKED PRINTED copies of the photos I'd taken at Anderson's house. He said, "I can't believe Anderson and Berry knew each other."

"Maybe there's some kind of Facebook group for people who feel they were screwed by an insurance company."

"Very funny."

"No, I'm serious. There are a zillion different groups, and it's a good way for people to share stories and advice."

"You want me to look into it?"

"Sure, but not right now. We need to be careful when we talk with Berry. We can't let him know that we're aware of his relationship with Anderson."

The phone rang. "Detective Luca, Homicide."

"Hi, it's Cybill, Cybill Gates."

"Hello, Ms. Gates. Were you able to find anything on Wade's husband, Frelig?"

"Yes. He rented a Nissan Pathfinder on July seventh out of our Pine Ridge Road location."

I jumped out of my chair. "John Frelig rented a car from Hertz?"

"Yes."

"Can you send me some proof of the transaction?"

"Uh, we don't have the hard copies here. I could take a screen shot, if that helps?"

I told her to text it to me.

"Frelig rented a car on the seventh!"

"It's got to be him."

"We have to look at the footage for a Nissan Pathfinder; see if we can get him entering the lot and at what time."

"Can the facial software recognize a car?"

"Not that I know of. There's software to tell you what make and model a vehicle is, but I don't know anything out there that could screen cars looking for a particular one."

"We have to look at all the video again?"

"Not we, buddy. If I can't get Chester to give me some eyes to do it, it's going to be you."

"It's okay, don't ask Chester. I'll do it. I don't want to get anybody else involved in this."

I smiled. "You don't trust anyone to do it?"

He shrugged.

"You're dead right, partner. In a homicide investigation, we can't take chances."

"Just following what you've taught me."

My cell sounded a text. It was from Gates. "All right, it's a 2019 gray Nissan Pathfinder. Plate number YZK 449."

45

While Derrick was reviewing the footage of the casino's parking lot, I was on my way to see Muscleman Belcher. He had some explaining to do about his whereabouts on the night Wade disappeared.

Rather than turn onto Vanderbilt Beach Road to enter the Pavilion Shopping Center where LA Fitness was located, I continued on Route 41, making a left turn across from Pelican Marsh's entrance.

Since I was in the neighborhood, it would only take a minute to drive past the Little People's School. Jessie was due to start in a week, and a recent arrest in Lee County had me unsettled. A deviant had been caught installing cameras in a girl's bathroom. A subsequent search of the YMCA in Bonita Springs turned up a pair of cameras in the boy's locker room. There were a lot of sick people out there.

The school's parking lot was empty except for a dark blue car with tinted windows. The man behind the wheel turned his head, rolling the window up as I drove by.

I made a U-turn and turned into the lot. As I approached

the car, the driver's window lowered, and I unbuckled the strap holding my pistol in place.

I moved the bottom of my jacket aside, making the badge on my belt visible. "You have business at the school?"

"Yeah."

"What kind of business?"

"I'm waiting for a—" He reached toward the passenger seat.

"Hold on! Both hands on the wheel."

"What?"

"Put both hands on the steering wheel."

He complied. "I'm a plumber, man. The lady wanted an estimate to put in a couple of sinks for the kids to wash up after painting."

"Let me see your identification."

The guy was legit, and I felt like an ass. I took the long way to see Belcher, heading west to Vanderbilt Drive. I needed the time and bay view to reset my mind.

Belcher was flat on a bench. Each manicured hand holding a dumbbell that would be tough for me to bench press. I counted the reps as I approached. He was up to nine when he began to struggle. A pair of spotters hovering over him were shouting, "One more! You can do it. Push! Push!"

He almost made it, but Belcher relented, and they took the weights out of his hands. I read the numbers on them at a hundred and forty pounds each. I took a second look; it was one hundred and fifty. It was good to be armed.

His back to me, Belcher sat on the bench breathing heavily. I walked in front of him, and he tossed his head back when he saw me.

"I never saw anyone do so much weight."

He shrugged. "My best is six reps at one fifty-five."

"You look like you're ready to beat that."

"After the competition."

If he didn't provide the answers I needed, there was a chance he wouldn't get to show off his body on stage. "We need to talk."

"Again?"

"Yep. The locker room?"

He nodded, grabbed a towel, and I followed. His skin looked like it would split if you touched it. Did bodybuilders get stretch marks, like many pregnant women, when they stopped working out?

A guy with a towel around his waist was shaving. He was the only one in the room. Belcher went to his locker and pulled out a jar of something red and took a sip.

He was wearing a green tank top that was one wash away from incinerating. He looked like he had no neck; his shoulder muscles started behind his ears.

"If I worked out like you and your buddies, there is no way I'd look like you guys. I'm convinced the only way to get into your category is by using something like human growth hormones."

"What did you come here for?"

"You taking steroids?"

"No."

"Where were you the night of July seventh when you spoke to Beth Wade?"

"I don't know."

"You sure you want to stick with that answer?"

"I think I might have been in the car."

"Where?"

"You think I remember something like that?"

"Damn right I do. Your girlfriend went missing that night."

"She ain't my girlfriend."

"Let me jog your memory. We have cell tower activity that proves you were on Immokalee Road past Collier Boulevard, traveling east."

"If you say so."

"I know so. You know what's out that way, don't you? The casino. The place Beth Wade was last seen."

"This is bullshit. I had nothing to do with that."

"You'd be more believable if you didn't turn your phone off to avoid detection."

"What? I didn't do anything. My battery died, that's all."

"You expect me to believe that?"

"I don't care what you believe; that's what happened. I'm going back to my workout. I think it's time I got myself a lawyer."

I watched his V-shaped back as he walked into the gym. He was as arrogant as they came. I wanted to wring his neck —if he had one—but I knew how that would turn out. One more piece of evidence against him would bring his cocky ass back to the ground.

I was behind my desk reading the murder book, the Belcher section. Had I missed something? A connection, a slipup of some sort? We had an Explorer that was the same color as his seen at the casino. I couldn't think of a way to clarify whether it was him or not and went back to reading. I was halfway through the second interview I'd had outside the gym when Derrick came in.

"Good, you're back."

"What's up?"

"Guess what I found?"

After Belcher, I had zero patience. "An efficient way to communicate?"

His shoulders slumped. "Sorry. A gray Nissan Pathfinder entered the casino's parking lot at four minutes after midnight."

"You get a plate number?"

"Couldn't grab it."

"When did it leave?"

"Three fifteen."

"Just the driver in the vehicle."

"Yep, and it looks like a male."

"It could be the husband, Frelig."

"Could be? It has to be him."

"It's three o'clock. Time to take a ride, and see what Frelig has to say."

"Oh, that meth snitch Bolo Lora called. He got out and wants to talk to you."

"He say anything?"

"No, just that he wanted to talk to you. Here's his cell number."

I punched the number in.

"Who's this?"

I knew it was Bolo from his smoker's voice. "Detective Luca. What did you want?"

"I got some more information for you."

"Spit it out."

"Before I tell you, are you going help me with my, uh, legal problems?"

"I'll let everyone know how helpful you've been. What do you have?"

"They moved Seke out of the casino."

"Who's they?"

"The tribe's leadership."

"Where is he?"

"On the Miccosukee Reservation. I'm telling you, he did it, man. They moved him to keep his ass away from the law."

"Are you certain about this?"

"Hundred percent, man. A hundred percent."

"Thanks for letting me know. You find out anything else, let me know. You're in deep trouble, and this is the only way out for you."

I hung up. "The Seminoles moved Seke out of Immokalee. It looks like they're stashing him on the Miccosukee Reservation."

46

It was early, earlier than I'd been at my desk in a while. I hadn't beaten Derrick into the office in months. I was looking forward to the coffee he always brought me, since I was sipping cafeteria java that must have been from the overnight shift. I reviewed a list of the previous day's arrests and complaints and set it down.

I was hoping the lab would be done analyzing the evidence from the Anderson home. They had promised it for today, and I wanted to have a handle on it before talking to Anderson. If it didn't come in by nine, I was going to see Berry first.

We hadn't been able to find a link between the two men, other than they both felt Wade had screwed them over on an insurance claim. The idea they conspired to kill Wade was a tempting one; Berry had served time for a serious crime, one that involved a conspiracy.

It would be easier to grab and subdue a feisty woman like Wade when there were two men. I studied the map of the casino and the surrounding area. Wade's car was just steps away from the woods that bordered the parking lot. It was a perfect hiding spot.

Had they surprised her, silencing her, and hooding her head before she could scream? As easy as it would be with a pair of abductors, she still would have been able to make a call for help before being overwhelmed. Rowan was in the parking lot at that time.

I leafed through the murder book for the transcripts of my interviews with Rowan. I'd asked him whether he saw anything, but he claimed to be glued to his phone. I never asked whether he heard something, but that would have been implied in my original question. If he heard something while looking at his screen, he would have been pulled away from his phone and looked around.

One other thing generally bothered me with conspiracy theories: anytime you added a person to committing a crime, you increased the risk someone would talk. One of my strongest beliefs was the only way to keep a secret between two people was when one of them was dead.

Still, I had to acknowledge that a network of criminals and gangs were able to operate far too effectively for my sensibilities. People planned and carried out crimes together all the time. Just because the risk was higher in the keeping it secret category, it didn't stop them.

I took the Pine Ridge Road entrance into the Vineyards. It would give me a chance to check out more of a community I'd only seen once. I drove north on Vineyard Boulevard, which ran along the interstate. A ten-foot-high wall wasn't for security; it was there to tamp the road noise. I wondered how effective it was as I approached the community's clubhouse complex.

Taking a short detour to feed my curiosity, I turned up its access road. There were a handful of tennis courts and scores of golf carts. People were streaming in and out of the club-house in tennis and golf wear. It was an active community.

A kid in a safari hat was pressure washing the Avellino Isles sign. It was one of my favorite things about Naples: it wasn't only green, it was clean.

Berry's red truck was in the driveway, which was a relief. He seemed surprised by my call, and the thought he might run had passed through my mind.

His hair was slicked back, highlighting his widow's peak. *Fox Business News* was on the TV, and there was a pile of papers on the desk in the family room.

"Working from home?"

He sighed. "Somebody's got to do the bills. People don't realize that an average renovation, nothing big, there's almost a hundred invoices. And that's not counting all the little crap the guys need on a job that they run to Home Depot for. Keeping track of it is a full-time job, and since the La Playa bullshit, I've been doing it."

He should only know the paperwork we had to deal with in my line of work. "I can imagine."

"I'd like to get all the contractors together and get every-body to agree to some kind of documentation or administra-tive fee."

He moved a can of Coke to the side, and we sat at the kitchen counter.

I didn't want to tell him that the antitrust folks would frown on such an agreement, but that was not my area of expertise.

"I'm going to get right to it. Where were you the night of July seventh?"

"I told you, I was home that night."

"Can anybody vouch for that?"

"I was home alone."

"So, you have no proof you were home?"

"How am I gonna prove that?"

"How do you know Tony Anderson?"

"Who? Tony Anderson?"

"That's what I said."

"Sounds familiar, but I can't put a face to the name."

"Come now. You know him."

"How do I know him? Give me a clue."

"He had a claim that was reduced by Beth Wade, just like with you."

"That bitch screwed a lot of people. But I don't know who you're talking about."

I didn't have a picture to show him. "That's odd, because he referenced you."

"Really?"

"Yep. He was arrested on another assault. It was a serious one, and a judge granted us a warrant to search his home."

As each word tumbled out of my mouth, Berry's face lost a shade of color, but he remained quiet. "We found a notebook with violent references to what he wanted to do to Beth Wade. He was watching her, and there was a clear reference to information he said you gave him."

"Me?"

"Yes, sir. He said you told him where she lived and that she worked from home and drove a white Mustang."

"Oh, hold on, now. That was nothing."

"How did you know where Wade lived and what car she drove?"

"I saw her once, at the car wash. I was at the Auto Spa, the one on Pine Ridge, and she was there too. We were waiting for our cars to come out and started talking."

"Really? I thought you were fighting with her."

"Not then. This was at the beginning, when she first stuck her nose in the claim."

"And she told you where she lived?"

"Not exactly. She said she stopped going to the car wash by Walmart, even though it was right by her house. I don't know where she lives."

I knew how he knew she had a white Mustang, so I asked, "And the fact she worked from home?"

"We were just talking. It just came up. I swear, it was just us bullshitting around."

"You expect me to believe that?"

"It's the truth. We were at a frigging car wash, for God's sake."

"You're a salesman, right?"

"What do you mean?"

"You go out and talk to prospective customers and make them feel good about choosing you to do the work they need."

"Yeah, that's about half of what I do."

"That means you're a manipulator. You say the right things to lead someone to hire you."

"I have a reputation, man. I've been doing this a long time."

"Reputation? You've served time. I don't think you'd want to be talking about that."

"I paid my debt to society."

"Did you get Beth Wade to tell you where she lived and worked?"

"No way."

"Did Tony Anderson ask you to partner with him to get retribution?"

"No. I'd never do something like that."

"You forget about trying to get rid of your partner?"

He wagged his head, and I said, "So, how do you explain what Anderson wrote, in an explicit manner, that you told him about Wade?"

"I don't know. I think we may have talked in the waiting room at Accurate one day."

"You met at her employer's office?"

"I think so. It's the only thing that makes sense. If it's how I think it is, he was really pissed off at her."

"So, you told someone who was enraged at her where she lived? That right there is a conspiracy."

"No, no, I didn't say that. I just mentioned that I had seen her at the car wash and that she said she lived by Walmart. I don't even know her damn address."

"Why say anything about the kind of car she drove?"

He hesitated. "I don't know how that came up. We were just talking . . . I don't know."

I didn't know either—about what to believe. If it weren't for him telling Anderson about her car, he could just be someone who liked to gab. He was a salesman, after all. I would love to clear one of the suspects and was banking that Anderson would help clarify Berry's role.

47

OUR LANAI FACED WEST, WHICH GAVE US TOO MUCH SUN between three and five o'clock, but the nightly sunsets were a trade I'd make again. I looked west; the sky was an orange-infused masterpiece. It was a perfect night. I ignited the barbecue, clicked the TV on and went inside to get vegetables to grill.

Carrying a pan of broccoli and one of portobello mushrooms, I stopped in my tracks. The news was showing a picture of a house with blue tarps on it. It was Tony Anderson's. I set the pans on the table and raised the volume.

A picture of Anderson filled the left side of the screen. As the newscaster said he had been arrested, a bullet list of items began to appear to right of his photo:

* In custody for assault
* Suspect in murder of Beth Wade
* Bomb-making materials found in his home

I knew the information would leak out, but who the hell told the press about what was found in the search? Chester was going to ratchet up the pressure on me. I patted my pants pocket, feeling my phone. I expected it to ring as I placed the veggies on the grill.

Jessie came out, carrying a pink stuffed animal. "Daddy, Mommy wants to know if you want the fish."

"Come here, you little peanut."

When she smiled, nothing else mattered. I hiked her onto my hip. "How's Katie the Kangaroo doing?"

"Give Daddy a kiss, Katie."

The toy smelled just as she did. "Thank you, Katie. Now, how about you ask Jessie to give her daddy a big kiss?"

"Oh, Daddy. You don't have to ask Katie." She yanked my head toward her and planted her sticky lips on my cheek.

Lowering her to the ground, I said, "I have to turn the veggies over. Go tell Mom I'm ready for the salmon."

I was anxious to eat but not to tussle with Chester over charging Anderson. He was the reigning number one, but I didn't want to rush. I had to be beyond certain. I'd lost months of sleep over the first homicide I handled and wasn't going to repeat the mistake I made.

Instead of demanding more proof, I had bowed to pressure. It was the worst decision I'd ever made. The kid we arrested hung himself his first night behind bars. If that wasn't horrifying enough, within weeks it was proven that someone else committed the murder.

It took me a decade and Mary Ann's help to get past it. As with most bad experiences, there was some good that resulted. The episode had made me exceedingly cautious before making an arrest.

———————

DERRICK HELD up the *Daily News* when I came in. The front-page headline read "Murderer? Terrorist?"

Alongside it was Anderson's mug shot, which took a quarter of the page.

I shook my head and grabbed the coffee on my desk. "I'm going into the lion's den."

"The sheriff?"

"Yep. He called me on the way in." I took a couple of quick sips and said, "Might as well get this over with. I want to go see Frelig after this." I put my coffee down and walked out the door.

"Morning, Frank."

"Good morning, sir."

"I heard it was your idea to do a search on Anderson's home. Solid work."

"Thank you."

"I assume you're going to recommend we charge him in the death of Beth Wade."

"It's too early for that, sir."

"Too early? Anderson's bail hearing is this afternoon, and the judge is Harris. That means a maximum of fifty thousand dollars bail." He lifted up the morning paper. "Anderson's going to be released, and the press is going to have a field day if we don't do something."

"I realize what it looks like, sir, but I can't make the jump—"

"What jump? Anderson had more than enough motive, twisted as it may be. We have the bomb evidence and his written intentions. What more do you need?"

"I understand, but forensics determined that the components found could have alternative uses."

"Alternative uses? If we let someone as unstable as Anderson out and something happens, we'll be run out of town before the coffee cools."

"That's what the report stated, along with the fact that no

explosives were found on the premises. I'd like to hold on to Anderson as well, but charging him with Wade's murder without an ironclad case that gets dismissed, or we lose at trial would be far worse."

"We'd build a case as the trial approaches. He may even plead guilty in some kind of a deal."

I wanted to ask him who *we* was. He should have said you. If we couldn't discover enough evidence to build a solid case and we lost, Chester would blame me. "If he didn't do it, he wouldn't plead to it."

"You said yourself he was a prime suspect."

"There is no question I have serious concerns about Tony Anderson. However, we're pursuing other suspects. I don't believe it is in the interests of the department to rush and charge Anderson until we are certain it was him. As an example, I just received interesting information on Magi Seke."

"What kind of info?"

"He's no longer working at the casino, and from what I gather, they moved him out to the Miccosukee Reservation."

"There can be a whole host of reasons. He may have wanted to move there himself."

"I don't know. That's where he was moved from after detaining that girl."

"We don't know if any of that is real."

"True, though a source confirmed it."

"What can we do to bring this case to a conclusion?"

"All we need is some more time, sir. That's it. In the meantime, assuming that Anderson makes bail, I recommend we keep our eyes on him."

THE CLOCK WAS COUNTING DOWN. Depending on the media reaction to Anderson's release, I guessed we had two weeks to wrap it up, as I got back to my office.

"How'd it go?"

"Predictable. Like I've told you before, Chester is concerned about the press and how the department is portrayed. Don't forget, he's got to go before the voters every four years."

"You got him to back off on Anderson?"

"The sheriff knows we don't have enough yet. He was taking a shot that I'd suggest we charge Anderson. He knew there was virtually no chance I'd agree, but he's crafty. If something goes wrong, he can say he wanted an arrest but deferred to the Homicide Department."

"He wants it both ways."

"Like every politician." I picked up the coffee I'd left behind. It was cold.

"You going to see Frelig?"

"Yeah, but I need a coffee first."

"I'll put it in the microwave for you, so you can catch up."

I opened my email and threw back my head. There were fifty-one messages. How the hell was I going to do my job? My method of dealing with tasks like this was different than most others. When there was a list to go through, I focused on the easy, quick items. It gave me a sense of momentum and accomplishment.

Scanning the box, I opened three I expected to be nothing more than acknowledgments. I wasn't disappointed. Two others were from companies hosting training seminars. I clicked through to check the subject matter and the speakers and hit delete.

The next was the daily report on arrests. It was something

my old New Jersey partner had trained me to check. I resisted doing it up north because the report was too long, but in Collier County, an average of fifteen people were brought into custody each day. It was a quick read.

There was a mug shot of those apprehended, their sex, date of birth, and whether they were still in custody. I had to do a double take. The next-to-last picture was of Ben Rowan, and he wasn't promoting tchotchke.

48

Was Rowan arrested on a DUI? I clicked on his picture for details. Rowan had been accused of sexual harassment and assault. He had posted a bond and was no longer in custody. I stared at his face for a full minute before checking the arrest number and pulling up the file.

A complaint against Rowan had been filed by a Rebecca Holman, a thirty-nine-year-old who lived on Coral Palms Way. The woman stated that she had been employed by Rowan and that he had made repeated sexual advances, which she rebuffed. When she rejected his last overture, she claimed that Rowan had grabbed her crotch and pulled her head to kiss her.

What the hell was wrong with this guy? How many more men would we find who were forcing themselves on women? As soon as Jessie was old enough, I would train her to use a gun. My bet was there wasn't a deviant who'd try to sexually assault a woman with a carry permit.

Derrick handed me the coffee, and I swung my monitor around. "Take a look at who got locked up."

"Ben Rowan? Sexual assault? That'll help his promotion business."

"I hope you and Lynn have a boy. That way you don't have to worry like me."

"I don't know, Frank. No matter what you do, there is risk. Like you said, you do the best you know how, and it will turn out all right."

I had told him what my father said to me? That had to be before Jessie came along. Now, I was seeing danger for her everywhere.

"I don't know if that's enough anymore." I grabbed my jacket. "I'm going to see Frelig."

EVEN THE LACK of traffic on Immokalee Road didn't lift my mood. Were sex crimes on the rise? Or was it because more women came out? Or was it the publicity around the subject? It seemed like new lines needed to be drawn on relationships.

Men might think something they said was playful, but it could be interpreted as suggestive or lewd when they tossed around comments that could go either way.

I pulled into St. Croix's driveway. It was a quarter to ten, and Frelig would just be getting into bed. The timing of my visit brought a smile to my face. I had to ring the bell three times before he answered.

Barefoot, Frelig had a Grateful Dead T-shirt on and gym shorts. He said, "Aw, come one, man. I just got off work."

"Sorry, this can't wait."

"But you got that Anderson guy—"

"You want to do this out here?"

A sigh worthy of a sixteen-year-old came out of him as he moved aside. We sat at the kitchen table. Pop-Tarts and

Nutella were on the counter. I thought only Europeans ate the chocolate spread.

"What do you want now?"

"I'm still having trouble with your whereabouts the night of July seventh."

"I told you, I was working. You know that." His cell phone rang, and he picked it up. "Hold a second, I gotta get this."

He spoke for a minute, reassuring the person on the other side that everything was taken care of and that the painters were coming tomorrow.

He hung up and said, "Sorry, one of my neighbors goes north for the summer, and the water line on his fridge went. It was a good thing he pays me to house watch."

"Money well spent."

"Measly fifty bucks a month."

"Getting back to the night in question. We haven't been able to verify your claim that you were way out east when you say a driver flagged you down."

"What can I tell you? It was late; no one was on the road."

"You had a fight with your wife earlier that day. Did you go to the casino to see her later that night?"

"No. I didn't go there."

"You didn't want to take the tow truck out there, did you?"

"I told you, I didn't go to the casino."

"Why did you rent a car on July seventh?"

"I didn't rent a car."

"Let me be more specific. An SUV, a Nissan Pathfinder, is what you rented."

"I don't know where you get your information from, but I never did."

"You're familiar with Hertz, the car rental company with the yellow logo, aren't you?"

"Of course I am."

"Well, they say you rented a vehicle from their Pine Ridge Road location on July seventh."

"That's bullshit. I was never there. Why would I rent a car when I have my own sitting outside?"

"I'm supposing that you did it to evade detection. You knew showing up at the casino in a big tow truck would attract attention, so you rented a car."

"And drove to the casino and killed Beth? Is that what you think?"

"It's one of the possibilities."

"That's crazy. I would never hurt Beth, and I didn't go to Hertz."

He was lying for sure about doing harm to his wife, as he'd been arrested for hitting her. He seemed adamant about not going to Hertz though. Was there a way someone could get around personally going to rent a car? Could they get someone to do it for them? But why go through all that and have it in your name anyway?

The Hertz office was ten minutes away. To avoid traffic, I took Immokalee down to Goodlette Frank, made a left and a right onto Pine Ridge. The traffic on Pine Ridge was much lighter the closer you were to Route 41.

The car rental agency occupied an old building across the street from Waterside Shops. The outdoor mall was so high end I wondered why they didn't spell shops as shoppes. It had more panache.

A customer holding keys was leaving as I entered. Except for a woman in her sixties behind the counter, the place was empty.

"How may I assist you? Do you have a reservation?"

Holding up my badge, I said, "I'm here on police business, ma'am. I need to verify some data on a rental you made on July seventh."

"Oh my. I think we're not allowed to give information, you know, because of privacy laws."

"That's correct. However, I already have the paperwork concerning the rental, from your head office. I left the documents in the office, but I have this." I showed her the picture Gates had texted me.

"I'm not sure that's proper authorization. Can I call headquarters?"

"You can, but all I need to see is a copy of the license used by John Frelig. You see, we're investigating a ring who seem to be making duplicate licenses and selling them. I won't take any of the paperwork, I just need to see if they're using the same technique. They've been very high tech about it. "

"That's terrible. I wonder where all this technology is going to take us."

"I know what you mean. The date is July seventh, the name is Frelig. He rented a Nissan Pathfinder."

"Hold on a moment. I'll pull the hard copies for you."

She was smiling as she handed the file to me. I found the copy of the license Frelig had used to rent the Nissan. It stunned me.

49

———————

I slammed the phone down. Derrick said, "What's the matter?"

"The Seminoles may be better at stopping information leaks than the old-time Mafia was. Nobody wants to say anything about Seke. This buddy of mine, we went to John Jay College, in New York; he's a muckety muck with a Dade County special task force. They have a lot of interaction with the tribe because of the Hard Rock Casino, and he can't get anything on Seke."

"Maybe they're figuring if he lies low on the reservation, we can't move the case forward."

"We're going to need something, something to trigger a reason to make them talk. Right now, all we have is Bolo Lara and the video footage."

"You know, last night me and Lynn were watching this documentary about this gang in Russia. The leader was a makeup artist, and he knew how to alter their looks to avoid facial recognition software from identifying them."

"Facial hair and a hat don't cut it anymore."

"According to what they said, it's actually easier than

you'd think. Large, dark sunglasses alone are enough most of the time, but these guys took it to another level. They'd add layers onto the face to change the biometric measurements."

"The thugs always seem to be a step ahead."

"The pace of change is exhausting."

I was about to say wait until he got to my age, when an image of Jerry Belcher, the muscleman, popped into my head. It was the time I had found him outside the gym sucking on his muscle-building potion. He was sitting at a table and was wearing sunglasses—large, dark ones.

"We need to take another look at the videos. Someone may be able to disguise their facial features, but they can't effectively hide their body type, especially someone the size of Belcher."

"That's true. Where do you want to start?"

"I'm going to see the woman who filed the complaint against Rowan."

"You think there's something there?"

"I'm not sure, but worst case, I learn something about people like Rowan. Why don't you concentrate on reviewing the video from July seventh? If you see someone the size of the Incredible Hulk, it could be Belcher."

"Can you think of anybody else with a distinctive body type? You said the hubby, Frelig, was flabby."

"Not enough to differentiate himself. Concentrate on Belcher. I'll see you later."

Since Derrick mentioned Frelig, I thought about him and our last talk as I walked to the Cherokee. Driving along Airport Pulling Road, instead of turning onto Golden Gate Boulevard, I continued north, making a right on Immokalee Road. It was a slight diversion. I'd take the interstate south, making up some time to see the woman who filed the complaint.

I circled the St. Croix neighborhood until I spotted a truck lettered Ace Painting and Paper. It was parked in front of a unit whose garage door was up. A white Ford Focus, whose hood was up, was in the garage. There was a cord coming from the engine plugged into an outlet. It was on a trickle charger. This had to be the place Frelig was home-watching.

Before getting out, I snapped a photo of the license plate. Approaching the apartment, I heard Spanish music leaking from the garage's open interior door. It was another example that if you weren't paying the electricity bills, you didn't care if the doors and windows were open.

Poking my head in, I startled a man in paint-splashed clothes.

"Sorry, didn't mean to surprise you."

"You the owner?"

"No, I live on the other side and heard about the damage. Is this the place that had the water damage?"

"Yeah, we changed some of the wallboard in here."

"He got lucky. Okay, have a good day."

I closed the door behind me and peered into the car. Nothing unusual. I opened the car door and popped the trunk. I looked in and froze. There was no carpeting. Had it been ripped out to hide evidence?

I sent a text to Derrick to look for a white Ford Focus in the casino parking lot surveillance after he was done looking for Belcher.

TAKING the last exit before Marco Island, I exited onto Collier Boulevard and took it to a small community called San Marino. Rebecca Holman lived on the ground floor of a multidwelling building on Marino Lane. There wasn't much going on architecturally, and I couldn't guess when it was built.

I didn't get the pea-soup-green color of the place, but it was neat, well kept, and assuming its location, likely inexpensive. As I rang the bell, I knew that at the right price I'd live in a sun-yellow building.

A voice behind the door said, "Who is it?"

Holding my badge up to the peephole, I said, "Detective Luca."

Two clicks sounded before she pushed the door open. A door that opened out meant it was built under the Miami-Dade improved building codes, placing it around ten years old. It made it easier to withstand high winds using the support of the door's frame.

"Hi, come in."

The apartment had low ceilings but was wide open. It was an inside unit with no windows on the sides and a tiny lanai enclosed with tall bushes. The combo restricted the light too much for my taste.

We sat in the kitchen, lit by a large florescent light.

"As I mentioned over the phone, I'm not directly involved in the complaint you filed; however, Ben Rowan may be connected to a case I'm working."

"I'm not surprised someone else filed charges. He's a pig."

"How long have you known Mr. Rowan?"

"About three months. That was when I applied for the job he advertised."

"How long did you work at Promo Pros?"

"I started the week after I was interviewed."

"When did the harassment begin?"

"About a month after I started working for him. It was

subtle at first. He'd make comments, you know. But I kept my distance instead of leaving. He knew I needed the job."

My temples pounded at the thought he would take advantage of her economic situation. "Tell me about the situation that led to the charge."

Her face reddened. "But I told it to the officer. I even signed a statement."

"That's fine, then. No need to go through it again. I know these types of violations are difficult and can be embarrassing to talk about, but the incident occurred on July third, didn't it?"

"Yes. The day before the Fourth of July."

"But you waited a long time to file the complaint."

"At first, I didn't know what to do. I was in shock, and then it was Fourth of July weekend, and I told one of my friends about it at a barbecue that Sunday. She gave me the courage to go public. I was going to go Monday, but I had to go for two tests up at the Cleveland Clinic. I'm a cancer survivor. They saved my life up there."

I caught myself before telling her about my bladder cancer but asked, "How long ago?"

"I've been in remission for six years now. They tell me I'm in the clear."

"Excellent." I was close to four years and still thinking about it at three in the morning.

She smiled. "Fingers crossed."

I gave a thumbs-up. "Please continue."

"I was going to go to the police on Tuesday afternoon, Wednesday latest, depending on how late I got back from Jacksonville. But before filing anything, I wanted to warn a young girl I worked with right before I left. So I called, and she told me Mr. Rowan took an unexpected trip to Asia. I was so angry and—"

"What do you mean by unexpected?"

"It wasn't planned, that I knew of, and I had just left. He would have had to say something to me, because when he wasn't around he trusted me to open and close the store. Probably because I was the oldest."

"Are you sure that the trip wasn't planned?"

"If it was, nobody who worked there knew about it."

Who would take a trip to Asia without planning? I was pretty sure he didn't need a visa to get into China, but he still would need to set meetings up. "And you're certain about that?"

"Absolutely. Why?"

"It's just surprising, that's all. Okay, so when you found out he was away, what happened?"

"Well, to be honest, I was, like, crushed. I know it's stupid, but I wanted him arrested, to see him put in handcuffs."

"I understand."

She wagged her head. "Let him see how it feels to be humiliated."

"I understand, but he was back for days before you filed a complaint."

"I had to go to Kansas. My mom has early onset Alzheimer's, and it's getting worse. Decisions had to be made. I moved her into place that specializes in it, but . . ."

It was another example of how unfair life could be. Here was a woman who had been stricken with cancer, has a mother with Alzheimer's, and was sexually assaulted by her boss. And I knew all that after just five minutes. Who knew what else she was going through?

50

DERRICK WAS TILTING HIS HEAD BACK, A SMALL BOTTLE OF eye drops in his hand.

"Staring at that screen getting to you?"

"You got that right. My eyes are dry as hell. But check this out. The lab made them from the video."

He handed me two images of a male in dark, oversized sunglasses. His body was similar to Belcher's.

"What do you think? It could be him, no?"

I looked at the way the shirt hugged his biceps, trying to recall the shape of Belcher's. "There aren't many guys with bodies like this to start with, and even fewer at the time and place of Wade's disappearance."

"Exactly. I mean, what are the odds?"

"I need to see the footage. I've seen Belcher walk and want to compare the two. It's one thing to disguise your face; it's a lot harder to disguise how you move."

"Sure. I didn't get a chance to check on the Ford Focus you texted me about. What's that all about?"

"I went to see Frelig, and he was adamant about not

renting anything from Hertz, so I took a ride to their Pine Ridge office. Guess what?"

Derrick smiled. "Okay, you got me."

"They rented the Nissan to a John Frelig who lives in Park Shore. It wasn't Wade's husband."

"What are the odds of that?"

"You're starting to repeat yourself."

"Sorry."

"Just busting. The Ford Focus is just a hunch. Frelig said something about a neighbor whose house he watches. I went by there today, and sitting in the garage on a charger is this Ford. And it has no carpet in the trunk. It could be Frelig used it. It would make so much more sense not having to rent a car."

"This is getting interesting."

"You think so? Wait till you hear about Rowan."

"What about him?"

"How about it looks like the trip he took was a last-minute thing. As you say, what are the odds of him leaving right after Wade's murder?"

"Has this ever happened before?"

"What? A person of interest takes a trip?"

"No. Having so many suspects. I mean, we've had three in the last two, but this is crazy; we have seven."

"It's a first, but I think we're down to six."

"Why is that?"

"Berry called me. He said he remembered that he ordered food through the Uber Eats app from Pelican Larry's some-time after ten on the seventh. I have a call into them to check the time."

"He still could've gone after that. She disappeared after two in the morning."

"No doubt, but it would establish that he was home if the

driver can ID him. Then we can use the Vineyards entrance cameras to track if he left and returned."

"He could have used another car."

"It's possible, but I don't think the Vineyards has the kind of traffic at that hour that would make it tough to vet each vehicle."

He nodded. "I'm with you."

"Then, come on, I want to see that video."

TWO SCREENS CAME TO LIFE. Frozen images of a bodybuilder filled both.

The lab tech, Peter Sample, said, "Here's the one of him on his way to the bathroom."

The area he walked through was loaded with people. The time stamp was 11:42 p.m. Schwarzenegger Junior weaved between people and disappeared into the bathroom.

"Rerun that." I took a step toward the screen and studied his movements. It could be Belcher.

Derrick said, "What do you think?"

"Tough to say at this point." I turned to Sample. "Let's see when he comes out."

The video sped up for a minute. "Here he is."

The muscleman came out and made a sharp left before moving out of sight. I got nothing out of it. "Let's see the other film."

"You got it."

The man on the other screen was in motion. He was walking between rows of blackjack tables. It was impossible to determine his gait. He was obscured most of the time and was zigzagging as he walked, disappearing down an aisle of slot machines.

"You want to see it again?"

If Derrick wasn't with me I would have declined. "Absolutely."

My mind wandered as I viewed the replay. It was useless. When the clip ended, I said, "Is there any way the lab can determine if this man has done anything to alter his appearance, with the intention of throwing off an attempt to identify him?" I knew it was a stupid question. I was trying to generate ideas.

"Not that I'm aware of. It would have to be something that looked unnatural, and that would make it a less-than-ideal disguise. That said, the sunglasses he's wearing, inside a casino, I might add, are widely known to be a tool to avoid recognition. Most people think facial hair, a hat, and glasses do the trick, but the software has evolved to digitally remove them. Oversized sunglasses, like he's wearing, and those that are dark, do work."

"Thanks. We'll let you know if there is anything else on this."

We took the stairs up. I said, "I don't know what to make of this. It was impossible to compare his gait with all the people there."

"That's one busy place. I never realized so many people went there."

"I don't get it. I work way too hard for my money."

"Agree, totally."

I pushed through the stairwell door onto our floor. "Something is bothering me. Why would someone go to a casino at night, wearing sunglasses?"

"And the only guy wearing them is built like Belcher."

"Couldn't this guy have used one of those Player's Club cards so we could ID him?"

"That would be too easy."

"We keep digging, and we'll nail this killer. I hate to ask you to do it, but we need to see if the Ford Focus that belongs to Frelig's neighbor went to the casino."

"No problem. I got it."

"But before you do that, go see that Uber driver. Make sure it was Berry that he delivered the food to."

"Sure."

"Thanks. I'm going to see Anderson. Might as well see where that leads before Chester starts asking questions."

51

CLEAN SHAVEN, ANDERSON HAD BEEN OUT A LITTLE OVER A day. He was wearing fresh clothes but a haggard look. It would take an innocent man a solid week of ten-hour sleeps to recover from a stint behind bars. With a minimum of an assault hanging over him, it was one of the few times I didn't have a firm opinion on when, or if, he'd return to what was normal for him.

I couldn't fiddle with the room's temperature because sitting next to Anderson was Barry Eichoff, the public attorney assigned to defend him. He was one of the few public defenders who didn't act like the police were gun-wielding yahoos. Eichoff was as fair a lawyer as I'd seen. Keeping him waiting wasn't fair. I would have to kick this off without the psychological edge I'd become superstitious about.

After a quick knock, I entered the room. We exchanged hellos, and I sat across from them.

"Gentlemen, thank you for coming in today."

"My client is anxious to clear the air concerning the Wade case."

"He'll have every opportunity, Counselor. Shall we?"

"Yes, I have to be in court in an hour and fifteen."

I flicked on the recording and recited the formalities.

"Mr. Anderson, you had a disagreement with Beth Wade over the handling of your insurance claim. Is that correct?"

Eichoff said, "We'll stipulate that my client was angry that Ms. Wade refused to approve a claim the underlying insurer initially agreed to."

"Good. Mr. Anderson, you were just released under bail proceedings. Can you tell us why you were arrested?"

"I got into a fight with a salesman from Fergusons."

"An altercation so violent that this salesperson ended up in an intensive care unit at NCH."

"Detective, the record of arrest contains the details. I'll never make my court appearance if we continue like this."

"That arrest led to a search of your home, during which we discovered materials that could be made into an explosive device." Eichoff opened his mouth to speak, but I cut him off. "I said, could be used. Now, why did you have such components in your house?"

"They've been there for ages. Didn't you see the dust on them?"

"Why did you have a box of material to possibly make a bomb?"

Eichoff whispered in Anderson's ear. After listening to the lawyer's advice, he said, "I wasn't going to make a bomb."

"You gave up on trying to blow Beth Wade to pieces and decided to smother her to death?"

"I didn't hurt that woman."

"Do you remember writing in your notebook that she should be dead? You should. You wrote it several times."

"I was mad, and I had a damn right to be pissed. She

screwed me over by sticking her nose in my claim. My house is a mess. She saw that."

"You were mad and blamed her. Is that right?"

"Yeah, it was all her fault."

"And you decided to take revenge. You found out where she lived, what kind of car she drove, and where she worked."

"I never did anything."

"I think you did. I think you thought that killing her would even the score."

"No, that's not true. I'd never do that."

"You'd never do that? You nearly killed a man over a barbecue."

Anderson slumped in his chair. "I didn't mean to hurt him."

"And you didn't mean to hurt Wade either, but you did."

"No, I didn't. Believe me, I didn't lay a finger on her. I'd never hurt a woman."

Eichoff said, "I'm sure you know that the incidents he's been associated with have never involved a female."

"Well, this one did."

"My client has repeatedly denied any knowledge or involvement in the circumstances surrounding the murder of Beth Wade."

"He can deny all he wants. We think he did it."

"I didn't. Please, you got to believe me."

I counted to ten then said, "The DA has authorized me to discuss a plea arrangement with you. If you admit to the murder of Beth Wade, we'll reduce the charge to voluntary manslaughter."

"No way, man. I didn't do it."

"I'd take the deal, Mr. Anderson. It's the best offer you're going to get."

"I can't admit to something I didn't do. I know I've lost my temper here and there, and I'm in a mess with this assault, but I never killed anyone, especially a woman."

"Counselor, I'd suggest you and your client discuss the benefits of the offer and get back to me. We'll give you four days to consider it. Have a good day, gentlemen."

I left the room believing Anderson wouldn't change his position. Why? Was it because he really didn't do it? Or did he believe we didn't have enough to convict him? I was going to have to tell Chester I delivered the offer. At the very least, I'd bought myself four days before he could start pressing me.

While walking to the Cherokee I checked my phone. There was a text from Derrick. It looked like Berry had been identified by the Uber driver as the one he delivered food to. The Uber Eats app had the delivery time as 11:09 p.m.

It wasn't an ironclad alibi, but rather than examine a couple of hours of the video of cars leaving the Vineyards, I was issuing a temporary pass to Berry. I didn't think it was likely, but if the other leads started to crumble, we'd circle back to the contractor with a record.

It was still early enough to catch Rowan while he was working. Pushing down the gas pedal, I reminded myself to keep my emotions in check.

52

Rowan was visible through the Promo Pros window. He had his back to the front of the store and was holding up a gold and blue pennant. When I entered, a skinny kid making copies said, "I'll be right with you, sir."

Rowan turned around, and though he was twenty feet away, I saw his posture collapse. He said, "That's okay, Ricky. I'll get this."

He took a step in my direction and hesitated before continuing. "Nice to see you. What can I do for you?"

Rowan was wearing short sleeves for the first time. His forearms were hairless, and he had a skinny red blemish on his left one. "I have a couple of questions for you."

"I'm in the middle of running a job." He checked his watch. "We have to deliver these pennants to the high school by five."

The thought of this pervert doing business with a school made my stomach churn. "No more than five, ten minutes max."

"All right, but that's all the time I have."

The same pictures of him and what looked to be his main

Asian supplier were on the walls. He hadn't hung the new one, though the only space was next to the new sign I liked that was up the last time I was there. It was an effective reminder to advertise. I was going to suggest that he put that message outside to draw traffic but didn't want to get offtrack.

"Before we get started, a cousin of mine, he and his wife are planning a trip to China. It's their first time. They weren't sure about what airline to fly. An American one or foreign? I mean, for me, I'd take an American one, but what do I know? Who do you take?"

"I like Delta. You can fly right out of Ft. Myers, connect in Detroit, and be there in under nineteen hours."

He said it like nineteen hours was nothing. "Really? Nothing better by driving to Miami or Tampa?"

"No. I've tried them all. Delta via Detroit on the way out and via Dallas coming home."

"Is that who you took on the last one?"

"Yep, I've been sticking with them. The points really add up."

He lost his color when I said, "A former employee filed a serious complaint against you."

"She left out the part that she led me on."

"It's never appropriate, or legal, to grab a woman's private parts without consent."

"That's not what happened."

"She's lying?"

"She was leading me on. I mean, she bent down, and you could see her tits, uh, her breasts were showing, and she just stood there, giving me a show."

"And you did what?"

"I thought it was an invitation, you know, so I tried to take her up on it. I guess I made a mistake."

"You guess?"

"At first I thought she was trying to, you know, play hard to get but . . ."

"You asked her to stay late that night, didn't you?"

"It was for work."

"What was so important that you wanted her to stay? Alone, I might add."

"We were busy; there was a job to finish."

"What job?"

"I think it was packing up a duffel bag we had made for Morgan Stanley that had a couple of giveaways in it."

"Ms. Holman was someone you trusted to open and close for you?"

"When I wasn't around. She was reliable and could do anything."

"Anyone could have filled the bags up; it didn't require any special skill set."

"I guess so."

"You had your eyes on her from the moment she came in for an interview, didn't you?"

"No, I didn't."

"You made lewd comments to her as soon as she started working for you."

"I have no idea what you're talking about."

"She needed the job, and you tried to use your position as her boss to press her into a sexual relationship."

"Nothing went on between us."

"Well, it wasn't because you didn't try to force it, was it?"

He crossed his arms over his chest. "I may have made a poor decision, but it wasn't like you're trying to make it."

"This place has a couple of cameras. Why don't we see how they portray the incident?"

He uncrossed his arms. "There's no video from that day. I

wish there was, but we don't have a digital system, so we record over every seventy-two hours."

Rowan thought he had all the answers. Had he planned the advance on Holman on the day before a holiday weekend, knowing that anything caught would be filmed over before it could be investigated? It showed a level of planning that made me question whether Holman was off on her assessment that Rowan's trip was a last-minute thing.

Getting back in my vehicle, I was praying like mad that Rebecca Holman would prevail and smack this sleazebag right onto the sex offender roles.

PETE JOHNSON, an officer I grew friendly with when I first came down to Naples, had retired after twenty years and took a supervisor's job with the TSA. Getting information without a warrant from an airline was iffy at best, depending on whom you asked.

Going with a TSA officer would help make sure I wouldn't need a warrant. Johnson was about to turn sixty but still kept in shape. If he hadn't lost his hair, he could pass for forty.

"You're looking good, Petey."

"Thanks, Frank. How's Jessica and Mary Ann?"

"Everybody is well. Jessie is growing so fast, it scares me."

He smiled. "Wait till they turn thirty, like my twins."

"I can't imagine."

"Me either."

"Crystal's engaged now. It must be exciting."

"He's a good guy. I just wish he wasn't a cop. I know I put Lorraine through a lot of sleepless nights."

"If he can get off the streets, make detective, it's safer."

He nodded. "But as you know, safer, not safe. If the pay was better, I'd tell him to come here. You just got to deal with the occasional nutjob."

"Seems kind of boring."

"It is, but that's okay. Chasing down scumbags got old."

"I hear you. I appreciate your help with this. You know anyone at the Delta ticket counter?"

"There's this guy Fred who plays ball when needed. Let's see what he has to say."

53

"ARE YOU FEELING OKAY?"

I climbed back into bed. "Yeah, just can't sleep."

"You worried about going to the doctor tomorrow?"

"No."

"You sure? Because there's nothing to worry about."

It was easy for everybody to say there was no reason for concern. The bottom line was, there was plenty to worry about. I'd had cancer. There was always the threat it would come back. "I know. It's not that."

"Stop thinking. Concentrate on your breathing."

"I'm trying to."

"You need to relax. If it's work, stop worrying about it."

"Sorry I woke you."

Rowan was what was keeping me up. The Delta Airlines rep confirmed Rowan's flight, but what was interesting was that he bought the ticket just the day before he left. Holman seemed to be right about it being a sudden trip. When I asked Rowan about it, he claimed he always waited until the last minute to buy a ticket, stating he was able to get the best price that way.

It was a strategy of sorts, but when I tried searching for airfares, half the time the cost was higher. It felt like a coin flip.

What was really bothering me was the fact I hadn't thought to ask Delta what Rowan paid. My TSA buddy advised against asking, as that was considered confidential. Airlines never wanted you to know what someone else paid for a ticket.

The more I learned about Rowan, the higher my suspicion. Now, with a sex charge hanging over him, I was seeing red.

That he'd forced himself on an employee was driving me nuts. I couldn't imagine Jessie being subjected to such a horrific situation. At least Holman had the good sense to quit and file charges. I would do my damn best to make sure Jessie would react the same way, but the statistics predicted a different outcome.

For a range of reasons, women were reluctant to press charges when they were violated. Some of it was shame. For others, economics were a factor, and there was too large a group for whom a lack of self-esteem kept them silent.

The subject of abusive men shifted my thoughts to Scott Dorsey, Wade's first husband. Two former wives of his were murdered. I had to dig into the first case. If it looked like he did it and got away with it once, maybe he went for a repeat performance, this time on Wade.

The mental lineup I visualized started with Seke, who seemed to have mental illness issues. Next was Belcher, who may have been pushed over the edge by the crap he was taking to build muscle. Then, at the other end, was Anderson and Berry. Their motive would have been revenge.

The suspects in the center, Dorsey, Frelig, and Rowan, were cowards who'd treated women like objects. I found myself hoping it was one of the abusers. We'd get one of them off the street, and I'd make sure eyes were kept on the others.

Either way, I was going to put an alert in the system, and if they so much as laid a finger on a woman, I'd make sure they'd regret it. I didn't make personal vows often, but this one calmed me down enough to let me drift off to sleep.

It was a combination of a clean report from the doctor and two cups of coffee that had me feeling better than I should have with three hours of sleep. Derrick had put a sticky with the telephone number for Rodney Long on my desk before he went to interview Frelig.

Standing behind my desk, I dialed the number. It rang six times before going to voice mail. I sat and left a message. Grabbing the murder book, I reread the interviews and Lee County file on Dorsey.

Closing the three-ring binder, I checked the time. It was ten forty-five. Jerry Belcher and his attorney were due at eleven. Fifteen minutes with the AC off wouldn't do much to make it unbearable, but with an outside temperature of eighty-six, it'd get uncomfortable quickly.

My preference was not to meet the person I was interviewing beforehand. I wanted as much as possible to be unfamiliar. Even fearful, if possible. People made mistakes when they were under pressure.

I looked through the two-way mirror. Belcher had a white T-shirt on and had his arms crossed over his chest. Even though he didn't have any facial resemblance, the way his muscles stretched his shirt, an image of Mr. Clean popped into my head.

Belcher's lawyer looked like a dwarf sitting next to him. His name was Clarence Reedy. He handled criminal law, but I never knew him to defend anyone accused of murder. I knocked and entered, wondering if that meant Belcher wasn't concerned or if he had made a massive mistake.

"Gentlemen."

Reedy rose and we shook hands. Belcher moved his chin in my direction. He wasn't even trying to be courteous.

I placed a file on the table and squared it. Then I opened it, picked up a couple of sheets of paper and shuffled them. I pretended to be reading. Three minutes passed, and Reedy cleared his throat. I stuck a finger in the air and wasted another minute before closing the file.

"Counselor, your client and Beth Wade had an extramarital relationship. Ms. Wade was suffocated to death and dumped in an irrigation canal."

"Affairs may be problematic in a moral sense, but it's not breaking any laws."

"Of course not. The night Beth Wade was last seen was July seventh. Merely a couple of hours before she disappeared, your client called her."

"They had a relationship. A phone call to a lover is nothing out of the ordinary."

"Mr. Belcher made the call in his car while traveling east toward the casino where Ms. Wade was enjoying herself on a night out."

Neither of them said anything, but Belcher shifted in his seat. He knew what was coming.

"Curiously, after that call, your client's phone went dark, leaving no trace as he traveled to Immokalee to meet with Ms. Wade."

"His phone died. It happens all the time. Assuming he was going to the casino is pure speculation."

"A car matching the blue Ford Explorer driven by Mr. Belcher was seen entering the casino parking lot."

"I'm sure there are thousands of blue Explorers in the area. Do you have explicit proof, with a matching license plate?"

Belcher had prepped his attorney. It was the smart thing to do. Lawyers hated surprises almost as much as detectives did.

"Take a look at this." I slid two pictures across the table of the man with Belcher's build.

"That isn't me."

Reedy said, "What proof is there that this is Mr. Belcher? Look at him; look at the picture. I don't see a resemblance."

"As he did in turning his phone off to avoid location detection, it's our contention that your client attempted to disguise his appearance by wearing oversized, dark sunglasses and applying layers of makeup to confuse facial recognition software."

"I'm sorry, Detective, I don't see how you can make a determination that this is my client."

"Come on, Counselor. How many other clients do you have with a build like that? We're working with techies, who assure me they will be able to prove it is him. So, instead of wasting both of our times, I'd instruct your client to come clean."

"Until such time that you can prove it is Mr. Belcher, we have nothing further to discuss."

54

Was I that readable? I thought Mary Ann had special powers to see into my head. She was good at it, but many couples had similar insights. When Derrick walked in with two cups of Starbucks, I figured it had to be me. He knew I rarely drank coffee in the afternoon. I had enough trouble sleeping as it was, and though it supposedly passed through your system in a couple of hours, I didn't need to play mental matador.

"Here you go, Frank."

"Thanks. I needed it today."

I greedily sipped it as he said, "Frelig was cagey. I asked him if Wade had said she had run into Scott Dorsey at the casino and thrown a drink at him. He gave me a look that, to me, meant he didn't know about it. But then he said she told him."

"He could be using it to deflect the focus from him to Dorsey."

"Exactly what I thought."

"Did you ask him why he never said anything about it before?"

"Yeah, he said he didn't think much about it."

"He didn't think an altercation between his wife and her first husband, just a week before she went missing, wasn't something to tell us?"

"That's what he said. I don't like Dorsey one bit."

"Maybe it's because he and Wade fought like dogs, and throwing a drink is no big deal in their world."

"Not in a public place. Anybody would be embarrassed having a drink thrown at them."

"Did you ask if he knew about Dorsey's first wife being murdered?"

"He had the same reaction as the drink throwing. I think he knew, but then he began acting like he was shocked to learn about it. He started saying we should be looking at Dorsey and that Wade had always said he was dangerous, blah, blah, blah. He didn't say anything new."

"We should ask Wade's mother if she knows if Frelig was aware of the first murder."

"Good angle. I'll check with her. I tried to probe if he knew she was screwing around with Belcher, but he didn't seem to know about it. How did it go with Belcher?"

"They stonewalled. He prepped his lawyer. But the video seemed to surprise both of them. They're demanding more proof. I'm racking my brain for something, but Rowan might have seen Belcher there. Who could miss a guy his size? If Rowan can place him there, maybe even talking to Wade, we're on our way."

ROWAN WAS TALKING to a skinny kid who was loading mugs into a box. He was wearing a white shirt, black dress pants, and a red tie. It looked schoolboyish. He turned away, shaking his head when he saw me, then strode over.

"I don't have the time today. A customer is coming in soon. If we can land this order, it'll be the biggest one in years."

"Good luck to you. I hope it works out."

"Believe me, I feel good about it, but I'm keeping my fingers crossed."

"I just have a quick question for you."

He sighed. "Okay, come on back."

On the center of his desk was a cooler emblazoned with a Kia logo. I guessed his big prospect was the Kia dealer with the annoying TV ads. They spent a ton on advertising, and though I couldn't stand their commercials, they got the word out.

"Nice cooler."

"I'm hoping they like the modifications we made. They're planning to give away one with each car."

"It's a good idea."

He ran his hand over the cooler's top. "It was my idea that interested them. I added interior lighting, a split top, a bunch of things, you know, to sex it up. It's miles better than the first one."

"I'm sure they'll like it. I wanted to ask you about someone who we think was at the casino the night Beth Wade disappeared."

"I told you about the guy I saw her talking to."

"Yes, but this is someone different. This man is a bodybuilder. Did you see anyone with a build like Schwarzenegger?"

"Yes, I'm pretty sure there was this guy. He was huge."

"Did he have glasses on?"

"Glasses? Uh, I don't remember."

I slid a picture of the man we had on video. "Does he look familiar?"

"I remember some guy wearing sunglasses inside. You know, some guys wear them when they play poker to hide their eyes so they don't give away anything when they're playing."

"Was it this man?"

"It's hard to say. I don't want to make a mistake, you know."

The skinny kid knocked on the door and stuck his head in. "They're here."

I stood. "Thanks for your time. Good luck."

I followed the kid out, saying, "I like the new cooler. Ben said he made changes to the original one. What did it look like?"

He pointed. "It's in that box, under the counter. Help yourself."

I pulled the box out and opened the flaps. An umbrella was sitting on top of the cooler. It was small, with a white top and purple body. A tag stated that it came in various sizes, but except for two depressions to set a cup in, it looked like every other one on the market. Placing it back in the box, I noticed the corner of a framed photo and took it out.

It was almost a mirror of the photos hanging on Rowan's wall. Standing in the middle of a dozen Asians, Rowan was smiling. But something caught my eye. There was something on his face. I brought the image as close to my eyes as possible, but his face was the size of a thumbnail.

The kid had his back to me. I slipped out my phone and took a picture of the photo and said goodbye.

Back in my car I pulled up the photo and zoomed in on

Rowan's face. They were Band-Aids. I was about to make a call when a text from Derrick came in. He had not only seen a Ford Focus that matched the car in the home Frelig watched for a neighbor, he thought the driver was Frelig, Wade's husband.

55

WADING THROUGH LUGGAGE-TOWING FAMILIES, I MET MY
TSA buddy under a sign listing departing and arriving flights.

"Hey, Pete, I can't believe how busy this place is."

"Tell me about it. A month doesn't go by without another
record number of passengers. There's a slowdown from the
high season, but as you can see, it's not much."

"I read they're going to expand the terminal somehow."

"Yeah, it's going to start any day now. The plan is to
centralize all the screening we do in one spot. There'll be
more lanes and it'll eliminate backups. They're going to move
the restaurants presecurity to postsecurity. It'll take time.
They have to bump these walls out, but better to do it now
than wait till it gets jammed up like most other airports."

"It's hard to believe the growth. When I came down, this
place was brand new. Now, less than fifteen years later, it's
got to be redone."

He started walking toward Terminal D. "Just about every
airport in the nation is obsolete. There hasn't been a new one
built in the States since the one in Denver, and that was
twenty-five years ago."

"Crazy."

We stopped at an unmarked door. Pete punched numbers in the keypad, and the door clicked open. I followed him into a cubicle with a large screen.

Pete said, "He came through at four fifteen. It's all cued up for you."

I sat in front of the monitor as Pete tapped on the keyboard, and a line of travelers came alive. Rowan was behind a woman who handed over her boarding pass and license to a TSA official. The officer scribbled something on her boarding pass and waved her through.

Wearing a long-sleeved, blue shirt, Rowan stepped up and handed his documents over. "Can you freeze it?"

"Just tap the screen."

I did and studied Rowan's Band-Aid-patched face. Two red scratch lines extended past the bandages. Did the injuries come from Wade's fingernails?

AFTER UPDATING Derrick on the Rowan TSA video, I asked, "What did the lab say about trying to clean up the muscleman video?"

"They said they were installing an update on some software they use. They're going to get to it as soon as it's up and running."

"What you can do these days is crazy. That app where you can see what you'll look like in ten or twenty years is scary. I know people think it's all fun and games, but that software is Russian owned. People are feeding their biometric data into it. I'm betting someone is going to be found using it to steal identities."

"It's a new form of phishing but more dangerous."

My cell rang. "Homicide, Detective Luca."

"Hi, I'm Rodney, Rodney Long. You left me a message?"

"Yes, thanks for calling me back. I wanted to ask you about Scott Dorsey and the murder of his wife Angela."

"They're finally reopening the case?"

"I'm looking into it and had questions about Mr. Dorsey."

"He did it."

"What?"

"He killed Angela. There's no doubt he did it."

"Why do you say that?"

"He was a jealous nutjob. Angie told me he threatened to kill her a bunch of times."

"Did she ever report those threats?"

"She said the cops never did anything, said that saying something wasn't against the law. Guess you guys were wrong, huh?"

I wondered if she mentioned anything about being battered by her husband. There was no record of her filing a complaint against Dorsey. It was so important for people to get it on record. Otherwise, there was no way to connect the dots.

"I understand you were with Angela Dorsey the night before she was murdered."

"Yeah, I was."

"Did Scott Dorsey call Angela that night, while you were there?"

"Yeah, he got all pissy when Angie tried to rush him off the phone. He said he knew I was there and went on a rant about me."

"Did you tell this to the police?"

"Of course, I told them the same things I'm saying now. They didn't seem to care. They were looking at me as a suspect. They kept asking about my record."

"The drug offenses?"

"Yeah, that's all they gave a shit about. And when a neighbor said we had a fight a couple of weeks before she was killed, they were ready to lock me up. It was such bullshit. They should have been all over Scott."

"I appreciate the information. I'm sure we'll be back in touch."

Talking to him raised more questions than reading the file Lee County sent over. If what Long said was true, why hadn't there been a more thorough investigation of Scott Dorsey? The murder book on Angela Dorsey would have records of each interview the police conducted. I needed to get my hands on it.

"What's going on?"

"That was the boyfriend of Scott Dorsey's first wife. According to this Long, he pointed a finger at Dorsey when she was murdered, but the Lee police never followed up. I don't want to jump to conclusions, but it kind of jibes with what I saw in the file."

"He's got a record, right?"

"Yep, and Long thinks that's why they never believed him."

"I don't know about that. We rely on quite a few unsavory snitches."

"No doubt. I'm going to see one of my wine buddies who's on the Lee force. You want to come along? He's a good guy."

"I'd like to, but I'm waiting on a call back from Wade's mother. Then I was going to go to the lab and see what's what on the video enhancement we want."

I WAS proud of the way Derrick was turning into a good homicide detective. When I was ready to pack it in, he'd be better than me. I'd like to think it was because of me, but a critical factor in being able to hunt down killers was the bulldog factor.

It was tough, slow going, and boring at times, but you had to keep following the leads no matter how minor they seemed. Derrick was determined, committed, and responsible. I couldn't take credit for those traits. It was his parents who deserved kudos.

One area he needed to develop was thinking outside the box. There was a fine line between wasting time on outlandish theories and peeking into closets others wouldn't. Maybe he was already thinking that way but was afraid to verbalize it to me.

It was up to me to encourage him, tell him how well he was doing. Stopped at a light on Bonita Beach Road, I reached for my cell to call him. Before I could punch his number in, the phone rang. It was Derrick.

"Hey, Frank, you got a sec?"

"Sure. What's up?"

"Just got off with Wade's mom. She said Frelig knew all about Scott Dorsey's wife being murdered. I don't know why the guy would lie about something like that."

"And why he never mentioned the drink throwing by Dorsey. I don't get it. It would point at some retribution by Dorsey."

"I don't think he knew about that. But the murder is puzzling. You think he's got some grand plan, like waiting till the heat got too hot and then throw this out there?"

And just like that, Derrick was thinking of remote possibilities. "If so, he should be writing novels."

"No kidding. I'm heading to the lab."

"Okay. I'm ten minutes away from the sheriff's office."

"If you don't mind me saying, what do you expect to get out of the old file?"

"Information. You never know what you'll find buried in an old case."

"I don't know. I know Dorsey was married to both of them, but I just don't see what we get out of it. We know he fought with them and was a jealous bastard. He was at the casino a week before she disappeared, getting a drink thrown at him. I just think we go with what we have and try to get more, but deal just with the Wade murder."

My pride told me to tell him I was the boss, but my gut told me the kid was right. "You're probably right on this. We have enough to go on. I'm turning around. I'll let Lee know what I found out."

"You don't have to, Frank. I was just trying to figure out your angle on it."

"I don't know exactly. I don't like anything about Dorsey. Maybe I let that screw with my focus. I'm going to see what Rowan has to say about the bruises on his face."

"Why don't we bring him in?"

It was a valid avenue to pursue. "He'll probably get a lawyer."

"You're right."

Being correct was always nice, but this acknowledgment was special at the moment.

56

Promo Pros was the quietest I'd seen it. Rowan was bent down in front of a printer, fiddling inside it. The skinny kid manning the front of the store waved hello to me.

"You here to see Mr. Rowan?"

"Yes."

Rowan turned around, his hands soiled with black ink. "As you can see, I'm in the middle of trying to fix this frigging printer."

The kid said, "Let me do that. I fixed it a week ago. The back drum probably needs to be cleaned."

Rowan didn't invite me in, but I followed him. He veered off to the bathroom, and I waited in his office. I scanned the walls for the newest photo, but it wasn't hung up. Why?

He came out of the bathroom drying his hands with a paper towel. "Okay, what now?"

"How'd did it go with the cooler?"

He frowned. "They said they'd think about it but wanted a lower price. It's always about the money."

"Sorry. I see you have pictures from your trips. Where's the one from this year?"

"I don't know."

"You're sure you didn't go on the trip at the last minute?"

"No, I told you, I always buy the ticket just before I go. It's a secret way to get the best rates. The airlines are happy to fill a seat and take a lot less for it."

"Did you get a bruise or scratch right before you left?"

His left eye bobbed toward his nose. "No, I don't think so."

"In the TSA video of you passing through security, you have bandages covering what look like scratches."

"Oh, those. I was clearing some brush and got scratched by a branch."

"Where was this?"

"A friend's house."

"When?"

"Right before my trip."

"Who's the friend?"

"Danny Lister. He lives on Livingston in Livingston Woods. He has a big piece of property and asked me to help him clear an area."

Up until he gave me the friend's name, I didn't believe him, but the way his friend's name and location rolled off his tongue, it sounded legit.

I WAS LOOKING up DMV records on Rowan's friend when Derrick came in shaking his head. He said, "It's not Belcher."

"They sure?"

"Yeah, they think the guy had bad acne and was covering it up."

"Why anyone takes steroids is beyond me."

"What do you mean?"

"The acne, it's a side effect from steroids."

"I didn't know that."

"What about the car?"

"Said they were working on it next. Said to give them an hour max."

"Good." I grabbed the phone and punched a number in.

"Danny Lister?"

"Yeah, that's me. Who's this?"

"Detective Luca, Collier County Sheriff's Office."

"Sheriff's office? What's wrong?"

"You're friends with Ben Rowan?"

"More like acquaintances, why?"

"Did he help you clear some brush around July seventh?"

"What?"

"Rowan claimed he helped you clear your property."

"Never happened."

"Are you sure about that?"

"I don't want to be a wise guy, Detective, but I live here, and I think I would know."

"Sorry for the mix-up, sir."

I could hear blood pulsing in my ears as I hung up. "Rowan gave me a line of bullshit on his scratches."

"Didn't he know you'd check?"

"I caught him by surprise. He was quick though. It sounded pretty good when he said it, but it's another lesson to check and recheck everything."

"He probably got them from Wade during a struggle."

"Rowan and Wade leave together, but they split up in the parking lot and disappear off the screen. Rowan's car leaves six and a half minutes later. Did he have enough time to approach Wade, subdue her, and throw her in the trunk?"

"That sounds like a stretch. We know Wade was a fighter."

"If he got in his car and drove to Wade's car, he'd save two minutes."

Derrick answered a ringing desk phone. It was a brief conversation. He stood as he hung up. "The lab said they're certain it's Frelig driving the Ford Focus."

"The one with the trunk carpet ripped out."

"Let's get moving and put two warrant requests together."

"Two?"

"I want Rowan's car and the one Frelig was driving to be examined by forensics. We have enough to get both. You write up Frelig's. As the husband at the scene of the crime, they can't deny it. The neighbor's address is in the murder book. I'll handle Rowan's."

DERRICK HAD GONE TO ST. Croix with a tow truck and a pair of marked cars. Everything needed to be handled properly to avoid any possible challenge in court. I opted to be present executing the warrant for Ben Rowan's car.

It wasn't that I felt he was more likely to have committed the murder. I knew it would be fun, and it was. I enjoyed embarrassing the pervert in front of his employees. When we showed up in force and I handed him the warrant, his cartoonish stammering put a smile on my face.

I was concerned that Rowan or Frelig might try and run. It would be a telling sign, and my request to have eyes on both of them twenty-four seven was quickly granted.

Chester had pushed the lab to prioritize the vehicles, telling me he wanted the case solved, but from what he told me when he learned of the dual request, I knew he was concerned that if we held an innocent person's car for days, the press would run with it.

It was eleven fifteen when the results came in. The presence of Beth Wade's blood and hair had been discovered in a place that surprised me. It was time to haul him in and make an arrest.

57

———————

We had him stewing in interview room two as he waited for his lawyer. He refused to talk without counsel. He had to know we found something, and to me, not talking was an admission of guilt.

When word came that his attorney had just walked in, I headed to the bathroom. My pee alarm hadn't gone off yet, but I knew I'd be tied up when it was time to go. I sat on the bowl, tickling my abdomen to get a flow going.

The Wade case seemed like it had taken too long, but in actuality it had taken less time than normal to get to the cusp of an arrest. I tried to figure why it felt like it had dragged, and the only answer that made sense was the sheer number of suspects and their propensity toward abusiveness.

Wade was combative, but that was no excuse. The world seemed more dangerous for a child than it was when my dad told me to just bring up your kid like you know how. Was it the exposure my job provided, putting me in touch with deviants and killers that made it seem worse? Was it all the media attention? Or had things really taken a downward turn?

Washing up, I remembered what Mary Ann had told me

when I was on a worrying rant. She said, "Do what you can to make it better. You'll still make a difference, even if you can't fix everything." Just like when my dad told me his advice on child rearing, I thought both statements were too simplistic when I heard them and brushed them off.

It took time for the words to sink in. They may have been simple, but there were no truer words spoken. Today was a day to put them to practice.

DERRICK and I settled into chairs across from Carl Moran and his client. My partner clicked the recording devices on and recited the formalities for the record. Moran was the son of a lawyer who ran a high-profile law firm that ran annoying ads claiming to be a lawyer for the people.

To me, it was nothing but a hustle by suits charging three hundred bucks an hour or grabbing a third of what someone was entitled to. The only people they were for were the ones in the mirror.

Though Moran was smiling, he knew his client was in trouble. There was no sense in wasting time wiping the grin off his face.

"Thank you for coming in today, gentlemen. I'll get right to it. Yesterday we executed a warrant to search and examine Mr. Rowan's vehicle, an automobile that was on the Immokalee casino property the night of July seventh and the early morning of the eighth."

Derrick slid photos of Rowan driving into and out of the parking lot.

"How do we know where these pictures were taken?"

Derrick said, "We can provide access to the casino's surveillance footage at an appropriate time."

"Mr. Rowan, how do you explain the presence of Beth Wade's blood and hair in your car?"

"That's impossible. It can't be."

"Here's the forensic report detailing the findings on the rear seat and floor of your car."

Moran, no longer smiling, picked up the document and set it down.

Rowan said, "I didn't do anything to her."

"The evidence tells a different story, Mr. Rowan. Here's what I believe happened. The two of you left together, and you had sexual designs on her."

As he shook his head, his eye began to tick.

"You went to your car and drove to Wade's Mustang and got out. Then you forced yourself on her, and she fought you off. Wade scratched you, maybe kicked you, and you slammed her head into the side of your car. Right here." I pointed to a picture of his car where there was a lip along the roofline. "We found a hair of Wade's stuck in the chrome. And the coroner said the bruise on the rear of her head likely was from an impact with it."

"That's not true."

"Maybe not all of it, but how else would Wade's hair get stuck on your car?"

"I don't know."

"You don't know? Come on now."

Moran said, "My client has denied knowledge of it. Badgering him won't help."

"Look, Mr. Rowan, do I think you killed Beth Wade? There's no doubt, and we have the evidence to support it. Do I think you intended to commit a homicide? No. I believe you made an advance on her, which she rejected, just like you did with Rebecca Holman. Only this time, Wade fought back physically, provoking you to respond by smashing her head against your car. She lost consciousness, and you panicked. You threw her in the back of your car. Then you suffocated her and dumped her body in an irrigation canal, clipping her fingernails before you did."

Moran said, "Irrefutable proof will be needed in a courtroom, Detective. You have a nice little tale here, but it's nothing more than that."

"It's a story where your client goes away for life, and you go back to your mansion. Now, you have a chance to help your client, because I don't believe he wanted Wade dead. She provoked him, but self-defense won't work here, Counselor, as it was an unwanted advance, something your client has a history of doing. If he confesses, we'll drop the charge to manslaughter."

Moran said, "Without any acknowledgment that my client was involved in any way in the passing of Ms. Wade, would the manslaughter type be involuntary?"

"Sorry, Counselor. While I believe the original strike was probably reactionary, he suffocated her afterward. I realize he may have panicked, but at this point, the offer is voluntary manslaughter."

"My client and I will need to discuss this further."

"That conversation will be taking place behind bars." I stood. "Benjamin Rowan, you're under arrest for the murder of Beth Wade. Derrick, read him his rights and cuff him."

58

THE FOLLOWING MORNING, DERRICK AND I WERE STANDING IN the back of the press room. Sheriff Chester was briefing the press on the arrest. He was in his element: there was an audience, and the news was good. Though he mentioned my name, it still bothered me that he took the lion's share of the credit.

It wasn't my ego; he never mentioned Derrick or the fact that we busted our tails to get Rowan. That bothered me along with how quickly Chester disowned any blame when things went wrong. In my book, a leader was someone who stepped up and took responsibility, shielding his people when the crap hit the fan.

Chester finished answering a question and closed the session. As we filed out, my phone rang. The number looked vaguely familiar.

"Detective Luca."

"Hello, Detective. This is Vine Strongheart. You left me several messages."

"Yes, I was trying to reach you."

"We were in the Beartooth Mountains. Sorry, there's no cell service, but that's a good thing."

"You're right about that. I understand you were at an American Indian conference."

"Yes, The National Congress of American Indians. Is that why you called?"

"No, I was investigating a crime, and we were looking at anyone who owned a yellow PT Cruiser, because there was a sighting of one at Gargiulo's on Immokalee."

"It could have been me. I have an outreach program to help farmworkers, especially the kids. We need to make sure they get an education, or they'll end up like their parents working the fields."

"That's good of you."

"I do what I can. We all should."

———

DERRICK and I were going through the murder book. We split the task up to make sure every drop of evidence on Rowan was orderly. The prosecutors would need it if it went to trial.

The word from the DA was that Rowan was going to take the plea and accept the voluntary manslaughter charge, but they were haggling over the length of a prison term, which could be as much as fifteen years.

My notes on Rowan's wife made me feel bad. The poor woman would not only go broke paying for Moran and Moran to represent her husband, she'd have to try and run Promo Pros. Her life was tossed upside down, but as tough as it was, she was better off without him. I hoped she had a friend who would help her see the light.

Derrick said, "I still can't believe the whole thing with Frelig's neighbor's car. He goes to the casino to see if his wife was cheating on him but ends up sitting there before turning around."

"That's why he was never seen inside."

"Crazy. I'll tell you, if someone would have told me they ripped out the trunk covers because a bottle of olive oil spilled, I would have thought they were lying."

"If it was a normal sized one instead of something from Costco, they wouldn't have to get rid of it."

"I told Lynn to stop buying the cereal from there. It's a giant box, and it doesn't fit in the cabinet."

"Some things they have good prices on, others are impulse buys."

"Big day tomorrow, huh?"

"Yep, Jessie's first day. I never thought you'd catch me making a big deal over nursery school, but we're even going out to eat afterward."

"Nice. Where you going?"

"Bayside."

"Fancy."

"We're going to use that gift card Mrs. Whitaker sent me for closing her husband's case. Jessie loves Venetian Village."

"Probably because there's a Ben & Jerry's there."

"We're definitely going to stop in there."

"Why don't you leave now? I've got it covered."

"You know, I'll take you up on that. Let me make a call to my buddy up in Lee first. I want him to follow up on the Angela Dorsey murder. There's something there. I can feel it."

The next book in this series is, The Grandpa Killer. Find it in eBook & Paperback.

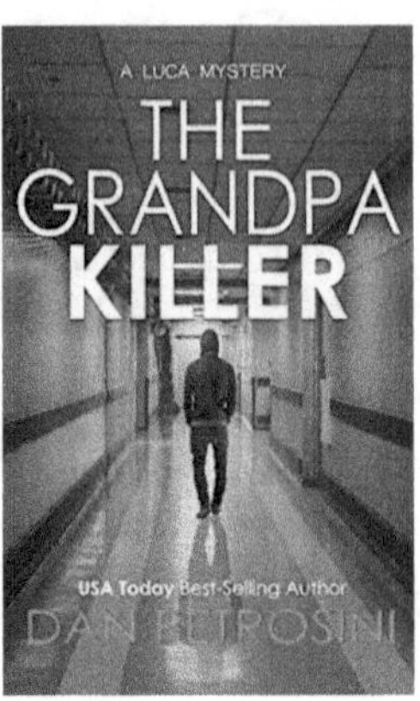

I hope you enjoyed reading this book as much as I enjoyed writing it. If you did, I'd appreciate it if you would write a quick review on Amazon or your favorite book site. Reviews are an author's best friend and even a quick line or two is helpful. Thanks, Dan

OTHER BOOKS BY DAN

Complicit Witness

Push Back

Ambition Cliff

You can keep abreast of my writing and have access to books that are free of discounting by joining my newsletter. It normally is out once a month and also contains notes on self- esteem, motivational pieces and wine articles.

It's free. See bottom of my website: www.danpetrosini.com

ABOUT THE AUTHOR

Dan is a USA Today and Amazon best-selling author who wrote his first story at the age of ten and enjoys telling a story or joke.

Dan gets his story ideas by exploring the question; What if?

In almost every situation he finds himself in, Dan explores what if this or that happened? What if this person died or did something unusual or illegal?

Dan's non-stop mind spin provides him with plenty of material to weave into interesting stories.

A fan of books and films that have twists and are difficult to predict, Dan crafts his stories to prevent readers from guessing correctly. He writes every day, forcing the words out when necessary and has written over twenty-five novels to date.

It's not a matter of wanting to write, Dan simply has to.

Dan passionately believes people can realize their dreams if they focus and act, and he encourages just that.

His favorite saying is – "The price of discipline is always less than the cost of regret"

Dan reminds people to get the negativity out of their lives. He believes it is contagious and advises people to steer clear of negative people. He knows having a true, positive mind set makes it feel like life is rigged in your favor. When he gets off base, he tells himself, 'You can't have a good day with a bad attitude.'

Married with two daughters and a needy Maltese, Dan lives in Southwest Florida. A New York native, Dan has taught at local colleges, writes novels, and plays tenor saxophone in several jazz bands. He also drinks way too much wine and never, ever takes himself too seriously.

He puts out a twice-a-month newsletter featuring articles, his writing and special deals and steals.

Sign up at www.danpetrosini.com